THE LOST TREERUNNER

THE LOST TREERUNNER

BRANDT LEGG

LAUGHING RAIN

The Lost TreeRunner (Justar Journal Book Two)

v2

Published in the United States of America by Laughing Rain

Cataloging-in-Publication data for this book is available from the Library of Congress.

ISBN-13: 978-1-935070-14-6

ISBN-10: 1-935070-14-2

Cover designed by: Jarowe and Eleni Karoumpali

PUBLISHER'S NOTE

BrandtLegg.com

This book is dedicated to Teakki and Ro

CHAPTER ONE

June 2101

"Grandyn!" Zaverly yelled. "This way!" Her screams were tainted with tears, strained with bitterness and regret. At twenty-three, she was among the younger surviving TreeRunners. Three years earlier, at the time of the government's "Doneharvest" crackdown, she'd fled with many other TreeRunners, a group of elite wilderness survivalist experts after the organization had been banned and its members rounded up for execution. Now the Aylantik Office of Intelligence (AOI), the state's feared stormtroopers, hunted the survivors, and Grandyn Happerman was wanted above all the others.

"Grandyn!" she shrieked again, tensing her gymnast muscles as the swarm drones closed in on him. Counting the seconds before she would swing down into the fight, she hovered more than thirty meters above, concealed in a man-made "tree-base" attached to one of the Amazon's giant kapok trees. The area was filled with stealth locations constructed of materials and wired-in technology that made them nearly impossible to detect.

He heard her calling his name as he ran barefoot through the thick jungle, dodging trees, his breaths coming in the controlled manner the TreeRunners had taught him since childhood. The chemical taste of a neurological-voiding-capsule, or "neuro-cap," in his mouth required added concentration to avoid swallowing, but TreeRunners were practiced in focus even more than in physical skills. Still, this being only the second time he'd prepared for the "final defense" as they called it, it took everything he had learned.

If killed or captured, the neuro-cap would dissolve and quickly mutate the cells of his brain, in a sense erasing his mind so that no knowledge would pass to the enemy, and if not already dead, the pill would kill him. Postmortem brain readings, known as said-scans, were one of the AOI's best sources of intelligence. In the era of androids, cyborgs, and Imps, humans implanted with computer-like processors, neuro-caps had been developed to work even on non-organic "people." At that moment, Grandyn wished he were not human, for then he wouldn't have to feel the certain death. But that eventuality, and ingesting the neuro-cap, might still be a minute or two away.

Before resorting to the cap he had other counter measures to try. TreeRunners acquired countless skills during their many levels of training, but this specialized knowledge had to be used sparingly, both to preserve resources and to avoid tech-tracing, the AOI's ability to track the fingerprint of any electronic device from the web of satellites monitoring the Earth's two point nine billion inhabitants.

As the hundreds of insect-sized drones closed within centimeters of his dirty, sweaty skin, the lanky twenty-one-year old dove through a deep root hole and released a Phantom-Shield Nano-device. It sent a perfectly replicated holographic version of him, including heat signature, into the same path and trajectory he'd been on. If the swarm drones followed it for at least three minutes he'd be safe. Temporarily.

The fall had not gone well. The location was familiar, as he knew every square meter of the forest. He'd even slept in this root hole more than once, but trying to time the drop and the deployment of the device while running at full speed made it a hazardous move. His medical sensor quickly told him he'd cracked several ribs, broken two fingers, and fractured a wrist. If the swarm drones returned, escape would be impossible. Hopefully Zaverly, the woman in the tree, had been able to call for help. He shifted the neuro-cap with his tongue, letting it rest against his cheek, and maintained his breathing.

Muddied and broken, shaking beneath twisting roots with leaves and bugs stuck to his sweaty body as the seconds pulsed slowly by, he recounted what had brought him to this desperate point.

Grandyn Happerman had helped his father, the world's last librarian, move the physical copies of more than one hundred thousand so-called "dangerous" books out of the Portland library before the AOI burned the last known remaining collection of printed books. A longtime family friend and well-known author, Nelson Wright, had helped them, but unbeknownst to Grandyn, Nelson's sister, Chelle Andreas, who was also assisting with the almost impossible task, was a highly placed revolutionary.

In the days following that successful book rescue, Grandyn's girlfriend Vida, and several friends had been killed by the AOI. He also learned the AOI had been responsible for his mother's death years earlier. And those same butchers either killed his father or had been holding him in some secret prison for the past three years. No one knew which was true.

Without time to recover from those horrendous events, he and Chelle were arrested. Normally execution would have been instant, but apparently he had a guardian angel because inexplicably, Grandyn found himself released. Thus began the three-year saga of fighting, not just for his own survival and for the chance to avenge the many deaths, but mostly because he was determined to find out what happened to his father, to destroy the AOI, and to bring down the Aylantik government.

As the tree guarded the TreeRunner, he silently recalled the decisions that had brought him to the Amazon.

For the first two years following the library's closing, Grandyn had been searching the Oregon Area for any trace of what had happened to his father. At the same time, the AOI had been scouring forests around the globe looking for Grandyn. However, the Amazon was the most difficult place for them to penetrate. With no word of his father, it seemed the best way to help him, was to stay alive. The Amazon gave him the best chance and Grandyn should have been safest there, but as the revolution grew nearer, possibly only weeks away, the AOI had stepped up its search efforts and brought the war to the most remote parts of the globe.

He stopped thinking as the pain took his concentration. He needed a plan. His breathing slowed, each noise analyzed, considering if it belonged in this jungle? Did he? The neuro-cap tasted bitter.

Damn it, Zaverly probably doesn't know where I am now, and I'm not sure my injuries will allow me to climb out of this hole, he thought. *What an irony . . . I escape my closest call yet with the AOI and end up starving to death in a root hole. What a way for a TreeRunner to end.*

CHAPTER TWO

Ander Terik fingered his gold AOI lapel pin and tried not to appear bored as the tall, severe-looking woman speaking circled back around to a topic he knew better than anyone. He'd been studying and searching for the fugitive Grandyn Happerman since he joined the AOI several years before. The AOI had kept the peace in the world for seventy-five years following a massive plague and war, which wiped out sixty percent of Earth's human inhabitants. The AOI acted as police, army, secret service, and intelligence for the Aylantik regime, which came to power in the aftermath of the horrible Banoff years and had ruled the world under a single government ever since.

Grandyn – the authorities simply referred to him by only his first name – was the son of two revolutionaries famous within the AOI, but quite unknown to the general population. He'd disappeared three years earlier and now occupied position number three on the Most Wanted List behind two women and ahead of his surrogate uncle, Nelson Wright. But Terik, assigned solely to Grandyn, had also researched the other fugitives to the extent that they might aid in his search for Grandyn, who at twenty-one was the youngest on the list and, according to their files, only two years younger than himself. Their closeness in age and Terik's degrees in forestry, botany, and arborist sciences had helped earn him the important assignment. Grandyn just didn't have the vast networks of revolutionary groups like People Against World Nation, known as PAWN, the Rejectionists, and the Creatives behind him. Grandyn Happerman was a TreeRunner.

The TreeRunners had once been a proud organization that had spawned great leaders and created lifelong friendships among many leading citizens. But that was before the events of the winter of 2098, when an uprising had nearly stolen the peace for the first time in more than seven decades. The AOI instituted something similar to martial law, called "the Doneharvest," which meant anyone even suspected of involvement with the rebels was executed or imprisoned without trial. Because of Grandyn's involvement, the TreeRunners had been outlawed and all members immediately sentenced to death. Most were rounded up within days, and even former members as old as sixty were terminated. But the most wanted of them all, Grandyn Happerman, had disappeared without a trace, and Terik was determined to lead the chase for the troublemaker whose entire family seemed bent on destroying the greatest society and longest era of peace in human history.

Terik looked up as the AOI Chief switched to English. It was her way of checking to see if everyone was paying attention. The Chief, a tough, cunning woman in her sixties with close-cropped gray hair, was always ready to win a fight, never imagining the possibility of a loss. Terik caught her switch immediately. He, like most upper level AOI agents, had been studying many of the dead languages because certain rebel groups used the old ones instead of the computer-created language known as "Com" that had been the official dialect of Aylantik since the Banoff. It had been largely based on English, but much more logically arranged. Other than for AOI agents, learning any other languages was illegal.

After struggling with some of the more obscure dead dialects like German and Chinese, he couldn't imagine why the world would ever need more than one. He'd written a paper on the subject at the AOI Academy, showing the inefficiencies and cause for conflict of multiple languages and currencies, arguing they had done nothing more than complicate and divide citizens' lives. He'd illustrated that crime rates had plummeted once physical currency had been outlawed and replaced by virtual funds known as "digis." The corruption of exchange rates and the elimination of untraceable deals made transactions fairer for everyone.

Now the Chief said something in Japanese and he heard a nearby agent say, "Torgon," which was profanity in the new language, because he couldn't open an AirView to translate fast enough and obviously didn't know a bit of Japanese. "Can't the Dragon Lady stop showing off and just speak Com like the rest of us?" the agent said under his breath. Terik ignored the insubordination.

Many saw Terik as too ambitious, too regulation-driven, and too vain. Some of that was true. He did everything "strictly by the book" – military haircut no more than twelve millimeters, Tekfabrik uniform, all-purpose-tread-transforming boots, and an intense workout regime that included live weapons, obstacle courses, and cliff climbing. Terik wanted to rise as far in the AOI as he could, and was willing to do anything to get what he wanted. In fact, he knew the only flaw in his records was the lack of a wife. The AOI liked family stability, and he planned to work on that part soon. The lean, six-foot tall, highly fit, and intelligent young man had no shortage of prospects.

Terik's AOI virtual-ID and personnel files showed his flawless record and rapid climb through the ranks. The twenty-three year old was everything they looked for in agents and a rising star within the Aylantik system. He had enlisted with the AOI in the early days of the Doneharvest and had performed heroically on several of his rookie cases. He'd also quickly distinguished himself in both physical and mental challenges, outperforming more seasoned agents on academic as well as field tests. "Just the type of soldier needed to track down these revolutionaries," a superior had noted. Another recommended him for the Grandyn Happerman hunt because of his seemingly natural endurance and closeness in age to the fugitive.

"Grandyn Happerman is a symbol to the rebels, and he possesses information which must be suppressed."

Terik nodded his head, his determination intensifying with each word the AOI Chief uttered.

"Make no mistake, ladies and gentlemen. Your future depends on capturing this dangerous man."

CHAPTER THREE

Lance Miner, the super-rich member of the A-Council, looked up when Sarlo, his assistant, walked in. The attractive and fit brunette had been with his company, PharmaForce, for twelve years, and had a mind perfectly matched for Miner's controlling, scheming ways. Sarlo also had higher principles than her boss, not that Miner was a bad man. She had once told her mother, "It's just that he sees such a big picture that he is willing to take shortcuts to improve the outcome."

Sarlo, like Miner, believed that he had the "weight of the world" on his shoulders, and that he alone could keep society from crumbling into something even worse than the pre-Banoff world.

Sarlo looked at the view. She adored most world capitals but called Buenos Aires her addiction. The culture, history, and beauty spoke to her, but it was the dance, passion, and fire that captured her. The city had grown dramatically in the previous twenty-five years, in part because of PharmaForce. Miner let her have the moment as she gazed out over the old historic district to the ocean. "I love my job," she said. The travel, a big perk, appealed to her, but Sarlo liked the proximity to power most of all. Miner

might not be as rich as his nemesis Deuce Lipton, but he knew
how to leverage his position so that most would agree he was
more powerful.

"I know you do," Miner said, flashing one of his charm-
drenched smiles. "We've been spending a lot of time down here
this past year, but I think we might finally be close to getting
him." He flipped an antique American silver dollar. It came up
tails, which told him things wouldn't go smoothly. *As if I need a coin
to tell me that*, he thought, slipping it back into his pocket.

By "him," Sarlo knew he meant Grandyn Happerman. Miner,
desperate to maintain the peace, had become obsessed with his
capture. Of course, he also wanted Munna, the one hundred
thirty-three year old woman who served as the rebels' inspiration,
captured. He would also have been happy to see Chelle Andreas
arrested and executed, but Grandyn had more significance . . .
much more. For months Sarlo had waited patiently for Miner to fill
her in completely, long ago learning not to push. He revealed facts
to associates as if they were rare gold coins. But today he had
promised a full update. "Today" usually meant he'd hit a wall in
his own thinking and needed her help unlocking more options.

"You still believe he's hiding in the Amazon?" she asked.

"The AOI is pursuing him there as we speak."

"But is it him?"

He frowned. Sarlo was obviously referring to the other times
they'd "captured" Grandyn, only to discover it was an imposter. It
seemed the TreeRunners were a loyal bunch. As part of their initiation and training, they'd repeatedly taken a blood oath of loyalty
to one another. That oath had caused many of them to pretend
they were Grandyn in an effort to confuse the AOI, and it had
been working. "We don't know for sure."

"But you said AOI. What about the Enforcers?"

The Enforcers, Miner's private army, had grown to more than
forty thousand as he tried to keep pace with Deuce's army, the
BLAXERS, thought to number fifty thousand. He had the

Enforcers shadowing the AOI in more than eight locations around the globe in a quest to find Grandyn before they did. Although Miner was the most powerful person on the A-Council, the secret committee which ran the Aylantik government, including choosing the "elected" World Premier, Miner couldn't make the AOI do what he wanted. Three years earlier things had been quite different.

Back then Miner had been on the verge of being elected Chairman of the Council, and was ready at that time to install Polis Drast as World Premier. But it had been Miner's greatest mistake, one of the few miscalculations he'd ever made. Drast turned out to be a traitor. He'd been caught in time, but not before severely damaging Miner's credibility and standing within the Council, effectively erasing two decades of work. Sarlo knew Miner had been extra-sensitive to being questioned since the Drast episode, so didn't push.

"The Enforcers are working some good leads," Miner replied. "But the little torg is like a ghost."

Sarlo wanted to ask for more current details why this twenty-one year old "kid" mattered so much, but waited. The hint of rainbows around the window's sides caught her attention. The special glass harvested solar energy, producing an almost imperceptible prism of light at the edges. It always relaxed her to watch the faint colors dance.

"I've read the reports, the sightings, and all the recon data," she said, unable to avoid walking to the window. Miner's private office, a mostly glass-enclosed penthouse, occupied the entire seventy-second floor of the PharmaForce Buenos Aires headquarters. "Grandyn has been spotted or pursued in Alaska, North Carolina, Oregon, Colorado, New Mexico, Russia, Germany, and in many parts of the Amazon. We know those aren't all him, but why are you so certain he's down here somewhere?"

"I'm not, but even the Imps agree that he's got the highest chance of surviving in the Amazon."

Sarlo, surprised by his admission, had been expecting a concrete data point that Miner had been relying on to keep them almost exclusively in the region for all this time. She also didn't like Imps, or "vampires" as she called them, people who had been implanted with DesTIn artificial intelligence systems, but Miner had increasingly relied on them during the past three years, perhaps questioning his own judgment after the Drast event.

"But is his survival more important to him than his cause?" Sarlo asked carefully. "After all, both his parents were eliminated by the AOI."

An android brought in drinks. They each liked citrus, lime for him, orange for her, with bubbles. He'd had a double shot of a caffeine-like stimulant added to his. He'd been up with night-mares again and needed the boost. As usual, the intense dreams were of war. Recently, these terrors had let up a bit and mostly occurred only while sleeping, yet they could hit him anytime. Sarlo thought they were more like visions. Miner didn't want to talk about them.

"Damn that Drast. He concealed the fact that the librarian's wife had been a revolutionary, or we would have been all over that closing. I should have known Deuce was involved. Hell, I wish Drast would talk to me."

"Even if the AOI would let you, and even if Drast would see you, he wouldn't tell you anything, and . . ."

He paced nervously. "What?"

"Could you stop yourself from killing him?"

"I would love to kill that torgon snake, but right now it's a few lines down on my to-do list. Nothing is more important than getting Grandyn." Waiting for her question, after a long pause, he smiled when it didn't come.

Taking his smile as a compliment, she stared silently down on the sixteenth century plaza. At the eastern end the presidential palace, the Casa Rosada, stood clearly visible, and the main balcony from which Eva Peron addressed the crowds seemed to glow in the midday sun. Thinking of the magnetic Evita, Sarlo shivered at the ease at which one person could change history.

"Grandyn can tell us what is going to happen," Miner said, bringing her back from a hundred fifty years of thoughts.

She turned to face him. "Meaning?"

"There are," he hesitated, "prophecies." He could immediately see the doubt on her face. "Keep an open mind." His dark eyebrows raised and he caught her curious brown eyes.

Sarlo was smart enough to know what she didn't know, and always listened before deciding on something. They had been through a lifetime of accomplishments, plots, and world-improving results during the past dozen years. She believed in him, and, in spite of the Drast event, she thought he was never wrong. Still, *prophecies*? That would be the farthest she'd ventured out on the limb with him.

"Prophecies?" she asked skeptically, this time aloud.

"Let me tell you a story that began more than nine centuries ago."

CHAPTER FOUR

The Chief continued speaking, occasionally in several languages, to more than four hundred AOI agents assigned to find Grandyn Happerman. With her razor-short gray hair and abundance of confidence, or was it arrogance, she seemed more like a military general addressing troops.

Normally conferences of this nature were done across the "Field," which might be best described as a descendant of the Internet. It connected all things and nearly everyone on the planet through their INUs, marble-sized supercomputers worn around necks. But the situation had grown so dire that all the agents had been summoned to Portland, a large city in the Oregon Area, part of the Pacyfik region, to hear from the AOI Chief in person.

Portland had been at the center of the storm since the closing of the world's last library, but it was more of a symbolic choice for another reason, at least based on the rumors. Polis Drast, the former AOI head of the Pacyfik region, had been arrested there outside his office. The official report said he'd been killed in the line of duty, but the AOI "silent-talk" said otherwise.

The AOI operated forty-eight prisons for the entire planet. The official Aylantik policy was that crime was unforgivable, and prison was not meant to be a place of reform. Inmates at those institutions were mostly allowed to remain alive for whatever value they might provide the state. If a criminal didn't have anything that could help the AOI, they were usually put to death. Low-level offences were handled with community service, house arrest, and fines. But serious crime meant a one-way trip to an AOI-max. Fortunately, Terik had a few contacts at the AOI prison located on an island off the coast of Vancouver, where he'd heard Drast was being held.

"Recent reports, updated minutes ago," the Chief continued, "show we're closer to Grandyn than perhaps we've ever been before." Terik looked for some kind of emotion on her face but found none. He realized that in his three years of working for her, he had never once seen her smile or heard her laugh, even during the most informal of occasions. "As I speak now, two separate sightings are being investigated. He will be found, and when that time comes, we must be prepared to eradicate his influence."

Terik assumed the Chief was wearing a Retina-synch, which allowed her to access data through what amounted to a micro-contact lens. He discreetly checked his INU and created a vivid holographic virtual monitor known as an AirView, which could be scaled from about the size of an index card to as big as a billboard. With the AirView open, which he made sure to keep small, his fingers quickly shuffled through real-time updates. In less than fifteen seconds he found the ones referred to by the Chief: swarm drones in pursuit of a high-value target in the Amazon, possibly Grandyn Happerman. But as usual, data transmissions from large forests were spotty.

How can no one fix this problem? he wondered, thinking of the regular use of the Field and data to and from the moon and Mars bases, but the Aylantik could not communicate across wilderness areas here on Earth. The second sighting, less surprising, had campers near Mt. Shasta reporting a group of suspected TreeRunners, including one positively identified by several people as Grandyn Happerman.

The agency had long believed Grandyn was still hiding in the vast tracts of forest in the Northwest portion of what used to be the United States. The world, now divided into twenty-four regions running north to south, currently had more forested land than when Europeans first set out to explore the globe six hundred years earlier. Grandyn Happerman had grown up studying and living in the trees. He could be anywhere. Terik wanted to be out there seeing firsthand what they'd found, instead of inside listening to his boss.

"TreeRunners, as you all know, still exist," the Chief said in a formal tone in which Terik detected more than a touch of bitterness. "We have banned the organization so that no more of these parasites will be trained and brainwashed. The AOI has punished thousands of them, but those who escaped, including Grandyn Happerman, are not just in hiding. They are, even now, plotting against the state. The information we've obtained from the brain scans of recent captures show that they, along with other rebel factions, are planning a major attack within the next ninety days."

"Why is Grandyn the key?" an agent asked.

"Did you not review the background material?" the Chief responded in clipped syllables.

"Yes, of course I did," the agent replied, laughing nervously. "It just didn't seem clear."

At the brief sound of his laugh, the Chief reacted as if she'd been slapped. Her head jerked in reflex action. It was so quick that most probably didn't notice, but Terik caught it, wondering if the humorless woman would be up to the pressure that was on its way. He shook his head. This poor dumb agent was going to be doing patrols in the middle of the boreal forest in old Siberia by the end of the day, but Terik had thought the same thing about the file on Grandyn, and suspected many of his fellow agents did as well.

Why did they want him so badly?

"Really?" the Chief asked indignantly, glaring at the agent. "In what way *wasn't* it clear?"

"It appears to center around his parents," the agent replied. "The mother was a lifelong member of PAWN and a historian."

Terik cringed at the reference to the largest of the rebel groups, "PAWN." People Against World Nation had already caused him serious problems, but now, according to AOI analysts, PAWN had joined forces with the TreeRunners and other groups, and were readying to start their long-planned revolution.

The agent continued speaking about Grandyn's parents. "The father, a librarian, stole a few truckloads of *physical* books. Neither seemed particularly powerful enough to threaten the peace, and certainly not the AOI. Then their son, a TreeRunner, joined PAWN at eighteen, allegedly becoming some kind of leader overnight."

Terik noticed the odd color of the sunlight that streamed in from one of the high windows and recognized it as the pink effect of the sound-proof nano shroud in place on the building.

The agent continued. "Although there don't seem to be any facts to support the idea that Grandyn is doing much more than hiding, and he's what, twenty-one now? Why would people follow him?"

"Great leaders are not determined by age," the Chief retorted. "History is filled with young adults who rose to power and changed the world: Augustus Caesar, Joan of Arc, Alexander the Great . . . a cause which people rally around, articulated by a charismatic person, will make that person a leader, no matter the age. Grandyn Happerman has both the cause and the charisma, as well as the pedigree, to lead. But more important than that, he has the skills. By all accounts, he excelled in the TreeRunners to a level not typically seen."

"But Chief, you still have not answered the question. Why is he the key?"

Terik almost laughed. The AOI typically held back information from their agents. Secrecy and distrust were hallmarks of the agency, and this guy was pushing his luck. But still, Terik admired his tenacity and wanted to know the answer, so he was silently rooting for him.

"The revolutionaries, as you might know if you have actually reviewed everything," the Chief replied, trying unsuccessfully to remain patient, "have Munna, their symbolic leader, Chelle Andreas, their tactical commander, and Nelson Wright, the former novelist, as their propagandist. But the man who can lead them into battle, who can employ guerrilla and terrorist tactics and is expert at survival and evasive actions, is Grandyn Happerman."

She scowled at the agent, who still seemed unsatisfied. Terik too, wanted the missing piece, he heard rumors from reliable sources that the librarian might have lived, if that was true, surely Grandyn's father could be used against him. Yet the file had Runit Happerman marked as deceased. He was about to ask, but the Chief made it clear she was finished.

"Now go find Grandyn so we can cut the head off the monster who wants to destroy our peaceful world. Go find the lost Tree-Runner." She swept her eyes across the room and gave her standard closing. "Peace prevails, always."

CHAPTER FIVE

Deuce Lipton listened in on the secure AOI conference. As the world's richest man and the owner of the companies that manufactured much of the technology that enabled the Aylantik's surveillance-state to monitor every breath taken by its happy citizens, he could also claim title to the most powerful man alive. However, Deuce was greatly outnumbered.

The A-Council, a secretive group of the world's elite, actually controlled the Aylantik, and thus the AOI. He, like most, had allies and enemies. Deuce spent considerable time trying to keep the scales tipped toward his friends, or at least in finding a balance.

He had offices around the world, though in recent years he favored those located in the western part of the North American continent. Most of his private workplaces included sophisticated planetariums built into the ceilings. He loved the stars, a trait he shared with his son, Twain. In the background, turned low, another of his passions was playing: Billie Holiday singing "You Better Go Now." Deuce found the old music, particularly Holiday, Bessie Smith, and Louis Armstrong, eased his stress like nothing else. He listened only on vinyl, and had a small and rare collection which he often traveled with. The old players weren't regularly manufactured anymore, but Deuce had them custom-made.

That he remained alive and had kept most of his wealth were testament to something more than alliances, accumulated power, or riches. He owed his continued existence to the enlightening words of his late uncle Cope. *"There is no greater force in the universe than the recognition of the dream and the knowledge that all energy emanates from one source. Whatever name you call it, this thing is best described as love."* That wisdom had guided Deuce during the tumultuous years since the Doneharvest.

His uncle had been a very unusual man, living his life in seclusion among the trees. He'd meditated and contemplated to the point where most would have considered him a mystic, although almost no one knew Cope Lipton had ever lived at all. But Deuce, and his now twenty-nine-year-old son, Twain, had called Uncle Cope "UC." UC had a way of seeing, of knowing things before they happened. The moments that followed his death had been so strange that Deuce still couldn't speak about it, not even with Twain, who had been the only other person present.

As he listened to the AOI Chief chastise the young agent for daring to question the official story about Grandyn Happerman, he worried about more than a revolution, more than the AOI or even the fate of the last remaining physical books in the world. Deuce Lipton, maker of the Eysen INUs, owner of the leading space company, StarFly, and the undisputed king of tech, worried about DesTIn, an artificial intelligence program that far surpassed the collective capacity of all the brains of human history. Technological singularity had been achieved, and the DesTIn network had been, for some years, improving *itself*, and now it had intellectual capacity and capabilities beyond human comprehension.

That frightening singularity event might have occurred fifty years sooner had the Banoff, in which billions had died in plague and war more than seventy years earlier, not interrupted the exponential expansion of many technologies. But now that it had happened and the artificial intelligence superiority existed, Deuce feared it might destroy all he was trying to save before he got the chance to realize his grandfather's vision of a society not run from the limited human perceptions, not interpreted by our five senses, and certainly not one created by machines, but rather originating in a place of awareness and enlightenment.

Blaze Cortez, perhaps the antithesis of the Liptons, had created DesTIn with the seemingly single aim to consolidate power and the world's wealth into his accounts. Deuce, now fifty-five, had known and studied Blaze, who was ten years younger, for decades, and yet couldn't say he really understood him.

The unpredictable man of Spanish descent had traced his origins back to kings, explorers, and conquistadors. He'd helped and hindered each side in the multifaceted conflict. Eight factions vied for control, each looking to be in the strongest position when the standoff inevitably broke into violence. Blaze had a mental roster of the players, arranged alphabetically:

AOI

Creatives

Deuce Lipton (BLAXERs)

Lance Miner (Enforcers)

List Keepers

Munna

PAWN

Rejectionists

Each group had utilized his services and equally been manipulated by Blaze, except perhaps the most secretive of the participants, the List Keepers. Interestingly, the List Keepers might have more in common with Blaze's peculiar genius than any of the other groups. They used information and technology in brilliant and precise ways to shape the world into their vision for it. They, like PAWN, predated the Banoff, yet they were so mysterious that no one could even prove their existence. But eventually, even they had come to Blaze, and he had been all too happy to do them a favor.

Deuce also kept a chart of the parties to the revolution in his primary INU. He used one of Blaze's DesTIn programs to extrapolate the data and variables to predict daily outcomes, and Deuce agreed with Miner that Blaze was key to the outcome because of his intersecting involvement with each of the parties. No one else had true ties to all of them, but Deuce's chart now showed ten groups with his notation on whether or not they wanted war and what alliance they would likely join if war came. Some believed Deuce would side with Aylantik, but that would be impossible for him to do and still pursue his grandfather's vision. It was in his best interests to allow that speculation to float, and although he didn't particularly want war, he didn't believe it was avoidable.

Aylantik

   AOI – peace – willing to kill everyone to get it

   Lance Miner (Enforcers) – peace

Rebels

   Munna – peace

   Creatives – peace

   Deuce Lipton (BLAXERs) – war?

   PAWN – war

   TreeRunners – war

Rejectionists – war
List Keepers – unknown

Wildcards
> *Blaze – unknown*
> *Trapciers (only rumored to exist) – unknown*

The wildcards could go either way, since no one knew anything about the Trapciers and Blaze would probably play both sides until a winner looked likely, at which time he would lean their way. But Deuce believed it would be the lost TreeRunner who would decide the outcome. His supposed ability to find the eight key books and unravel the prophecies was critical to either side, and fortunately the AOI seemed, so far, to be missing that point.

Grandyn's three-year vanishing act, as impressive as it had been, was, according to the DesTIn program, about to come to an end. Few people understood how Grandyn Happerman had been able to hide all that time while being aggressively sought by so many, but Deuce knew the answer.

Only the List Keepers could have saved Grandyn, and that fact gave Deuce his greatest hope for the future.

CHAPTER SIX

The minutes passed in the root hole like dripping sap. Grandyn considered exiting and running the other way, trying to get back to Zaverly. There was room in the tree-base, and climbing up tall kapok trees was one of his many talents, but his injuries would make that extremely difficult and, even if he could, it might endanger her. There could be another wave of swarm drones, or even an AOI platoon of real-life agents, or "grunges," as the rebels were fond of calling them.

The dense forests presented so many problems for the AOI because only DesTIn-enabled equipment could be utilized. Anything normally done over the Field wouldn't work with the forest-blind, a term given to the phenomena of the inability of the Field's to penetrate forested areas. The high tech arsenal typically available to hunt fugitives became useless in the battle against TreeRunners, and specifically in the quest for Grandyn. Swarm drones and grunges were the only options. Neither had proved effective, but in recent weeks the AOI high command had sent in thousands of grunges, newly trained in forest reconnaissance and engagement. There had also been news from PAWN that the AOI had developed a new DesTIn-based detection weapon designed specifically for forest work. The level of DesTIn-based weaponry had been advancing rapidly, the hunt for TreeRunners having fueled the race among manufacturers. DesTIn artificial intelligence programs allowed it to work without the need to communicate with human controllers.

While exploring his options, he heard the sound of cutting wood. Sawdust filtered down on his head as a red light blinked through the tangle of heavy roots and floating particles confirming his fears.

A new piece of AOI hardware had found him, and no path of escape existed.

He'd lost his communicator in the run and couldn't call for help. There wouldn't be time anyway. The only thing remaining to do, in preparation for certain death, was to check his ID chip. Secured into all Aylantik citizens, it detailed a comprehensive profile from parents, date of birth, health and financial records, education and job history, and other data no one even knew about. The chips were managed by the Aylantik Records Circle, and were updated at regular medical visits required by the government, but most people knew everything went straight to the AOI. A chip could be read only by a government reader, but they were all equipped with a quick ID system.

The noise grew louder. The machine had cut to within a meter of him. He swirled the neuro-cap in his mouth, ready to bite.

His eyes were filled with dust as he squeezed the skin on his neck around the chip. They were programmed, in case of emergency or death, to provide name, government number, and emergency contact information. He pressed his. The name Grandyn Happerman, 18346-083 appeared on a tiny virtual monitor, or "AirView," projected out through his skin. The contact had been blank, but in the final seconds before death, he decided to send one last attack against the AOI.

He touched the AirView and filled in the contact line with a series of numbers and letters that only a TreeRunner could decode. His final efforts might or might not prove useful to the revolution, depending on whether the right person ever received the information.

He grabbed a rock twice the size of his fist and readied it. The AOI's attacking machine would be armored, but there was usually a weak spot; a lens, electronics, sensors, something. Even if he were killed before biting the neuro-cap, it would dissolve the instant his body temperature dropped. He clenched the rock and wiped the grainy dust from his eyes.

The menacing, gray-metal-wrapped machine was almost through. He could see the red lights clearly now, like animal eyes. Its cutting blades resembling a shark's jaws, and the hovering heat emitting jets could have been legs. The mechanical monster hummed like ten thousand mosquitoes as it cut through the huge roots.

Will the blades kill me? Or will the on-board laser weapons do it? he wondered. *Either way, this is going to be ugly.*

Thirty-two-hundred-kilometers away, at an air-conditioned AOI command center, a top official monitored the situation. While they still couldn't control equipment inside the forest or manage long-range communications, new technology allowed satellites to monitor movements of the "mechanical monster" over a direct link. The screen showed the exact location of the Collins-HG3, its blade deployed, a target in sight. They might even get an image. But it didn't matter. Based on the information received, a platoon of grunges would be there in less than six minutes.

"Looks like we got lucky," a technician said to the commander.

"Luck? We have thousands of agents deployed in that hellish jungle. I've been increasing the numbers weekly for months." He glared at his subordinate. "*I* made this torgon luck." His frustration came from not being able to see the action, and because his superiors had threatened his career rested with Grandyn Happerman. He was the fifth AOI official to head the search in three years. The other four were now "retired."

"Do we have any idea what it's cutting through?" he asked.

"No," the technician answered dryly. "At the risk of stating the obvious, based on his location, it's probably a tree or trees . . . wait, it just stopped."

"Stopped? What the hell is it doing?"

"Defending itself."

CHAPTER SEVEN

After the Chief's speech, Terik skipped a summary presentation and took a detour before going back on official duty. The Flo-wing, a super-fast combination helicopter/plane, delivered Terik to the AOI prison, off the coast of Vancouver, in twenty minutes.

Hilton Prison seemed a throwback to Alcatraz, a pre-Banoff penitentiary he'd once read about. The cold stone buildings were built from the same rock that the waves pounded against on the inhospitable shores of the six-point-thirty-square-kilometer island. Five guard towers climbed from a crisscross of walls and tangles of razor-wire, left over from the days when automated electro-pulse weapons and sonic-sensors made escape impossible. No inmate had successfully broken out of an AOI prison in more than five decades.

Instead of taking a LEV, he walked the short distance from the landing pad, trying to decide how far he was willing to bend the rules to get what he needed. An old friend greeted him at the first gate. "Good to see you, Osc," Terik said, grabbing his friend's upper arm in a friendly greeting.

Osc had always looked like a Swedish ski champion to Terik, and had, in fact, skied on the Pacyfik amateur team in the Aylantik

Games. The two had met in the AOI training academy and hit it off as if they'd known each other forever. Osc had originally been assigned, along with Terik, to hunt Grandyn, but at the last minute he'd been switched to the very boring Hilton Prison with the promise of a transfer after a year.

It had been almost eighteen months.

"Is he here?" Terik asked, absently rotating his AOI pin.

"Yeah, his name's changed to Lex Evren," Osc said. A flock of seagulls flew low and the two men looked at each other, wondering if they were monitoring-mimic-drones, or just birds. "You really don't want to go through channels?"

"No. As I said in my message, my supervisor has made it clear that Drast was killed. The AOI's veil of secrecy on this one is hung from the top. I think only a handful know he's alive."

"And you really think it's worth risking your career to talk to him?"

"He was there at the start, working both sides, and he knew where Grandyn was. If he's ready to talk, I want to hear it first. Imagine my career if he tells me all that he knows."

"And why would he? The top brass has been in here at least forty times since I got transferred and he hasn't told them a torgon thing. And he's somehow beating brain scans. It's got them terrified."

"I'm going to play it differently. I've lived and breathed this case since the training academy. I know stuff most of the agents don't." Terik smiled. "I'm going to offer Mr. Evren something no one else has before."

"What?"

"Can you get me in?"

"I think I can get you and him in the same room for about eight minutes. Will that be enough?"

Terik nodded. "It'll have to be. Thanks."

"The visit will be monitored, but humans won't review it for weeks."

"I'm not worried about that," he said, flashing a silver button.

"Is that . . . ?"

"Yeah, a Whistler XTC. It'll block any monitoring."

Osc looked at him with raised eyebrows.

"Sometimes I need to interrogate someone without worrying about what my superiors are going to think."

Osc nodded. "So what are you going to offer Evren?"

"That I can save who he cares most about."

"Grandyn?"

"No, he doesn't care about Grandyn. He cares about Chelle Andreas."

"That's dangerous stuff."

"He loves her."

"And you can save her?"

"No, but that doesn't make a difference. All that matters is that he thinks I can."

"Why would he believe that?"

"Because I know what to say, and because he's locked up in here and I'm an AOI agent with high clearances, assigned to one of the most important cases, only a step away from Chelle Andreas, and I'm free to roam the world in pursuit of Grandyn Happerman."

"You're a gutsy guy, Ander. Hope you can pull it off without getting sent here yourself."

CHAPTER EIGHT

The roots collapsed down on him amidst a shower of dirt and sawdust. Somehow, while being buried alive, he managed to hurl the rock against the mechanical monster. It hit the reinforced side with a scraping clang. His last chance missed sensors, lenses, and anything else that might have been sensitive enough to slow the killing machine. The rock came back down in the continuing falling storm and hit him like a forceful kick to his stomach. He didn't need his health sensors to tell him another rib had cracked.

It's over, he thought, positioning the neuro-cap between his teeth. Just as he was about to bite down on the deadly pill, Zaverly's voice cut through the noise and grit.

"Grandyn! We're here," Zaverly screamed, her voice desperate. "Grandyn!?"

The AOI attacker spun and fired, and a battle played out in a fog of rubble and chaos. The metal monster flew a couple of meters above the root hole, engaging his would-be rescuers. He watched as it raged synthetic artillery and lasers against them for almost two minutes. Shots volleyed back and forth. Wood was exploding everywhere, dirt and rubble pouring in, jagged, like a rain of daggers.

"Get out Grandyn!" Zaverly shouted above the din of trouble. "Can you move?"

"I think so," he moaned, totally unsure as he began shifting inside his likely grave, feeling drugged and stuck in a steamy sludge.

The machine exploded above, showering more lethal debris. One long metal piece gashed his leg while another, glowing hot, burned his arm. Zaverly swooped in on an Airslider, a jet-propelled scooter equipped with laser munitions. "Come on Grandyn, you're not dead yet!" she said, clawing through the dirt and splintered roots, then pulling him roughly on board.

"Torgon!" he cried out.

"A 'thank you' might be more appropriate," she said, cracking her knuckles, a habit that always annoyed him. "Sorry there wasn't time for a stretcher and painkillers Grandyn. The grunges are minutes behind." As if to punctuate her point, flames shot above their heads. "Damn, they're scorching us!"

With nowhere else to go, she steered the Airslider up through the fire. The dangerous maneuver into the burning heat took their breath. The flames grabbed at them and, with no protection on their upper bodies, their skin melted and burned, but they were clear for the moment. Zaverly banked the Airslider unhesitatingly into narrow openings between thick and twisting trees. It was one of the reasons she'd drawn the Grandyn assignment. She had no fear.

The other TreeRunners who had helped locate him and fight the machine were now fiercely battling with an AOI platoon, six rebels on Airsliders against thirty heavily armed agents. The AOI weapons were the latest tech, and the only hope the rebels had was that their opponents were on foot. Zaverly knew what would happen, and she desperately wanted to go back and help. In her opinion, saving Grandyn was not worth the loss, but she believed in the revolution enough to follow orders, even when it made her sick.

Forty minutes later they were in an underground bunker receiving medical attention along with water and rations. "Grandyn, you're inhaling that stuff. Slow down," she said.

"I was dead. What am I doing here?"

"I wish I knew."

Another TreeRunner came in and reported that all six they'd left battling the AOI platoon had been killed.

"Torgon!" Zaverly looked at him. "Will you be able to sleep tonight Grandyn?" she asked, shaking her head. "What *are* you doing here?"

"The only good news," the other TreeRunner said, ignoring the tension. "Two AOI agents survived, and our snipers picked them off from twenty meters up in a tree as they tried to evacuate."

"Damn it Grandyn, why do they let you out of the bunker?" Zaverly said, as if she hadn't heard the "good" news. "You're a torgon death magnet."

He looked down, unable to tell her that his guilt and outrage exceeded hers. But as much as he liked Zaverly and was grateful for what she'd done on this and many other days, he could not tell her his secret.

When the technician told the AOI commander that the Collins-HG3 had been destroyed, he began to prepare his resignation. An hour later, before he'd been able to submit it, word came of the full loss of life and his INU lit up with a zoom from the AOI Chief.

"Terrible day for the families of our fallen," she said bitterly.

"Yes, Ma'am."

"But I'm convinced this was him. The rebels responded too fast. They fought too hard and had too many assets in place to protect him. Congratulations, Commander. I know you're fighting blind, but you've done the impossible: you found Grandyn in spite of our handicaps in the jungle. You now have my full authorization of redeployment and resource pull. Finish what you started. Bring me Grandyn dead or alive, but I *must* have his body."

CHAPTER NINE

Nelson Wright looked at his beautiful sister as a concerned older brother. Chelle, the rebel leader, looked thin, and much older than when he had seen her two years ago.

"I look that bad?" she asked, catching his worried stare.

"Yeah. You appear more like our grandmother than my sister." Nelson, a simple, eccentric novelist, had been one of those most responsible for the current state of the world.

Three years earlier, he'd been the mastermind behind stealing the last physical books before the AOI destroyed them. Ever since, and unbeknownst to most of its citizens, the utopian Aylantik society where everyone had a job, food, free and comprehensive healthcare and access to the Field with its unlimited entertainment options, had teetered on the brink of a worldwide rebellion that would end seventy years of peace and shake the accepted view of history. Nelson, believing one should be suspicious of perfection created by anything other than nature, actually wore eyeglasses to protest the Aylantik Health Circle's policies providing perfect teeth, skin, and vision.

"I'm sure I don't look good either," he said.

"You never do," Chelle responded with a quick smile and a

tone that sounded as if she wanted to laugh but couldn't. Dappled light came through high branches as they walked the narrow trail in a safe section of forest in the central California Area mountains.

"No, I don't," he said, sipping from a flask. Nelson, a gifted and bestselling author, had scripted much of the struggle, the search for truth, and had even left a veiled revolutionary trail to follow in his published works. But more than that, the often drunk and always pastry-eating, scruffy, teddy bear of a man, had influenced the participants, on all sides.

Apart from Chelle, he personally knew Deuce Lipton and Blaze Cortez, and counted all three Happermans as family. He'd also become a confidant of Munna, the hundred and thirty-three year-old symbol of the revolution. He may not have yet met Lance Miner and the AOI Chief, but they had both read all of his books, even some unpublished ones. For all his importance, everything he'd seen and done, it was the recent year he'd spent with the late Cope Lipton living among the redwoods that had shaped him the most. Nelson Wright now stood as a changed man from the one who fanned the flames in the early days of the struggle.

"But after my year in the wilderness with Cope, I look better on the inside."

"Your year in the wilderness, that always strikes me as funny. We all live in the woods most of the time. It's our best chance for staying alive."

"I know, but it was different, *very* different, with Cope. I wish you understood the magic."

"Do you?"

"No, but I accept it. More than that, I rejoice in it."

"What about Twain?" Deuce's son had also lived with Cope during his great uncle's final year.

"He was impacted differently, and he's still out there following Cope's path."

"I wonder what Deuce thinks of that."

"The Liptons are a special lot," Nelson said. "I expect he knew

Twain would follow Cope, even before he was born."

But Nelson, while documenting the wisdom and magic of the man they called UC, was still trying to figure it all out. He'd poured much of it into new writings, many of which had been snuck onto the Field, hoping to influence a new legion of thinkers and to document the hidden history buried by those who feared it. And to that end, Nelson had taken to starting esoteric debates and long, meandering, intellectual, spiritual-infused conversations with everyone he encountered. It was a vain effort to recapture his talks with Cope, for after his passing, the void cut large within Nelson's world.

"Why did you come Nelson?" Chelle asked. "You know it's not safe."

Nelson lit a bac and sat on a fallen tree. "You know why."

"AOI killed two more TreeRunners today," Chelle said.

"Grandyn?" Nelson asked, filled with panic.

"No, but we still can't find him." She fanned the smoke away. "Like I've said a hundred times, if we can't find him and we're his friends, then the AOI isn't going to find him."

"I want the books."

"They have hundreds hunting him," Chelle said, ignoring her brother's request. "Grandyn needs to come in and let us protect him."

"Like we protected his parents?" Nelson asked, knowing that mentioning Harper and Runit Happerman would disturb Chelle.

"Cheap shot, big brother," Chelle said angrily. "Those were different days! A-And you know damn well Harper wasn't under our protection," she stuttered. "And Runit was a casualty of the Doneharvest."

Nelson knew Chelle had loved Grandyn's father, and she knew he'd loved Grandyn's mother. "We both have a lot of regrets from those times," he said. "Especially at the end with the library. Runit and I never put things right. I owe him the protection of his son and those books."

"*We* owe him," Chelle said. Her voice reflected the strain of trying to keep those promises when Grandyn didn't want their protection. In the course and confusion of the early days of the Doneharvest, the books had been scattered. "But you know how complicated it all became after Runit . . ."

Her thoughts lingered back three years as if it had been a thousand. So much had happened since then, but that burning, bloody gash in her heart, still noisy and toxic, made it seem like yesterday.

In the months following Runit's disappearance, the AOI's Doneharvest crackdown resulted in thousands of arrests and executions. Chelle and Grandyn had been first among them, winding up in AOI custody, but Polis Drast, then head of the Pacyfik region, had released them. As one of the most powerful people in the Aylantik government, he'd been playing a dangerous game. Hand-chosen and backed by Lance Miner to be the next World Premier, Drast was only months away from achieving that goal when the AOI figured out his plot. Drast had been planning to use his position as World Premier to disassemble the AOI and undo the restrictive policies of the Aylantik.

"Any word on Drast?" Nelson asked quietly.

"Just rumors."

Chelle recalled the time when she met Polis Drast in college, she a student and he a young professor. The two shared a common philosophy for reform and would often talk late into the night. Nelson's early writings, as well as those of authors he'd brought to their attention, had heavily influenced them. Drast had been the more ideological of the two. He thought the government too restrictive, that the AOI was more brutal than even Nazi Germany's Gestapo.

"I still see him the way he was back in school. Do you remember his passion?"

"Yeah, he was a great speaker," Nelson said. "I always thought he was going to get you all arrested."

"A close friend back then said that I was an extremist by any government definition, but Polis was an extremist by any extremist definition."

"That's true. But you both put it on the line, and once you met Beale Andreas the team was unstoppable," Nelson said. "But Beale is dead and Polis is too, or he's rotting in an AOI prison wishing he was."

"You know, Polis never got over my marrying Beale."

"I know."

"Polis had already proposed."

"I know."

"I told him I wasn't the marrying kind, but he thought it was because he was older than me. It wasn't that either. I didn't care about his age. The truth is, I was afraid of him. He had so much torgon passion."

Their ideological debates might have all gone the way of late night college talks had a recruiter not found them. At the time PAWN, enjoying a lax period in government monitoring, had begun aggressively recruiting. It didn't take long for the underground to find Polis Drast and his star pupil, Chelle Wright. Soon the recruiter introduced them, and the still relatively unknown author Nelson Wright, to members who enlightened them further on the crimes of Aylantik. Eventually the three of them learned enough that their initial feelings of discontent were replaced with a burning desire to take down the government.

Over many months they developed a loose plan, independent of PAWN. They took into account the three paths to power. Chelle would enter the business and financial world, while Drast would go into law enforcement and politics, and Nelson would use his talent and flare for writing to influence greater numbers. If they succeeded, they would have a grip on all aspects of the requirements for revolution – rebels, money, and military.

They were young, she recalled, and hadn't a clue what they were up against.

CHAPTER TEN

"There was a man named Clastier," Miner said to Sarlo as he paced the Jatoba-wood floor of his Buenos Aires penthouse office. He liked the sound his expensive shoes, crafted from leather-like Tekfrabrik, made when he walked on it, like a soft click. "Before him, Saint Malachy, an Archbishop in the old Catholic Church, born a thousand years ago, saw things in the future that later came to be. And there have been others."

Sarlo, sensing a long monologue, sat in one of the ultra comfortable tru-chairs, which not only conformed perfectly to the sitter's anatomy, but delivered gentle massage and acupressure while harvesting body heat for energy.

"You see, the Banoff plague and war had been prophesized centuries ago," he continued. "But none were as specific and accurate as Clastier's."

"Wait, if the Banoff had been predicted, why couldn't it be stopped?" Sarlo asked.

"There were those who prophesized about World War II and assassinations of powerful leaders. Knowing something might happen is one thing, believing it is another, and quite different altogether is actually doing something about it. Sometimes it's a matter of faith, and then there's the issue of SDE phenomenon, meaning a suppressed destiny always expands."

Sarlo stared at her boss, a man she believed she knew extremely well. "When did you get so metaphysical?"

"It isn't metaphysics, it's by any means necessary," Miner said, staring back. "There cannot be a war." He paused and stared out the window for half a minute. "But if war does come... we *must* win."

It was the first time she'd ever heard him admit that war might be unavoidable. "Did you get this from the Imps?"

Sarlo had been impressed with the knowledge of the group of four Imps Miner had made a habit of consulting. He'd even put them on the payroll. But she didn't trust them. Something about their being part human and part machine made her uncomfortable.

"The same Imp who told us about Deuce Lipton's uncle."

"But we never found him, we never—"

"We might not have found Cope Lipton, but he was real. You know we intercepted that conversation between Deuce's son and daughter talking about him, and there are the references in Nelson Wright's unpublished work."

"But none of that is verified. It could all be one of Deuce's counterintelligence moves."

"Yes, it could. But it's not. What if the future is there to be known?"

"What is this? A science fiction novel? One of the burned books from Portland that caused us so much trouble?"

"That's just it. They saved the books."

"I know the librarian, his son Grandyn, Chelle Andreas, and her brother, that author Nelson Wright, got fifty or sixty thousand books out before the AOI crew got in there to do the burn, but what are you saying?"

"I'm trying to tell you that hundreds of years ago people prophesized, *accurately*, about the Banoff and other matters . . .

including the rise of Aylantik, the Doneharvest, and a revolution."

Sarlo studied him as she rose from the tru-chair. Obviously he believed the unbelievable things he was telling her. "A revolution?" She moved her hands in a quick gesture and a needle beam of light appeared. The air temperature in modern buildings was optimized to the body temperature of the occupants, but Sarlo liked it a tad warmer and quickly made the adjustment by touching the light.

"Yes. In our time. A revolution that is about to occur, and if we can find the prophecies we will know how to win."

"And that's what the librarian was really trying to save?"

"It doesn't matter what he was trying to do, but yes, he probably thought that was all it was about. But Deuce Lipton knew because of his Uncle Cope, and he knew because his grandfather, Booker Lipton, knew about the prophecies."

"Wait, back up." She touched her INU and an AirView came to life between them. "You're telling me that Booker Lipton who was, back then, the wealthiest man in the world, had these prophecies that predicted the Banoff, and did *nothing* to prevent it?"

Booker's photo appeared in the air. Below him, a photo of Deuce's father, Spencer Lipton, and next to him a blank silhouette labeled Cope Lipton. Below Spencer was a photo of Deuce, and below him Twain and Tycen Lipton. Next to the family tree was a similar chart showing the known holdings of Deuce. It was enormous, representing major corporations in key industries, and even in the vastness of what it showed, they both knew it was incomplete, a fact that constantly infuriated Miner.

"I don't know what Booker Lipton knew about the Banoff," Miner said. "I hardly see why that matters now. He's long dead, and so are his sons."

"Booker was lost at sea in 2060, but no body was ever recovered," Sarlo said.

"Are you being serious? Are you trying to imply that Booker is still alive?" Miner asked incredulously. "Booker was born in 1975, he'd be one-hundred-twenty-eight years old. Impossible!"

"And how old is Munna?" Sarlo asked, raising her eyebrows. "I'll save you the math. Munna is reportedly between one hundred thirty-three and one hundred thirty five."

"We don't have time for this fanciful talk."

"Really? Then please, let's continue the conversation about prophecies and saints."

He couldn't help but laugh. "Hell, I don't know what I believe, Sarlo. But I know there are things in this world we can't explain. Like how could Munna live to be so old? How come the Field can't penetrate into any large forest? How the hell did the universe begin?"

"Big Bang," she answered as a troop of at least thirty AOI agents with jet packs flew past the building. The formation was more than a hundred meters from their windows, and a common sight, but no one really liked it. Drone flyovers happened so often that most people didn't even notice them.

"And before the Bang?"

"Have you read the prophecies?" she asked, trying to rein in their winged conversation.

"No."

"How do you know they exist?"

"The Imps, and not just them. I have countless intercepts going back to the days immediately following the librarian's looting of the books, when he was urged by Deuce to search for them. And even . . . " He hesitated.

"What?"

"They predicted the Eysen."

"So? It's a huge invention." Sarlo, knowing the Eysen-INU to be the most revolutionary object ever invented by humans, wasn't surprised.

"They predict its *discovery*, not its invention."

"What? Booker Lipton invented the Eysen."

"No. He *found* it."

"Where?" She couldn't believe how strange this conversation had become.

"I don't know, but he found it and reverse-engineered it."

"This is some sort of fairytale made up by the Imps at the direction of Deuce."

"I don't think so. The prophecies are said to have come from Eysens."

She scoffed, walked around the room, stopped at the window, and then whirled back around to face her boss. "If that's true, then we've got a bigger problem than PAWN and the so-called prophecies."

"What could be bigger?" Miner asked.

"If the prophecies came from an Eysen that Booker didn't invent, then his grandson, Deuce, may have that Eysen. If he does, then he already knows the future."

CHAPTER ELEVEN

Inmate Evren entered the room and looked at Terik with total disinterest.

"I'm AOI agent Ander Terik. I have a few questions for you, Mr. Evren."

"I was napping."

"Sorry to bother you, Mr. Drast," Terik said.

The use of his real name got his attention. In all the time he had been there, the AOI had sent eleven different agents to harass and interrogate him on dozens of different occasions, but this was the first time anyone had ever addressed him by anything other than Lex Evren, or "dirt bag," or "good-for-nothing-treasonous-bastard," or some other equally unpleasant term of endearment. It was also the first time he'd ever seen an agent so young.

"New tactic?" Evren/Drast asked.

Terik held up his Whistler.

Drast nodded knowingly and looked around suspiciously.

"I need your help," Terik said quietly.

"You need *my* help?" Drast asked. "Are *you* in hell? Are *you* in an AOI prison? Because if you aren't in one of those synonymous places, then you don't get to ask for help because freedom, by its very nature, affords endless opportunity and limitless possibilities. Prison, on the other hand, steals everything!" He looked into Terik's eyes with steely penetration.

The outburst surprised Terik. "I don't have much time," he said firmly.

Drast laughed. "You don't have much time. Oh, the irony. The torgon irony."

"I need to know if you still have access to your data?"

"My data?"

"It was reported that all your data was destroyed when you died." Terik gave Drast a hard look, as an attorney might do while trying to lead a witness on the stand. "Was it?"

Drast glanced at the Whistler. "Do your superiors know you're here?"

"No." He subconsciously rubbed a thumb over the gold AOI emblem on his Tekfabrik shirt.

"You're a fool." He shook his head and got up, but then sat back down. "Why are you here?"

"I want your data. Specifically, everything you have on Grandyn Happerman."

Drast laughed again. "My, oh my." He rubbed his hands down his cheeks. "Trying to be a hero are you, agent Terik?"

"Can you help?"

"Why do you think I would help you with something like that? That is crazy, and contrary to what my former AOI colleagues might think of me, I'm a careful man. Do you know I was going to be the next World Premier? Do you think that kind of thing happens by accident?"

"Look Drast, I'm short on time. Tell me what you want."

"Is this the AOI asking? Or some reckless and cocky young man?"

"Take your pick."

"Why don't you tell me what I want," Drast said, looking into Terik's eyes.

Without dropping his gaze Terik whispered. "Chelle Andreas. You want Chelle Andreas."

Drast nodded slowly, but didn't speak for at least twenty seconds, never taking his eyes off Terik. "And how can you give me Chelle Andreas?"

"Well, obviously I cannot bring her here to you, but I can get a message to her, and from her back to you."

"Careful, boy. You're talking treason."

"The message would have to be non-conflict-related. Strictly personal. I would read it and her reply."

"Do you know where she is?"

"Yes," Terik lied, he hoped convincingly enough.

Drast thought for a moment and then smiled. "Messages," he said.

"What?"

"Not one message, but messages, plural, as in a continued correspondence."

"No way."

"No deal then."

"Even one exchange would be incredibly risky."

"Well then, go shake in a corner somewhere, but if you've got any balls, boy, then cut the deal. Get what you want and retire a hero."

Terik looked at his INU. He had just over a minute left. "How many messages?"

"I want a dialog with Chelle. As much as I'd like to know she's okay, and for her to know the same about me. That's just not enough for what you're asking. But an on-going conversation with her, that might be worth the treasure you seek. That might be worth the private files I can give you on Grandyn Happerman."

"*And* the related parties," Terik added.

"You can have the three Happermans and the TreeRunners. You shouldn't need more than that."

Terik saw his seconds ticking away. "I want Nelson Wright and Vida Mondragon," he said.

Drast stroked his chin. "Fair enough. Come back tomorrow and I'll give you the first message to Chelle and tell you how to access the first of the data files."

"The first?"

"You want six data files. I'm not giving them all to you at once. I want to be sure the messages get out and back in first. I want to be sure you really can reach Chelle."

"No. You're in no position to bargain. You give me the message with the six data files. You have my word I'll get the message to her."

"You're wrong. I *am* in a position. You want what I have far more than I want your services."

"I don't think so."

"Try me."

"With all due respect Drast, the Chief may decide to execute you at any time. I can't risk everything I'm risking and then have you turn up dead. It could just as easily be that they transfer you to another prison that I can't access."

"Don't worry, agent." He said the last word as if spitting it in two hard syllables. "They aren't going to kill me until they're sure I can't hurt them."

Osc came to the door and gave a firm out-of-there signal.

"Okay. I'll be back tomorrow."

"Excellent," Drast said. "Now you be careful. And remember, making a deal with the devil is never what it seems."

CHAPTER TWELVE

Chelle recalled the feeling she had one day when she, Drast, and Nelson were attending a secret PAWN rally in Vermont, the autumn after she graduated.

"Nelson, do you remember that October in Dorset?"

"Sure, why?"

"It felt like anything was possible. Like we could really change the world."

"And we have."

"Well so far all we've done is make a mess of it." She thought of the disastrous fates of Beale, Runit, Polis, and of all the others who'd already died in the quiet rebellion. "But I believe we're right, and we can still prevail."

"Peace prevails, always," Nelson said shrilly, mocking the Aylantik's motto.

"But according to Munna and Cope Lipton, what I felt back in Dorset was destiny."

"According to UC, destiny is a multi-layered force, always changing. In some ways your true destiny is every conceivable thing that could happen to you during the course of a lifetime." He paused and looked at her, seeing the new lines of age in her face, thinking about how she'd been as a girl, following him around, asking questions, demanding things be done a certain way. "But it most often is the thing we're passionate about. Or at least, that is the vehicle in which we travel to our destiny. For me, it's writing."

"And mine?"

"I'd have to say it is your sense of justice. That is your vehicle."

She nodded, as if satisfied with that assessment. "And my destiny?"

"To help right the greatest wrong ever wrought."

"I hope you're right."

The years since college and that sense of justice had been hard on Chelle. After finding and marrying Beale Andreas, a man who shared her passions and dreams and had his own brilliance, he became the first casualty within their circle. Suddenly, reality crashed in on their private conspiracy, making everything more personal, more dangerous, and victory more essential.

Beale Andreas had grown rich and powerful as a private banker and dealmaker to the elite. In the beginning, they never could have imagined the fortune he'd amass, the success that never swayed or deterred the couple from their mission. If anything, the vast wealth made them more determined because they knew where the easy funds had come from – the manipulation and exploitation of the masses. But along the way, Beale discovered too many secrets held by the powerful super-rich, and one of them got him noticed by the AOI, who did what they always did when there was even a hint of a threat. They eliminated him.

Drast too rose to unimagined heights, climbing quickly through the ranks of the AOI, so that by the time of Beale's assassination, Drast had been made Pacyfik Head and was able to protect Chelle, but not their wealth. Just as he had erased their connection from their college days, Drast could only save Chelle by making sure she was severed from all Beale's files, accounts, and data. Her sense of purpose and anger intensified as she became completely immersed in the revolution and took on more and more at PAWN. Drast did his best to reduce the level of her security risk and used his influence to keep her far lower on watch lists than she otherwise would have been.

Drast had become so good at keeping them all under the radar that when the AOI Chief finally caught onto him, his arrest came as a great shock. Although he had prepared well for such an eventuality, he didn't expect it. Even the day before they came for him, he'd been working on the agenda he would implement once elected World Premier. He seemed to have the confidence of Lance Miner right up to the end, and was only months away from "ruling the world" when the shock of his disappearance had disrupted the entire revolution. Among the few that knew the events were related, some suspected Blaze Cortez had been the one to discover Drast's duplicity and gave evidence to the AOI Chief. Chelle always believed it had been their own mistake, thinking something must have slipped through during the Doneharvest that gave them away.

"And what of Polis's destiny?" Chelle continued her questions to Nelson. A gray fox sauntered across the trail twenty meters ahead of them, checking out the strange people not usually found in this part of the forest. It studied them for so long that Chelle worried it might be a monitoring-mimic-drone.

"He has had the heaviest load to bear," Nelson said. "It is not easy to live a double life, and at the levels of power he was dealing with . . ."

"Life and death, every day," Chelle agreed, thinking back on their once grand plans and how close they'd come.

Just before the Doneharvest, they were weeks from bringing the revolution into the open. The books were the catalyst, and once safe the rebellion would explode with its own momentum. Some of the rebels, including Chelle, acted recklessly in those heady days of all-or-nothing stakes. They had underestimated the AOI's response, believing that Drast would be able to temper any

push-back from his high office. But the AOI Chief acted outside
the normal bounds of established agency protocol and made unex-
pected unilateral decisions. She was a tough woman who trusted
her instincts more than any INU or DesTIn-generated report. At
the time it was unlikely she had reason to distrust Drast, but she
might simply have thought him not up to the monumental task of
putting down the first major uprising in the world-nation's
seventy-five years.

The Doneharvest had been brutal, without regard for public
opinion or consequences. The AOI had crushed every flicker of
discontent. They burned and killed and took few prisoners. They
were fully authorized by the A-Council to overstep and encouraged to err on the side of abuse of power. It got even worse after
Drast's arrest a year into the devastation, and no one seemed sure
if he was still alive. The official story was he'd been killed in the
line of duty, but Deuce and PAWN had separately verified that
he'd actually been arrested. Beyond that, the stories ranged from
execution to imprisonment, no one could get a straight story.

Chelle had spent the intervening two years searching for
answers to what happened to the men she'd loved. After losing
her first love, Beale, and Runit likely dead, she clung to the hope
that Drast, the only other man she'd ever shared her bed with,
would be found alive. If so, she'd find a way to free him. It seemed
that searching was all she did, but not just for Drast. Nelson had
heard whispers that Runit had survived, but Chelle had seen him
that day, his body so battered, and could not believe he lived more
than a few minutes after the siege. As much as she would have
liked to, she could not accept that Runit might still be alive.

Grandyn was another mystery of the Doneharvest, and then
there were Runit's books. Suddenly everyone wanted them. Deuce
and Miner both had competing teams searching, as did PAWN,
and it was unclear if the AOI, which had reportedly discovered
and destroyed the books, was still looking for more. The AOI burn
and subsequent round up of the stolen books had happened under

Drast's watch, so there was a question of how many, if any, were actually destroyed.

"We have to find Grandyn. It's all going to happen soon, and I don't want him out there alone when the blood starts spilling," Chelle said. "You've got to talk to Deuce."

"I'm sure he's had people searching."

"Screw searching. Tell him to *find* him."

"Deuce doesn't operate quite as freely as he once did."

"I know that, but the man has satellites. He can find my missing bracelet from thirty thousand meters above the earth, he can find a lost TreeRunner."

Nelson hadn't told her about everything he'd learned from the year he'd spent with Cope Lipton. Cope had shared more than just existential knowledge and mystical wisdom. Nelson had gleaned things from the prophecies which made it clear that they needed Grandyn for much more than to keep him safe. They needed him to win the revolution.

CHAPTER THIRTEEN

Grandyn took a deep breath. He'd needed to do what he was about to do for a while, but with each passing day, with the urgency of the gathering tensions and the desperate searches, it became harder for him to even think about doing it. At the same time, every day it became more necessary. Sitting in an empty bedroom of a rundown house on a secluded street, he pushed the button.

The zoom connected in audio-only mode. Infinite-encryption worked on video as well, but Grandyn liked to be what he called "drastically cautious." He'd learned to manage paranoia as an asset. Grandyn didn't speak at first. Hearing Nelson's voice, after so long, reminded him of all that he'd lost. Worn-out words of his dad's floated into his memory, like every time he'd quote dead authors to make his point. Grandyn smiled and almost laughed.

Finally, just as Nelson was about to give up, he spoke. "Nelson, it's me."

Now it was Nelson's turn at silence, and then he almost whispered, "Is it true?"

"I've been drunk for about a week now, and I thought it might sober me up to sit in a library," Grandyn said.

"It is you!" Nelson exclaimed, recognizing the line from *The Great Gatsby*. "Shoot, Grandyn, it's good to hear from you. I've been half afraid you really were dead."

"I can't say I haven't thought about it a thousand times. There's been no word of my father so . . . "

"I know, but some say he lived."

"And I'll keep searching. But if he's dead, and if I knew my parents existed somewhere beyond this world, and if I could get there, I would happily leave this lie we call life. But I don't know either of those things, so all that's left for me is tearing down the Aylantik facades and to find those maggots responsible. And I will find them, and then I'm going to kill them." Grandyn surprised himself. He usually tried for more control, but Nelson was perhaps now the one person on earth who knew him so well, their history was a shared one. They spoke the same memories.

"Isn't it funny? You want to make them pay and they have all the riches that have ever been," Nelson said, as he sat in the back of a LEV van, one of many PAWN had outfitted to move key members around.

"They'll pay with more than gold."

"I live for that day," Nelson said excitedly, but then softened his tone. "Listen to me, Grandyn. If your dad didn't make it, then I believe he and your mom do exist in another dimension, and I also think it is possible to reach it."

"O-kay," Grandyn said slowly.

"I know it sounds crazy, but I'm writing a book about all this wild stuff. About an amazing mystic I spent a year with. You wouldn't believe what this guy showed me! And now I'm with Munna. I'm writing about her too. You've got to see all this."

Grandyn knew Nelson to be "out there," always searching for a hidden truth, always pushing for possibilities, but he didn't need another distraction, especially one that sounded like a fantasy. "I'd love to hear more about it sometime, but I'm more concerned with the Aylantik right now. Even if what you say is true, they won't allow those topics to be explored, let alone published."

"You're right about that. They've done so much damage, far beyond their mass killings. It's like Munna says, If they'd only put all the energy and resources they've used to control and retain power into studying the mind and the possibilities of its connection to the universe, we'd all be our own wildest dreams."

Grandyn had no time for metaphysical or philosophical discussions and quickly changed the subject. "The TreeRunners have been victims of the mass killings. The AOI is trying to exterminate us, and they're getting damned close to doing it."

"I know. I'm sorry."

"It's my fault."

"That's not true."

"Oh, it is so beyond true."

"Where are you? We're in Idaho Area. It's safe here. Can you come?" Nelson asked. He battled his worry for Grandyn every day, along with drink and other destructive habits, but Nelson had long been infatuated with worry. His writer's mind played life like a chess match, always seeing many moves ahead. "I miss you."

"I miss you too. But traveling isn't easy these days, as you know."

"I can arrange it," Nelson said. "Chelle is here. After two years of making sure we were not in the same place, she has come."

"Why? It's too dangerous. Especially this close to the Exchange."

The "Exchange" was the code word for the second start of the revolution. It had actually begun back when the books were taken from the last library, but the AOI had successfully initiated the Doneharvest, which wiped out enough of PAWN's infrastructure and membership to halt the revolution before it could even really begin. After three years of learning how to endure during the Doneharvest era though, they had built a coalition of Creatives, Rejectionists, TreeRunners, and others, ready to go again. Another big difference this time was that they had secured the full support and financial backing of Deuce Lipton.

"She needed to see Munna in person. They've never really gotten along. I mean, they respect each other, but . . . well, it's a long story. But my relationship with Munna is helping."

"To tell you the truth, Parker isn't a big fan of Chelle either," Grandyn said, speaking of the woman who headed the TreeRunners. "But she and Chelle are actually a lot alike. Strong women leading male-dominated groups. They've each got great strategic minds and—"

"They both lost their husbands to the cause," Nelson finished.

"Yeah," Grandyn said, thinking of his dad and how much he had loved Chelle. "How is she?"

"Actually this is all taking its toll on her. It would do her good to see you. The connection to your dad and all."

"It's not a great time."

"Shoot, it's the best time. You're the most important TreeRunner, and you could help smooth things out with Chelle and Parker. You could meet with Munna. I sure could use your company right now, and I want to show you what I'm working on."

"I really can't."

"There's something else Grandyn. Your dad left some unfinished work, and you and I are the only ones who can complete it. You know what I'm talking about?"

"Yeah."

"Then you know it could make the difference in the revolution . . . decide who wins. Us or the AOI."

"If you're talking about Dad's 'missing eight works,' I can hardly see how they matter anymore."

"Oh they matter, Grandyn. Your dad gave up everything for those works, but there's even more. Those books hold secrets you can't believe."

CHAPTER FOURTEEN

Grandyn and Nelson stared at each other.

"I heard the AOI intercepted the books when PAWN was moving them," Grandyn said. "That the books were destroyed."

"No. The books made it." Nelson replied. "They're scattered, but they still exist."

Grandyn felt weak and sighed deeply. His father's books had survived. It was hard to believe. "Are you sure?"

"Grandyn, I am certain. We're working on finding them now, but I need your help. Nothing you're doing out there is more important than what we need to find in those books. Your mother and father began this . . . let's you and I finish it."

"I don't know. It's hard—"

"Grandyn, they are hunting you. They aren't going to lock you up, they will kill you on sight. Last time you were captured, there were powerful people in position to help you. We don't have that advantage now. Shoot, I don't even know how you've kept alive *this* long."

Grandyn heard Nelson exhale and could almost see the smoke. Hardly anyone smoked, cigarettes were not even manufactured anymore, but a few private farms sold a similar tobacco product called "bacs" that was without a filter, longer, and thinner than the old-fashioned kind. Nelson had smoked them for decades. One of Grandyn's earliest memories was playing with the ashes.

"You're still smoking? How are *you* still alive?"

"I'm serious, Grandyn. How have you eluded the AOI and PAWN all these years?"

"You might say I have some powerful friends of my own."

"You must. I've twice mourned your death only to find out weeks later that the reports were mistaken."

Grandyn moved the shade just enough to see out the bedroom window as he heard a drone fly close by. "Sadly, those were friends of mine. Other TreeRunners murdered for my crimes."

"Torgon that! Crimes cannot be committed against laws that are unjust. Do you recall what Thomas Jefferson said? 'If a law is unjust, a man is not only right to disobey it, he is obligated to do so.' Gandhi agreed. 'An unjust law is itself a species of violence. Arrest for its breach is more so.' We're on the right side here." His voice riled. Grandyn could picture Nelson's blurry eyes come clear like they did whenever he made a point he was passionate about. He loved Nelson and his crazy abandoned lust in this their over-regimented world.

"And I agree, but since you brought up Gandhi, he also said, 'The law of nonviolence says that violence should be resisted not by counter-violence, but by *non*violence. This I do by breaking the law and by peacefully submitting to arrest and imprisonment.' We're on the verge of embarking on a planet-wide revolution. It is *certain* to be violent, *and* bloody. So be careful whom you quote, Nelson. Next thing you'll be saying is 'God is on our side.' How many wars have started that way?"

"I'm with you. I spent a year with a man who preached non-violence *ad nauseum*. And try bringing up war to Munna."

"Have you discovered yet how she's lived so long? Amazing."

"She sure is, and I'm not sure even she knows, but it's got something to do with increasing our mind capacity to comprehend beyond our senses," Nelson said as an AOI patrol LEV went by a bit too slowly. "And that's the thing. Aylantik has hijacked the world and we have to get it back. We all have different reasons for wanting them out of power, and mine have changed a lot over the years, but the bottom line is we're on the wrong track."

Grandyn did miss Nelson and their conversations, and he believed getting together with Munna, Chelle, and Nelson on the eve of the Exchange could be very important for the revolution. Another drone fly-over. This time there were five, which meant they were AOI. They always flew in multiples of five.

"I wonder if I could get Parker to come with me."

"She will if Deuce tells her to," Nelson said, excited that Grandyn was considering it. "Deuce was a TreeRunner."

"Seriously? Wow," Grandyn said. "How come the AOI hasn't killed *him* yet?"

"Well, there are many answers to that question. But, like you, he entered the TreeRunners at age five, and his wealthy parents didn't want him getting favorable treatment, so they put him in under a fake identity. No small trick, but . . ." He paused to listen as he heard voices nearby. "It was deeper than that. I've learned a lot about his family over the past few years, and they knew."

"Knew what?"

"About all this. Even about your dad."

"What are you talking about?"

"There were prophecies. Grandyn, we *have* to get to the books. You and I are the only ones who have a chance to uncover their meaning."

"The revolution is coming. We don't have time for old predictions."

"It's all connected. We can't win without the books, Grandyn. It's always been about the wisdom in the books. After the loss of your mother, the only things that mattered to your father, were you, and the books. Let's bring them together again, for your dad. Runit believed that the books were worth saving because of what they contained. He just didn't yet fully understand how much they contained . . . the great secrets that have been hidden from humanity."

CHAPTER FIFTEEN

Miner received word of the escalation in the Amazon Area. It felt like the nightmares that had haunted him most of his life were coming true. War . . . how could he stop it?

"The AOI thinks they have him," Miner told Sarlo. "The commander is working on a 'dead or alive' order."

"What is this, the wild west?"

"We must get to him first."

"Why?"

"He can find the prophecies."

"How are you so sure?"

"Because they are still hiding books, and because they are protecting him, and because his father was the last librarian. He grew up in that library . . . He knows."

"I don't want to sound pessimistic."

"Really? Why should today be any different?"

"Sorry if being the voice of reason is a detriment."

"Say what you were going to say," Miner said, almost smiling.

"That all sounds a bit circumstantial."

"Maybe, but there is something else. The Imp said that the prophecies contain a passage about the prophecies themselves.

About their being discovered in this time. Damn it, they are *going* to be found, and we have to be the ones in control of that." He rubbed his 1988 silver dollar. It always made him feel connected to the power his family had held for more than a century. "It has to be Nelson Wright, Grandyn Happerman, or Deuce Lipton who get to them. Obviously Deuce isn't going to help me, and we've got people looking for Wright, but it's urgent with Grandyn because the AOI wants him dead."

"How do the Imps know all this?"

"They have access to two things we do not." He paused, as if she should already know this, and he believed she should. They'd been together so long that he felt as if their minds were connected. His wife trusted him, but others might have been jealous of an attractive woman spending so much time with their husband. Miner did want her, but had long given up on the conquest in favor of maintaining their perfect business chemistry. Still, on the days when he was tired, he wondered if he could juggle the two.

"Which two things do the Imps have access to?" she pressed, moving her toned body closer. "Or is that secret also contained in the prophecies?"

He smiled. Not so much at her sarcastic line, but at how she managed to defuse him. "Imps can enter every data base on the planet. It doesn't matter how secure, they get in. There is stuff about these prophecies in there. It's buried deep, and I don't know where, but the prophecies weren't a total secret. People wrote about them, they were investigated, but somehow they got suppressed. There have even been several large-scale discrediting propaganda campaigns about them over the centuries."

"And the Imps sift through all of that?"

"Yes, but their biggest advantage is the same reason they can be trusted with all the data. Remember what the Imp told us in Denver?"

"That Imps are perceived as being less than human and it's made them social outcasts?"

"The part after that," Miner said, pointing a finger at her knowingly. "That their accelerated intelligence has created vast amounts of mental capacity and mind expansion which in turn has led to something far deeper than someone without an implant could achieve . . . awareness."

"Of course, I do remember that," Sarlo said, backing into a tru-chair and crossing her legs. "It was that monologue . . . here, I'll play it." She tapped her INU and manipulated a mini AirView. A second later the Denver Imp's voice filled the room.

"There are so many things that you have no idea about, dreams which remain on your tongue when you speak, unappreciated in crossing the sea of imagination. Places to travel to when there is no one left to blame, hidden realms where invitations were long engraved but now gather dust, unopened."

"You've been obsessed with Imps and prophesies ever since," Sarlo said. "If I didn't know better, I'd say that freak put a spell on you."

"Maybe he did, but you were there. You saw how he controlled all those AirViews simultaneously with only his eyes and how colored sparks and pops flowed around us like some kind of light-ning storm ballet." Miner waved his arms and swirled them around as if trying to recreate it. "Go on, play the rest."

"You want to know about Lipton." The recording of the Imp's whispered voice still gave Sarlo chills. *"Lipton,"* it echoed.

"How do you know?" Miner asked on the recording.

"It was amazing," Miner said as they listened to the recording while the Imp sang a song.

"He's weird," Sarlo said, not for the first time. "They all are. I prefer my humans without a computer crunched into their head. I like people real."

"Then you were born in the wrong century. Shh, listen to this part," Miner said, pointing to her INU.

The Imp's voice rolled out again, sounding more alive on the recording than it had when they were standing next to him. *"That greater capacity of mind allows us not just to access all the knowledge of humankind, my dear. It provides us the ability to find the channel and frequency to touch the source."*

"The source?" Sarlo's recorded voice asked.

"The human mind, free of distractions, practiced and open, is capable of reaching higher planes. I'm connected to the infinite knowledge of the universe."

"You're half-machine," Miner had said.

"The machine simply frees my mind," the Imp said. *"Why do you think we get the implants? To get rich?"*

Sarlo recalled the shabby little cabin where the Imp resided. No, it certainly wasn't getting rich, although that would have been easy enough for all of its access. She suddenly thought of the Imp as some kind of futuristic monk.

"Tell him," Sarlo said on the recording.

"I am a better man," the Imp said. *"Accept that. If I can help, then I must already know."*

"Prove it," Miner's recorded voice said. *"Tell me where my question begins?"*

"Booker Lipton. What happened while he was gone?"

As they listened, they heard Sarlo gasp, and both recalled the moment when the Imp confirmed that Booker Lipton, Deuce's grandfather, had a secret second son who had grown up hidden from the world, free of the burden of his father's wealth, and had instead pursued a different path to power. Indeed a different *type* of power. Cope Lipton knew of the prophecies, and was also part of them. As were Deuce and Munna, and so was Miner. The final stages of a centuries-long battle for the direction of the human race was being played out.

"It doesn't matter how crazy it all seems," Miner whispered to Sarlo while standing just centimeters from her. "This is destiny. No matter what we believe. Big things are happening. If we don't find Grandyn and those damned books, we will be run over and forgotten, but if we get to them first . . ."

He stared deeply into her eyes. Their working relationship was substantiated by a unique bond, forged across years of experience in watching and manipulating world affairs.

"Then destiny will be shaped by our hands."

CHAPTER SIXTEEN

Terik had a few chances to get to Chelle. It was a trade-off of sorts. She was more valuable to the AOI than Grandyn, but he didn't have all of her files at his disposal. There were other agents pursuing her, more experienced ones with greater resources, but Grandyn was within his scope. If he could end the AOI search for Grandyn, then the priority would shift to Chelle and PAWN, and he'd be assigned to lead it.

Terik thought for a moment, staring out at the nearby mountains and the millions of acres of trees. *If I can get Drast to cooperate, I can change the outcome of the coming war.*

Osc met him again. "I was able to get yesterday's recordings overwritten, but I'm not sure how many times I can do this."

"I appreciate it, brother. You know what's at stake."

"Of course."

"Then find a way."

Osc nodded. A couple of minutes later, Terik stood facing Drast, who seemed to look five years younger.

"Agent Terik, so lovely to see you today."

"I don't have much time."

"None of us do." Drast's smile turned serious. "Here is my

message," he said, handing Terik a single page covered with small print written in all caps.

Terik barely glanced at it, knowing he would read it later. "And my data?"

"You will find what you need in area eighty-five."

"On the AOI system?" Terik asked, alarmed.

"Yeah, don't worry. Here's the key. No one else has it." He handed him a tiny slip of paper that appeared to be from a candy wrapper. Drast had carefully written dozens of letters and numbers on it. They seemed random, but Terik was sure they were not.

"I wasn't counting on this still being in the AOI system. How do I know this isn't some sort of trap?"

Drast laughed hard. "Do you forget who I am? I ran one of the largest AOI regions in the world for longer than you've been alive. I know everything about you Agent Terik. Now, deliver my message, and try to find some courage before you come back next time." Drast stood and pounded the door. The escorting guard opened it and immediately took Drast back into the bowels of the prison.

"What happened?" Osc asked. "You had more time."

"I insulted him," Terik said. "I didn't mean to."

Osc looked down the steel corridor where Drast had just disappeared and then back to Terik. "Are you sure you're doing the right thing? You could end up joining him in here. It's not a nice place. You have some image of it as a hellish lockdown of hate and punishment? You have no idea how lovely that image is compared to the brutal reality of what this is." He grabbed the scruff of Terik's shirt.

Terik, stunned, pushed back. "What's your problem, man?"

"I want to be sure I have your attention. We've known each other a long time. If you wind up in here, this place where misery and despair go to relax, where men lose their minds in the madness of torture, isolation, and abuse, you'll regret everything, and you'll know that nothing was worth it . . . Hilton Prison is proof that hell exists."

"I won't ever wind up in here."

"How are you so sure?"

"Because they'll never let me live that long."

"All I'm saying Ander, is this place is worse than death. Don't insult Drast. He's doing the hardest time you could believe. Use him to achieve your objectives, cheat him, rob him, call him a traitor, whatever, but give him the respect he deserves for even surviving this torgon island."

Terik looked back down the hall. "You're right. Thanks." He paused and looked at his old friend. "These are tense times. I'm feeling the pressure and I appreciate your warning. Not many people would bother the way you just did." He hugged Osc, patting him on the back.

"It's cool. One day we'll look back on all this and cry."

Terik laughed. "I hope that's true. See you in a few days."

For years, there had been tensions between Grandyn and Parker, the woman who led the TreeRunners. Grandyn didn't blame her for the animosity. Because of him, the TreeRunners entire organization had been outlawed, thousands of its members hunted and killed. Then there were the recent losses, dozens of TreeRunners who had died in the campaign to protect him. Grandyn's refusal to tell Parker his exact whereabouts complicated their relationship further, but she knew of his vital importance to the revolution, a cause she had only reluctantly joined when the AOI tactics in killing so many of her friends made it clear that the perfection of Aylantik's system was not everything it appeared. It was through no fault of his own that the AOI wanted him dead, and the TreeRunner oath meant he must be protected, so Parker did everything she could to thwart his pursuers.

Deuce Lipton was frustrated with Parker because, as a Tree-Runner himself, and the main backer of the revolution, he felt he had a right to see Grandyn. He needed Grandyn's help with the books, and he felt his BLAXERs could do a better job of keeping Grandyn safe. Deuce had asked many times for access to Grandyn. Had Parker known Grandyn's exact whereabouts, the oath still would have prevented her from sharing, even with another TreeRunner.

It was as if the founders of the TreeRunners had known the trouble they would one day face and anticipated this eventuality. Interestingly, unlike most institutions, the founders of the Tree-Runners had not enshrined themselves into the group to be cele-brated and memorialized. In fact, no one knew for sure who had begun the secretive organization. Its history was something like the mist which rose above the morning river through the redwoods.

Long before Grandyn had contacted Nelson, the fugitive-writer had also pressed Parker to help him find Grandyn. It was about eight or nine months after the Doneharvest crackdown had begun, and at the height of AOI brutality toward TreeRunners. Parker, of course, knew about the book theft from the Portland Library since it had been the origin of the trouble between the AOI and the TreeRunners, so she wasn't surprised to learn that the books were important to the revolution.

"We need Grandyn to help us interpret things contained in the books," Nelson had told her.

She'd already heard the same thing from Deuce. "It seems there are many people after Grandyn and these books. Not just the Aylantik. Several *different* factions of the rebels want them too."

"I was with Grandyn and his father when the course of these books began. Grandyn is like a son to me, the books belong—"

"Do you even *have* the books? And does Grandyn know what he is to do?" she'd asked.

"We have the books that we need," Nelson lied. Only some

were accounted for. Nelson was practical enough to not care too much if PAWN, Deuce, the Creatives, the Rejectionists, or even the List Keepers got the books, as long as it wasn't Miner or the AOI. But he believed he knew best, that the books were still part of his destiny, and Nelson truly loved Grandyn. "Grandyn will know what he needs to when it's necessary."

"But you must tell him everything. It's his life at stake," she'd said, knowing she would never forget Nelson's answer.

"We've kept him isolated from the core information, just as we do everyone. Secrets can only be pried from people who know them."

It was the last part that changed how she operated the Tree-Runners, and she issued it on all future official directives. "Secrets can only be pried from people who know them."

CHAPTER SEVENTEEN

Three years earlier, at the start of the Doneharvest crackdown, the AOI had intercepted as many as a third of the books. PAWN had been attempting to move the books not already claimed by Deuce Lipton. In the days following the Portland Library's closing, PAWN began moving shipments from the old barn where they'd first been hidden. Only a portion arrived at the PAWN bunkers in the northern California mountains where shelves were waiting.

It may have been a lucky break for the AOI, or they might have been tipped, that answer remained unclear. But government agents confiscated enough books to fill a small storage facility on the outskirts of Sacramento. The AOI scheduled a burn for the ill-fated books, and less than thirty-six hours after the last seizure, the tiny warehouse was burned.

Apparently though, unbeknownst to even the agents on the scene, the place had been emptied, and the one-of-a-kind literary treasures were saved yet again. Drast had had them covertly moved in the night to a secret location.

It was only after Drast's arrest that the AOI began searching for more books, but in reality no proof of books existed, since it was impossible to know how many were originally taken from the library. They weren't even sure whether Drast, who had greatly exaggerated the number he recovered and "burned," had really destroyed them or not. But they wanted Grandyn, because in the rebel movement there were two symbols, two rallying points: Grandyn and Munna. Each represented a type of truth the Aylantik could not tolerate.

Grandyn stood for information and history, while Munna embodied health and spirituality. Both needed to be extinguished in order to defeat the rebels, and for peace to prevail, always.

Now the AOI thought they had a break. Grandyn was hemmed in on Mount Shasta. They'd been close to catching him before, even believed they'd killed him several times, but the TreeRunners used look-alikes and decoys. Even while they pursued a "rock solid" lead on Shasta, other AOI units were involved in trapping a positively ID'd Grandyn in the Amazon. Each team had to assume their Grandyn was the real one. The commander on Shasta was sure of two things. Grandyn couldn't be in two places at once, and this time they really had him . . . on Shasta.

The agent projected several photos of the fugitive TreeRunner from an INU. The campers, three men and three women, all agreed. "No question. That's him," one of them said. "Is he some kind of serial killer or something?"

"No, sir," the agent responded, delighted to have a positive ID. "We're not at liberty to disclose his crime, but he is considered armed and dangerous."

The campers looked at one another. "Break camp," one of the guys said. "We don't need to stay another night until they catch this guy."

The AOI agent nodded as if this were a wise choice, one that might have been made for them if they hadn't come to the decision on their own. A few minutes later, two more agents ran up.

"Check this out," one of them said after getting a good distance away from the campers. "It's an INU we just confiscated from a hiker."

Seven AOI agents stood looking at an image that promised to get them all promoted. It was a clear shot of Grandyn Happerman.

"When was this taken?" the agent in charge asked.

The junior agent brought up the metadata on a separate AirView. "It's less than an hour ago!" They looked at one another gleefully.

"Zoom it, now!" barked the one in charge. "Pull everyone in. Let's go." The metadata also showed the GPS coordinates. "Grandyn was less than a kilometer from here forty-eight minutes ago. He is not going to get away."

There were now two confirmed sightings of Grandyn thousands of kilometers apart. The AOI Chief received the update as she walked offstage and immediately ordered an investigation.

"This is ridiculous! How can we not find one lost TreeRunner? A twenty-one year old *boy* is making fools of the most efficient intelligence organization the world has ever known," she snapped at a subordinate. "Let's hope one of these Grandyns turns out to be him. Either way, I want full details of how they are foiling us."

Mount Shasta became infested with AOI. Flo-wings, swarmdrones, and hundreds of personnel descended on the wilderness in the biggest manhunt since the Banoff. Roadblocks and satellite tracking assured he didn't get away by road. Air traffic had been shut down to all non-AOI flights. Twelve hours later, there hadn't been a single new sighting. More platoons were brought in, along with an AOI General. Half an hour after he was onsite, the Chief zoomed.

"Our Amazon sighting went bad. That Grandyn escaped," she said, looking as if someone had just slapped her. "What's your news?"

"Not much better I'm afraid," the General said. "It's as if he just disappeared."

"The Amazon could have been anything, but we got multiple positive IDs on Shasta and a photo. He's there somewhere, probably been there for three years. It's only one hundred thirty kilometers from his last known location in Southern Oregon."

"We've just started doing imaging sweeps to see if we can uncover underground bunkers. But it's a big area, and because of the trees and other unknown interference, we can't get much from the air."

"I'll keep a feed open," the Chief said. "I'm staying with this real-time."

He ran. But it wasn't like "normal" running. TreeRunners almost glide through the woods. From their earliest days in the clan, they are taught a meditation of survival until they develop a sensorial instinct. One of Grandyn's first clan leaders told him, "You must run so quietly that the wind won't even hear your steps."

TreeRunners spend months in the forests learning to exist like an animal. Practice and repetition are used until their skills are honed to those of Native Americans and other prehistoric people. Living without technology, without anything, TreeRunners acquire what their leaders refer to as the seventh sense: resourcefulness. By the time they are thirteen, all TreeRunners must build an entire cabin with nothing but their hands. The undertaking begins with a solo TreeRunner making stone tools, then using sticks, mud, leaves, peeled bark, and other natural materials until a one-room house complete with fireplace is constructed. They're also experts in starting fires with sticks, and camouflage. A clan leader would say, "If the deer don't fear you, you will have nothing to fear."

And TreeRunners run . . . they run, fast and light.

CHAPTER EIGHTEEN

Blaze Cortez stared at his twenty-four lieutenants, seated around a large, round table constructed of a clear composite material which allowed the incredible array of electronics embedded inside to be visible. His inner circle consisted entirely of men, and he'd given them each a code name. Gawain, Lancelot, Percival, Galahad, Bors, Kay, Gareth, Bedivere, Lucan the Butler, Griflet, Yvain, Morholt, etc., all names of King Arthur's Knights of the Round Table. Blaze, quite fond of the story, had, in spite of the ban, several hundred books dedicated to the legend, which he insisted was not mere myth.

"Gentlemen," he began. "We seem to have lost a TreeRunner. And not just any TreeRunner, but a very important one."

They all knew this. They knew about Grandyn Happerman. They knew about a great many things because the majority of them were Imps. The six that were not were something even more dangerous . . . "CHRUDEs" or Cloned Human Replacement Unit DesTIn Enabled.

CHRUDEs, although not invented by Blaze, certainly owed their existence to him, since the "brains" that controlled them were the most advanced DesTIn systems ever created. Equally impressive were the outerworks, so human-like that the CHRUDEs actually looked far more like people than Imps.

In order to get the skin perfect and maintain complete secrecy, Blaze had acquired longtime chemical maker, Dupont, which in 2102 had celebrated three hundred years since its founding as a gunpowder mill. But even more remarkable were the lengths Blaze had gone to give his CHRUDEs an authentic quality by installing a "bloodstream" just under the "skin," so that any point in the body could bleed if cut. The bleeding could simply be stopped based on medical probabilities analyzed by the unit's DesTIn. Eyes and tongues took years to get right, but were now flawless. CHRUDEs even breathed. Blaze designed, and was extremely proud of that system, which incorporated a fan used for cooling the unit's electronics. Precise engineering made the CHRUDEs' weight that of their human equivalents. While they were not capable of eating, they could take in liquid, which was stored, transformed to the appropriate color, and discharged normally at any later time – a detail to make sure that in any situation they would pass as human. All these features, as Blaze liked to say, "made CHRUDEs anything but crude." By any measure, including body temperature, they would appear and act human.

Morholt, one of the CHRUDEs, spoke up. "If we are to locate Grandyn, we must *enlist* the help of the *List* Keepers," he said, adding, "no pun intended."

Blaze smiled. They were incredible. "More human than humans," he had said often. In fact, they were superior due to their immunity to all illness, even death. The pun might not have indicated CHRUDEs' superior intelligence, memory, and recall, but it showed the subtlety of the DesTIn systems. No one could tell the difference.

"But the List Keepers are intent on keeping Grandyn to themselves," he answered.

Galahad, an Imp, interjected. "Of course they know of the prophecies?" he asked.

"Yes," Blaze answered.

"Then we must assume they want Grandyn in order to gain access to the prophecies so that they will possess the determining knowledge." Everyone knew the "determining knowledge" referred to the information allegedly contained in the prophecies that would show either side which steps were necessary to win. Blaze was about to counter his presumption when Galahad continued. "But this would mean that the List Keepers want to win the war, or care who wins the war, and that is not the case. I believe the List Keepers want to avoid conflict. They want the prophecies not to use them, but rather to make certain that no one else gets them."

"Yes," added Lucan the Butler, another Imp, "The List Keepers have, for so many decades, plodded along, trying to create the world they envision one pixel at a time."

"They have a fear greater than losing a war," Blaze said, and he believed this completely, but it troubled him more than anything else. Because for all his knowledge, the tremendous access he had to data of every type, and his loose alliances with every major party to the conflict, Blaze had no idea what the List Keepers feared. The organization was far more secretive than any he knew, including the A-Council that actually ran the world. "Anybody?"

All of his "knights" looked around to the others. No one had a theory as to why the List Keepers, who so diligently had been trying to defeat Aylantik since even before the Banoff, would risk letting them win when there had never been a more opportune time to end their reign. Blaze considered this one more reason to get Grandyn.

There were almost no lights in the room other than the considerable illumination coming off the table, and because Imps and CHRUDEs preferred cooler temperatures, it was also chilly. Blaze didn't mind. Tekfabrik utilized his body's natural thermal output to keep him warm, plus he always wore an old-fashioned blazer, custom tailored and mocked by all behind his back.

"Grandyn is a TreeRunner," Blaze began, "and yet it is not the TreeRunners who hide him. Sure, they make great sacrifices to try to protect him, but even they don't know where he is."

Bors, a CHRUDE, interrupted. "If he is important to the List Keepers, then we must readdress their black holes."

Although among the power elites, it was generally assumed that the Imps could penetrate any INU and Field defense. However, there was one system they had yet to infiltrate. The List Keepers shields, dubbed "black holes," were legendary among the Imp community. Every Imp, almost as a matter of unofficial initiation, had tackled and failed to get anything from the List Keepers. Their black holes were so incredible that they had earned their name due to the complete absences of even a presence. Many Imps were convinced the List Keepers were a myth.

The only proof of their existence was Blaze Cortez. He had confirmed to a certain few Imps that the List Keepers were real. It had been done only in an effort to find someone who could break through the black holes. Word filtered through the Imp world after Blaze promised incredible rewards to the Imp who could show him the way into the List Keeper's system.

"The best of us have spent light years searching for the way in," Percival, an Imp, said. "Perhaps the List Keepers leave no footprints because they have no electronic or digital presence."

There were some disgruntled noises around the table at such an outrageous theory. The List Keepers were, in fact, believed to be an INU-based organization, stealing, injecting, manipulating, and reviewing data as the ultimate weapon. Several knights spoke at once, before Blaze, deep in thought, waved his arm to silence them. It was almost a full minute before he spoke.

"Percival, perhaps I should change your name to Merlin." Blaze smiled to the point of nearly laughing. "The List Keepers leave no footprints because they do not walk in the digital realm."

CHAPTER NINETEEN

Ander Terik's lean physique hunched tensely over the Grandyn Happerman file he'd obtained from Drast. His eyes darted at any sound, fearful that his AOI supervisors could somehow see what he was doing. But it didn't matter; the revelations contained in Drast's data went so far beyond the *standard* AOI Grandyn file that he couldn't turn back. His sweaty fingers squeezed the sharp points of the AOI pin he always wore.

Drast hadn't given him everything he needed, but it was still more than enough to shock him. Grandyn's mother had been one of the leading pioneers of the revolution movement in the modern era. Terik knew that PAWN had been around in some form even before the Banoff, but the organization had operated in deep stealth mode for more than seventy-five years. Their actions of quiet, methodical base-building appeared almost as if they knew it would be seven decades after the Banoff war until their strength would grow enough, and the conditions would exist to try again. There had never, in human history, been such a patient revolution, and it had been a long, silent war.

Terik read the reports and realized that an open war, following such a muted period of dissent, would erupt horrendously loud. With massive damage and casualties likely on both sides, the revolution, regardless of the outcome, was sure to forever alter the peaceful utopia they had come to know. He watched, fascinated, as images and footage of Harper Happerman filled AirViews around him.

Strange, he thought, *her son never knew about her pivotal role in shaping the revolution that would define his life.* Her claims that the Banoff had been intentional, although presumably never made outside of PAWN, doomed her to an early death. There was stunning detail contained in Drast's files. *How could the AOI know of these accusations and yet no official denial or material refuting them had been made part of the record?* Drast would have had to ask that himself, probably many times.

Terik could see that the Grandyn file he'd been given when he was assigned to the case, the one he'd been adding to and working with all this time, was only about five percent of what Drast's contained. He wondered if the AOI Chief, or even the current Pacyfik head, had all the data Drast did. After pondering that question, he decided they couldn't possibly have everything he was looking at, but they certainly had a lot more than they gave the agents.

When he reached the end, a section that detailed the days after Runit Happerman engineered the theft of the books from the Portland Library and his reported death, and Grandyn's arrest, Terik knew not even the AOI Chief could have access to those parts. It showed photos of books, and outlined Grandyn's "escape" from AOI custody and his disappearance, yet it detailed very little about what happened to his father.

Now that Terik had the facts of Grandyn's life, he needed to decide what to do with it. He'd obtained the information illegally, which put his whole AOI career in jeopardy, and therefore his life was also at risk. In some ways, he had learned more than he wanted to know.

How important is it to advance in the AOI? The deeper I dig, the more there is to confuse me. The more layers, the more lies I find. But how trustworthy is Drast? His agenda might be bigger than everyone's.

Drast's file outlined clear links to Nelson Wright, and alluded to more connections with his sister, Chelle Andreas, Deuce Lipton, and Blaze Cortez, but much of it was a quagmire.

He needed to talk to Drast again, and this time he needed to convince him to give up everything. Drast could be executed at any moment. His data was too valuable to expire with him, yet it would, if Terik couldn't convince or bribe him. Terik might even use that data to propel his own career inside the AOI. He knew that Drast was a much smarter man than he was, but these were different times, and if the AOI survived the looming trouble, then Terik wanted to be a top gun in the agency. Drast's files would help him achieve that.

His fingers fidgeted the AirViews. Lost in thought, his mind was troubled that he wanted something he wasn't sure he should, or could, have.

Terik also worried that in the meantime, the files, if he could get them all, might prove more dangerous than he could handle. But that was a risk he had to take. He had suspected for some time that Drast was still working with the rebels, but the files had made him sure of it. Now the question was by what means?

Terik believed that getting information out of a super-maximum-security AOI locked-down prison was impossible. Guards were subjected to the strictest AOI background checks and monitoring. They were, like his buddy Osc, full-fledged AOI agents vying for better assignments. The Field was blocked at all AOI detention facilities, and there were daily searches for micro devices and weekly sweeps for nano level equipment.

How is Drast doing it? Terik wondered.

A few high ranking guards, in order to insure "Evren's" safety, were aware of Drast's true identity. Beyond that, only the top echelon of the AOI leadership even knew that Drast was still alive.

Maybe ten people in the world know he's here, Terik thought. *Could one of them be an Aylantik traitor as well? If I can get to Chelle, I may find my answer.*

CHAPTER TWENTY

Grandyn considered his next move carefully. He'd nearly taken this step three times in the past, and on each occasion he'd deemed it too risky. But in these final days before the Exchange, the tension permeated the air and affected his every breath. He could no longer ignore one of his father's final wishes.

Grandyn selected an invisible section of his INU. Twelve different "old-fashioned" passwords had to be entered just to reach the retina and fingerprint scan areas, and then he was FRIDGed, a Facial Recognition Identification Grid, and finally the INU placed the infinite-encrypted zoom.

On the other end, Deuce Lipton smiled as he saw the zoom come through. He'd been expecting this contact every day for the last thousand days.

"Grandyn, thank you for getting in touch," Deuce said to the young man he'd never met but whom he knew so much about.

"Mr. Lipton, my father asked me to do this."

"I know he did. Runit was a brave man. He changed the world. And please, it's just Deuce."

"It doesn't feel like he changed anything."

"Oh, never doubt it. Runit Happerman did change the world. The world just doesn't realize it yet."

"But the books?"

"They've survived. We don't know their exact location yet, but we think we have most of them accounted for. I've been trying to bring them all together again since the Doneharvest began. The timing of your zoom is fortuitous, as I'm getting close. If all goes well, we'll have Runit's books brought back together within weeks."

"So Nelson was right. The books have survived." Grandyn knew he'd have to find a way to get to them. "Why did my dad think I could help with the books, and why did he want me to contact you?"

"I should think that would be obvious. You grew up with the books, and your dad told you what to look for. He knew I would have them. I promised him I would keep his books safe," Deuce said, surrounded by stars, as usual. He'd been in his posh office reviewing satellite images and data from the outer planets. His passion for space was sometimes the only thing able to ease the stress of the deteriorating world situation. "We need your help."

"That's all fine if we're not in the middle of a revolution and if I'm not one of the most wanted men on the planet," Grandyn said. "You must employ plenty of smart people who could find what you're looking for. Maybe even get a computer program to analyze the contents of all the books."

"Grandyn, you know full well that we're not looking for an ordinary passage here. Not some simple paragraph written by a normal author. These are codes, imbedded into the letter, the language of the books, even the construction of the physical object itself."

"Doesn't sound like a job for a TreeRunner who never even went to college."

"One tree, ten thousand leaves. One trail, ten thousand paths. One runner, ten thousand followers." Normally, hearing Deuce recite the TreeRunners' secret motto would have surprised Grandyn since it's known only to members, but Nelson had tipped him off to Deuce's TreeRunner past.

"Do you still run?"

"Mostly a walker these days, but I don't miss a chance to get into the forest whenever I can."

"It's different when you have to hide in them."

"Does it take away some of the mystical nature of the trees?"

"No, not at all. It adds to it. I always loved the woods, but now that I am totally dependent on them, I feel that it's the only place I belong. There's total trust in the trees. Sometimes . . . I know this sounds strange but, sometimes it's like trees are more human than we are . . . Does that make sense?"

"Completely."

"I don't know if I can do what you need, Deuce. Even if you *can* get all the books together, it's eight books out of more than one hundred thousand."

"It's 112,804 and I've got 51,003 of them hidden on an island. Grandyn, I've had a team of experts searching for the secrets, and they've been using every kind of tech I can find or invent, even DesTIn . . . but they've come up empty."

"How long have they been on it?"

"A year and a half."

"And you think *I* can do it? Even if I had some magic formula, I wouldn't have the time. We're about to go to war."

"I know, but Grandyn, you're the one. You can do this."

"How can you be so sure? Just because my father said I could?"

"No, because *my grandfather* said you would."

"Wasn't your grandfather Booker Lipton?"

"Yes."

"And isn't he dead? I mean, long before I was born?"

"Yes. But Grandyn, he had access to things."

"Prophecies?"

"Yes. You know about them?"

"Nelson told me."

"My grandfather sent me a letter. Rather, he gave it to my uncle to give me on a certain date in this year. He mentions your father and you, by name. He said—"

"How could he have mentioned us by name? The letter was written before I was born, maybe before my father." Grandyn heard a noise outside and checked his Whistler. The little house had cameras hidden on the parameter. He checked and saw nothing.

"Like I said, he knew things."

"Why didn't he just put the prophecies in that letter?" Grandyn asked.

"Because he didn't have them all. I know about the ones he did have, but those have all happened already. They don't do us much good. The ones in the books are about the future, and they'll show us how to bring down Aylantik."

"If the prophecies are real and they show that we beat Aylantik, then we have nothing to worry about."

"Whatever definition of prophecies you're working from, I assure you it does not apply to these," Deuce said. "These prophecies constantly change until they actually happen."

"What?"

"It sounds far-fetched, I know."

"It sounds impossible." Grandyn quieted as he heard jetpacks. Typically AOI agents, the only ones authorized to fly jetpacks, flew only in heavily populated areas. But for weeks Grandyn had noticed the stepping up of patrols. He needed to get back to the woods.

"Yet they exist," Deuce said.

"Do they?"

"Yes."

"Inside the books from the Portland Library?"

"Yes."

"How can they change if they are printed inside a book?"

"I don't know."

"Because they don't," Grandyn said, "and you want me to risk my life for a myth?"

"Your father did, and your mother, although she probably didn't know about the prophecies, she did believe in the cause they are rooted in, and she died for it."

"Then we've already given enough Happerman blood."

"Your family has certainly done more than their share. But Grandyn, you think this is just about ending the brutal reign of the AOI and knocking the Aylantik out of power, but this is about so much more than that." Deuce looked off into the stars displayed above his head. "This is about changing the way we live . . . the technology that has made me rich, all its luster and convenience is but a distraction. We've been entertained for three hundred years while our birthright has been taken from us, hidden and obscured by cheap and easy *things* and imaginary fulfillment.

"What is our birthright?"

"To be as powerful as a star. To live free as an expression of love."

Grandyn thought Deuce was talking over his head. He didn't want to be in the conversation any longer. "Let me think about it."

"How can I find you? We're running out of time."

"You're a TreeRunner. You'll find a way."

"Grandyn, please. We have more in common than just being TreeRunners. They killed my father too."

"I'm sorry, I didn't know," Grandyn said sincerely. "They've killed a lot of fathers. More than anything, I want to stop them from killing more, but there are many ways to kill a snake. I'm already working on a few."

"There is only one way that will succeed. I need your answer."

"I'll be in touch."

When the connection went dead, Deuce screened for the originating location of Grandyn's call, but he wasn't surprised, given the List Keepers involvement, that it proved impossible. There had not been much in Deuce's privileged life that required patience, but he needed every patient breath he'd ever had for the greatest challenges he'd ever known: the revolution, the books, and Grandyn Happerman

"Saying nothing, that's enough for me," he whispered into the starry sky as Bessie Smith sang "Nobody Knows You When You're Down and Out."

After the zoom, Grandyn sat with his head in his hands, unsure what to think, what to do, what answer to give, but mostly he thought of his father, and refused to accept that he was really gone.

CHAPTER TWENTY-ONE

Zaverly had been a TreeRunner for almost nineteen years. She'd joined at age five and wanted to spend her life in the woods. Although most members used the TreeRunners as a stepping-stone into the world of business or even AOI service, she was hoping to remain in the group and train future recruits. But then the AOI shut them down, killed everyone they could find, and continued hunting the survivors ever since. Even AOI agents who were known to have been former TreeRunners were quickly executed. The AOI Chief had been very clear, "once a TreeRunner, always a TreeRunner," and Zaverly knew it was true.

She'd blamed Grandyn for all the bad that had come the way of the once great organization. If he hadn't recruited members to help steal books, the AOI might not have come down on them all. But at the same time, she was in awe of him. Zaverly, lean and muscled and almost one point eight meters tall with long dark hair, had no shortage of male admirers in the remote jungles. But beyond that, the olive-skinned beauty was popular for another reason. Her ability to fight. She never, ever, gave up.

He stared at her as she popped her knuckles one by one just by extending her fingers and bending them in a certain way. The noise unnerved him, but it was part of how she unwound. He'd seen the routine many times. The double-jointed gymnast bent and contorted in ways he didn't think possible, in ways that *shouldn't* be possible. He had to close his eyes when she bent a foot behind her neck while the other one remained on the floor before cart wheeling into the reverse position.

Zaverly might have been the most determined person he'd ever known. How she got that way at such a young age was something she didn't like to talk about. Something had made this twenty-three-year old a tempest. Her looks were a natural camouflage in the dark jungle, as if she'd been born there, but it was Zaverly's earthy eyes that stopped people. They contained a fire, both literally and figuratively, as her irises exploded in yellow and brown flecks. A warrior had been his first impression, but that had been based on her physical appearance. Once he got to know Zaverly and experienced her fiery personality, he came to believe he'd never meet a tougher fighter. She seemingly didn't know how to give up, couldn't stand the word "no," and didn't tolerate anything less than giving everything.

Zaverly saw those same traits in Grandyn, although in a softer, smoother form. His intensity drew her to him, and she hated him more for it. For a girl without weakness, Grandyn Happerman, the man she'd been assigned to protect, was as close to one as she got. Having to deal with him, a man she wanted to go away, a man she had to save, a man filled with mystery, was making her crazy. Added to that, her loss of control made her even angrier.

Finally alone, Zaverly looked at the man she'd just saved again as she read the names of those who had been killed to make their escape possible.

"Grandyn, you can't keep going out there. I'm not coming for you next time. We're all going to die!"

"I don't want you to keep coming after me."

"You're so damned noble. Do you think that impresses me?"

"I don't care what impresses you."

"You should, you ungrateful torg. Do you know how many times I've saved your life? Do you know how many have died so that you could go on living, so that you could cost more lives, and more and more and more!?" She pushed him into a wall.

"Umpf," he said sinking to his knees.

"Oh, damn, your ribs. I'm sorry, I forgot."

"Leave me alone," he said, shaking off her attempts to help. "You think I'm a death magnet? Well, I don't want any of this."

"Then why do you go out there?" she said, trying to help him up.

He pushed her hand away. "I'm just following orders. If you don't like it, why don't you complain to the supervisor?"

"I have . . . lots of times."

"Well then deal with it or quit."

"You know no one quits the TreeRunners."

"No. Not since the Doneharvest. Dying is the only way out."

"And you've been a big help in that department."

"Torg off, Zaverly."

She glared at him.

"Four and twenty-six," he said.

"What's that supposed to mean?" she asked spitefully.

"You've saved my life four times . . . and twenty-six people have died to keep me alive."

Her eyes filled, and that was the exact moment she fell in love with him. "You know?"

"I see every face."

"Why do they send you out?" she repeated, desperate for a rational answer that could begin to make sense of the deaths. "You must have asked them. I mean, you're an amazing TreeRunner, but there are many others who are better. We need the twenty-six who have died protecting you, more than we need you out there."

"True," he said, "but the AOI declared war on the TreeRunners, and as soon as that happened we became allied with PAWN, the Creatives, the Rejectionists, and everyone else who wants to see Aylantik fall."

"I know that."

"Of course you do, so think about what it means. We're at *war*. It may not have been declared yet, the general population may not know it yet, but sides have been chosen and people are dying."

"What's that got to do with you?"

"I took an oath and I follow orders. If our leadership and that of our allies says Grandyn Happerman is a symbol of the revolution or has some special purpose, then I'm not arguing. And if they deem it strategically important to keep sending me out into the jungle for whatever reason, then I'm going to do it, because those people are a whole lot smarter than me, and they see something you and I can't when we're buried beneath all these trees."

"What's that?" she asked, her eyes glued to his.

"While we only see the trees, they see the forest."

Grandyn sat by himself, something he did all too often, and wondered when it would end, all the deceit that had surrounded him since his father's last day or, the last day he saw his father. The trees offered lonely protection, but it was the TreeRunners who were paying with their lives. He'd asked Parker to provide a list of the next of kin for anyone who had died in the service of the "Grandyn Mission," and he had quite a file. One day he hoped to be able to talk to the families, the spouses, the brothers and sisters, and in several cases the children of the people who had sacrificed themselves for him. Parker had told him repeatedly that it was for the cause, not for him, but her words, merely designed to make him feel better, meant nothing.

After discovering Deuce was a TreeRunner and talking with him, Grandyn felt sure that the trillionaire had been the one who initiated the Grandyn Mission.

Clearly, Parker has refused to tell Deuce where I am, he thought, *although she's rarely known herself, but he must have convinced her to make sure I was kept alive at any cost. It has to stop. Maybe if I go to Deuce's island and try to figure out the books, all the dying in my name will end.*

But he knew there were other risks. Grandyn had had many missions of his own, and he'd been working with the inner strength and drive that comes from a single-minded dedication to revenge.

Along with his personal vendetta, two other things pushed him. He owed his life to those responsible for saving him and keeping him hidden, the List Keepers. He didn't know much about the highly secretive group, but he could feel their power as he survived and eluded the biggest manhunt in AOI history. Then there was his allegiance to the TreeRunners. Most of his peers, who had not been TreeRunners, were finished with college. But more than seventy percent of his TreeRunner friends from pre-Doneharvest days were now dead.

Grandyn's life had become more complicated than he could have ever imagined. He recalled the day he escaped AOI custody and Fye, the List Keeper who'd taken him in, had said, "Grandyn, you're just like a cat. You have nine lives."

Yet here he was three years later and it seemed more like twenty-nine lives.

He'd grown to love Fye, and she had to know it, but he was afraid to express it, or even to show it, because everyone he'd ever loved was lost. When he was a little boy his parents used to tell him love was the most powerful force in the universe, yet all his love ever seemed to do was get people killed. He didn't want to think about love, he didn't want to think about anything other than revenge, and as he sat on the damp log, he shivered, somehow knowing that the real trouble still lay ahead.

CHAPTER TWENTY-TWO

Lance Miner stood on the roof of his office building in Buenos Aires. He'd installed massive Whistlers – screening, mirrored panels – along with a host of electronics and nanotechnologies, that would make monitoring and eavesdropping impossible. Still, he whispered as he spoke to Blaze Cortez through a single-use, quantum-secured, infinite-encrypted INU. "In the era of total surveillance, complete monitoring, and anti-privacy, paranoia is no longer a disorder. It is an absolute necessity," Miner had said to Sarlo when the rooftop protections had been added to all his buildings.

Miner flipped his coin as they spoke. Blaze followed it with his eyes. "Oh, an old piece of money that is. One hundred and thirteen years ago, 1988, yes," Blaze said. "The Philadelphia mint struck 5,004,646 of the coins while San Francisco made 557,370 for a total mintage of 5,562,016. They contain one ounce of .999 fine silver. The Americans were oddly the last place on earth to adopt the exceedingly superior metric system. I must say that's a lovely coin. The obverse shows a design originally created by Adolph A. Weinman, while the reverse depicts a heraldic eagle. Those Americans with their symbols and patriotism. Too many of them wound up in the Aylantik government. Anyway, nice to see something from the days when money still had a physical form, even if it wasn't backed by anything more than a dirty promise."

Miner, accustomed to Blaze's expositive rants, ignored it. "You claimed three years ago to know where Munna was, and we got nothing," Miner said. "How do I know that this time you're really going to come through?"

"Let me remind you that it was I who was the first to confirm Munna's existence when the AOI and your own Enforcers were convinced she was just a myth. 'It's impossible a woman born before the Banoff can still be alive, and no way she's over one hundred and thirty,' you said to me. Ha! And here she is now, at one hundred and thirty-three, leading PAWN and about to embark on a war that will certainly cost you your precious peace and perhaps even take down your entire way of life."

"We still can't find her."

"Then I should also remind you that I was more than willing to tell you her exact whereabouts three years ago when I knew. But Drast, who became a traitor you might recall, wouldn't pay my price, and now I guess we know why, don't we?"

Miner didn't need reminding. He'd been lucky to survive the Drast affair. Polis Drast had almost become World Premier. He was, by a long measure, the highest-placed official who'd ever been arrested by the AOI. The fact that he'd been groomed and backed by Miner had opened a long investigation into his affairs that continued even now. Miner was the most shocked of all at Drast's duplicity, yet he missed Drast because he had been his best road into the inside world of the AOI. Miner still had plenty of low-level informants, but he needed much more than the limited access they could provide. Now he had to rely heavily on Blaze, a man he knew he couldn't trust.

"You're a strong man Lance, I'll give you that. Drast's betrayal would have finished a weaker person. What did it feel like? Were you tempted to jump off a bridge? You're talking to me from a roof right now, aren't you?" Blaze asked. "Does all this talk of Drast screwing you over make you want to walk to the ledge and step off? Because if it does, I wouldn't blame you. As I said, it would have killed someone weaker."

"Shut up, Blaze," Miner said calmly, silently furious he had to deal with such a slippery rogue. At least the Imps were basically honest, but Blaze was an unclassifiable villain, at once Miner's greatest asset and also a nearly invincible foe. "I need to know where Grandyn Happerman is."

"Everyone wants to know that." The world currency had become secrets, and they were brokered in power trades by those who could discover where the leaks and cracks were. The AOI knew "everything," so the relatively few things that escaped their notice were of great value. The Doneharvest and the imminent revolution had only increased both the market, and the price for such information, and no one was better connected and equipped to profit from the current climate than Blaze. "I must admit, not even I have that golden nugget at the moment. But you can be assured that I have been working on it and I have a number of leads, one in particular that is extremely promising."

"You'll no doubt be selling that information to the highest bidder?"

"Naturally."

"Contact me first."

"Of course, of course," Blaze said, smiling so that his voice sounded overly cheery, but then he switched to an urgent, admonishing tone. "You aren't going to be able to stop this war Lance. It's bigger than you or me, bigger even than Deuce." He couldn't resist the dig.

A formation of five, mid-sized drones buzzed overhead.

"You may be right. But even if I can't stop it, I can make damn sure I win it."

"Do you think so? Have you run the simulations?"

"I have."

"Then you're using different inputs and variables, because everything I see says that if the Aylantik wins, then the world is nothing like the one we enjoy today. An AOI victory may be worse than a loss."

"What makes you think I'm talking about AOI winning?"

"Ah, interesting," Blaze said, sounding delighted. "Yes, you have your own army . . . the Enforcers, and just as important, you have your own treasury, but you also have your own enemy. One with a larger private army and a much larger treasury. What is it you plan to do about Deuce Lipton and his BLAXERs?"

"I'm sure you'd like to know my plans so that you could sell them to Deuce, but you need to be careful. If you've run enough simulations, then you should know that you don't come out well in any single scenario."

"Don't worry about me," Blaze said, laughing. "I'm not even real."

"I don't doubt that," Miner said, not even cracking a smile. "Speaking of real or not, is Munna dead or alive?"

Another contingent of drones flew close by.

"Munna is still breathing last I heard."

"And Cope Lipton?" Miner watched Blaze carefully.

Blaze seemed genuinely taken aback. "Cope Lipton?"

Miner wasn't sure if the response meant he was surprised that Miner knew about Cope, or it was because Blaze didn't know himself.

"Yes, is Cope still living?" Miner repeated and watched more closely as Blaze discreetly moved AirViews and piled data and images into digitally layered heaps around him. He suspected that meant Blaze had not known about Cope, but he could just be scrambling to find out how Miner had obtained such priceless information. "You do know who I'm talking about, don't you?"

"There's a time to discuss this, and it isn't now," Blaze said, sounding nervous, something Miner had never known him to be.

"I have an urgent matter to attend to, so we'll have to continue this later. My humblest apologies and all that."

Miner nodded, still trying to read Blaze's response. "Okay, but I need Grandyn. A twenty-one-year-old punk *cannot* be permitted to bring down the greatest society in the history of the world." Miner slapped the side of a Flo-wing which was parked next to him. "And I want Munna too. She can't be allowed to live any longer. One-hundred-and-thirty-three is too long even for me, but for a meddling, pre-Banoff, living-in-the-wood-like-Robin-Hood revolutionary, it's a torgon century too long!"

Blaze nodded, still looking shaken, and then disappeared. As Miner stood on his roof with Buenos Aires stretched out to the ocean below, it suddenly hit him.

Munna was the living, breathing embodiment of the prophecies. She knew Cope, had probably known Booker, and had found some secret fountain of youth. Grandyn might be able to figure it out, find some treasure map concealed in the books, but if anyone already had the keys to finding the prophecies and could decode and apply the actual meaning of the predictions they contained, it was Munna.

CHAPTER TWENTY-THREE

Grandyn remembered the day he'd met Fye. It had been at the end of a three-month saga, which had begun with helping his father and Nelson get the books out of the library. After being captured by the AOI, Grandyn found himself magically released into the custody of Fye, a woman he immediately felt comfortable with, a woman who would change his life in many ways, a woman who was actually the only reason he'd lived this long, and a woman he loved more than anyone or anything else.

As devoted as Fye was to the revolution and Grandyn's shared dream of the destruction of the AOI, if it came down to it, they would both give up the cause for each other. But that was a fantasy world, because if they ever walked away from the cause, the only thing protecting them would be the wind, and that changed directions every day. They knew they'd never last an hour out there alone. Grandyn and Fye shared a complicated fate made simple by the realization that if they didn't continue to risk their lives to change the world, they would die, and the world's weight would crush the soft progress they'd made.

Fye had taught him what she was allowed about the List Keepers. In a time of secret organizations, there was none more so than them. The List Keepers had the keys to all information, and through painstaking methods few knew and even less understood, they could manipulate it so that almost any intangible thing could be changed, or even made to disappear completely. But their real talent, what made them such a threat to the Aylantik, was their ability to use those results, combined with other tactics, to affect tangible things, including people.

Grandyn remembered back to the time after Drast had arranged his release. When she'd finally told him her name, hours after getting him out of custody, he thought it was some sort of code-name, not something parents would actually burden a kid with.

She glared. "Fye," she had repeated. "As in 'fight' or 'fire.'"

"As in 'fine.'" He shrugged, with the lightest laugh.

She laughed back.

"I like you, Grandyn Happerman," she had said. "I like you so much so that I'll never call you that again."

He'd looked at her, puzzled.

"The AOI is going to hunt you, and you'd be amazed how much of a trail a name leaves. By changing your name, we cut eighty-eight percent of your footprints out of the system."

"I thought it was illegal to change your name."

"It is. Now you know why."

"Then how will you do it?"

"We'll break the law . . . don't worry." She smiled. "We do it *all* the time."

"But you said Fye is your real name."

"It is. No one has ever heard of me."

"How come?"

"I was born outside the system. My parents are List Keepers, as were theirs." Her expression had seemed proud. "We'll start with giving you nine different names, complete with identities and histories you'll need to memorize."

"Why so many?"

"Because most of them will wind up dead," she said, pointing to the names.

"Fye, what exactly do the List Keepers do?"

"Ever since the Banoff, we've been trying to fix things . . . one bit of data at a time." She doodled on a pad, he'd seen her do it a lot. She didn't draw pictures though, instead it was always numbers and letters and he couldn't make sense out of it.

"How do you fix things?"

"It's a long story. I'll tell you later, but it's hard to comprehend. It's really big," she said, making the word "really" last for four seconds.

"That pad is paper, and if I'm not mistaken, that's a pencil," Grandyn said. "I guess you like antiques."

She just smiled.

CHAPTER TWENTY-FOUR

They spent a lot of time together over the next few months, and in the stress of their situation of trying to survive as revolutionaries in a world set against them, their passions swelled in the drama of the cause.

Fye was a bit of a mystery, an important member of an organization that seemed to exist only in whispers and shadows, but he'd been captivated by her from the beginning. Whenever she looked at him her expression hid things, things he wanted to know, as if her every glance said, "I have stories to tell you when you're ready." She was different from Vida, his girlfriend the AOI had killed at the start of the Doneharvest. All his girlfriends had always been dark-skinned, passionate brunettes. Fye, light in every sense – sandy blond hair, soft green eyes, pale complexion – had a gentle spirit. Her plain appearance and simple prettiness belied the real source of her power: Fye had a brilliant mind. She never told him her age, but he guessed her to be around twenty-five. He couldn't reconcile her youth with her genius. He once asked her how she'd gotten so smart. Fye blew it off.

"All List Keepers are smart, I'm nothing special." And he could tell she meant it. Fye had no false modesty. In fact, he'd never known anyone as confident. *That must come with being so smart*, he thought. *People like that believe they can handle any situation.*

Fye also had a way of looking at people as if she could see all their pain. Even people Grandyn thought were jerks, Fye saw something good in them, something maybe long-lost or buried deep, but she saw it. He always had the feeling that she would do anything to help anybody, but sometimes being a List Keeper prevented her from going out there and actually helping.

In the years that he'd known her, the List Keepers had seen to his safety, and in all that time he still hadn't learned what they did, who they were, and how many existed. He had met a few others, but they were even more secretive than Fye. It often bothered him because he trusted her completely. She had his life in her hands, but she didn't seem to trust him. Still, he believed her, believed in her goodness so totally that he let it go. *One day, if we all live long enough, she'll tell me the rest. She'll show me everything,* he thought.

But that was a fairy tale hope, because as the war grew closer, their different missions meant they were almost always apart. The risks were constant, as every day someone they knew was arrested or killed. In the tension of the unraveling situation, she was the calm that kept him from going on a suicide mission just to kill AOI agents. He would surely have been long dead without her. She had made him lost to the world, but just as important was what she had taught him.

Grandyn recalled the last night they had together. She'd shown him three things that had weighed heavily on his mind ever since.

"What is it?" he'd asked as they walked into a large dark room in an underground data center located deep below the forests outside the Yosemite Earth Park.

She pushed a rare physical button, almost everything now virtual. The room came alive with AirViews, and he realized it was the largest interior space he'd ever been in, probably one hundred by two hundred meters. "Who are all these people?" he asked as the air around them filled with faces, images, names.

"They are the victims."

He looked around as the images flashed hundreds of thousands at a time, as if he were on a crowded city street. "Victims of the AOI?"

"No, that's much smaller, and we have that too. These," she paused, "these are the victims of the Banoff."

He stood silent, his words stolen by the spectacle. They surrounded him, millions and millions now, threatening to smother him. Children, so many children and people, beautiful, smiling people, just living life. Stills and film, color bits of life sliding all around. Faces, millions of eyes, some looking into his as they passed.

"How?" he gasped.

"Are you okay?" She held his arm. "I know I should have warned you, but it seems more fair to let them tell you, not one of us descendents of the survivors. But I know. I've seen them fourteen times now and it's still unbearable. Most people don't even survive as long as you their first time. Most people don't come back again."

"How?" he repeated.

"How did they compile all this?"

"No, how could they destroy all this on purpose?"

"It is a cold evil that did this, and the worst part is they knew before they did it." Fye looked at Grandyn. "You don't know, do you?"

"Know what?" he asked.

"They didn't just create the Banoff. The killing didn't stop seventy-five years ago."

"I know the AOI kills people all the time. They killed my mother, remember? And my father, I still don't know . . . "

"I'm not talking about the AOI and their enforcement executions."

"Then what?"

"The AHC."

"The Health Circle?"

"Yes. The inoculations, their treatments, the booster shots, everything they do is part of the system."

"What system?"

"*The* system." She opened her arms wide. "The system that they use to keep everyone in check, to get the birth and death rates where they want them, the way they quietly eliminate troublemakers, how they soften thinking. It's all planned."

He stared at her blankly.

"Don't you *get* it? Grandyn, *no one* dies from natural causes."

The terror of the revelation washed over him like a toxic wave. He didn't think any innocence remained in him, yet somewhere in a previously untouchable place within the last surviving purity of trust in his species, his innocence was shattered, and in that instant, Grandyn thought he might pass out. A sick feeling came with that toxic wave and it crippled him.

"They're still killing us," he whispered in a strained voice filled with agony and grief.

"Yes," she said, freshly devastated at seeing the effect the revelation had had on him. Fye had grown so used to the knowledge that she'd forgotten its brutality, its soul-crushing impact. But now she remembered and she realized it had been slowly robbing her peace.

"Why!?" Grandyn cried. "Why do they do this?"

"I don't know," Fye said quietly. She knew all the intellectual reasons for their continued atrocities – greed, power, control – but her heart was unable to understand how they justified any of the mere existence of their so-called Eden. "Even if they'd succeeded in creating paradise, even if that was their initial aim—"

"But it wasn't."

"I know, but even if it was, there can be no paradise if half the people are killed at the entrance gates."

"And if they keep killing to make it perfect for the rest of us. Torgon, I just don't know how they think it's okay, and I sure as hell don't know how to process that information into my own psyche." Part of him wanted to unlearn it. He knew it was impossible, and the strong part of him, the brave and true part, savored the information even while it choked and suffocated him.

CHAPTER TWENTY-FIVE

The long-anticipated meeting had been hastily arranged. All parties involved were anxious to leave as small a digital footprint as to the where and when of a gathering so important. They were also anxious for another reason. They all wanted the same thing, yet followed completely different paths to get there. Perhaps even more important was the resolve each had that they were the most correct, while the others were making a terrible mistake. And so began the first meeting of the top allied rebels in three years.

Grandyn, the last to arrive, found Munna, Chelle, and Nelson waiting in a brilliantly camouflaged cabin. The combination of natural foliage, nano-camo, and other Tekfabrik made it impossible to see the structure until less than a meter away from the all but invisible front door. Inside, antique, overstuffed leather sofas and chairs fit the location, but they were artifacts in the modern world of tru-chairs and over-holds. The handmade plank tables were neither wired for electronics, nor adjustable at the touch of a screen. The cabin was one of Nelson's favorite hideouts. Rustic and comfortable, the place exuded the same feeling Grandyn had about the inhabitants.

"The prodigal son returns," Nelson said, putting down his glass of wine and starting toward Grandyn.

"Nelson, you look great!" Grandyn said with a hug.

"Shoot, you've learned to lie well, haven't you?" Nelson patted him on the back.

"Nelson, you do look great compared to how you looked this morning," Chelle said, then pushed her brother playfully out of the way. "Let me get a good look at you Grandyn. It's really you. Three years we – and half the AOI – have been looking for you, and here you are. You look so much like your father."

"Hi ya Chelle," he said smiling, while giving her a lighter embrace than his "uncle" had received.

"I'm good enough," Chelle said. "Better now seeing you really are alive."

"TreeRunner," a strong, high pitched gravelly voice Grandyn would have known anywhere called out. Chelle stood aside, and Grandyn saw Munna sitting in a straight, ladder back chair, looking a bit smaller than he remembered. "Could I have a word, TreeRunner?"

"Of course Munna." Grandyn strode across the room and knelt on one knee next to her.

Munna took both his hands. "It is true that the world has been searching for the lost TreeRunner for more than one thousand days and nights. And it is true you have done many terrible things to remain unfound, things you never would have thought, and you're ever so troubled." She stared into his eyes until they filled. The soft, crinkly skin of her hands felt warm, her grip firm and strong. "You've done what you had to. You're young. You must let go of the guilt. If you carry it around, you'll never grow as old as me."

She was like a grandmother he'd never known. Wise and able to keep him safe, able to teach him things. And something else, she could *forgive* him. Munna was no ordinary person, anyone in her presence could sense it, even if they didn't know her age.

Munna had a way of looking at a person, as if she could see their every thought, and not just the current ones, but everything. The whole history of their thoughts. Her ancient eyes looked like mythical battlefields covered with flames and blood, exploded earth and loss. Her touch conveyed the better part of a century and a half of wanderings. She knew parts of the world that didn't exist in books anymore. She remembered things that others might never know, and in her deep-rooted connection to the past, even without the prophecies, Munna could sense the future as if she had already lived it.

"Forgive yourself," she whispered to Grandyn while squeezing his hands almost painfully.

He gasped involuntarily at the release she'd somehow granted him. Munna smiled and let go of him.

"We have to talk about the Exchange," Chelle broke in. "There isn't a lot of time here. The agreement was for no more than three hours."

"I didn't agree to the time limit," Nelson said. "And if we couldn't find common ground on the length of our little get-together here, I certainly don't think we're going to reach an accord on something as frightful and magnificent as a revolution."

Chelle shot her brother an annoyed who-asked-you look.

"I don't know what you think I can add about the Exchange," Grandyn said.

"You're a TreeRunner, and, I suspect, a List Keeper. We cannot win without the support and participation of both groups."

"Well, I can speak for neither party," Grandyn said as Nelson handed him an apple. "Parker is in charge of the TreeRunners and I'm not her favorite. I'm not even close to the leadership. As far as the List Keepers, I'm not remotely smart enough to be one, and even if I could acknowledge my connection, it would have no influence."

"Are you really going to stand here and pretend you aren't

aware of your influence?" Chelle asked. "By the way, the apples are from me. They're organic."

"Thanks," Grandyn said, taking a bite. "Influence is something one earns. I've been on the run for three years. Some might call me a coward . . . hardly worthy of being considered in a monumental decision such as this. What did Nelson say? 'Frightful and magnificent.' That does sum it up."

"Does he know about the prophecies?" Chelle asked Nelson, then, without waiting for an answer, turned back to Grandyn. "Of course you know about them. Can you find time?"

"Ah, the prophecies," Nelson said. "That's the real reason for this meeting. At least, as far as I'm concerned."

"That's not true," Chelle said. "We're here because it's weeks from the start of the Exchange and the outcome of it is already known. We need to find and understand the prophecies if we're going to win the revolution. You cannot separate the two. The prophecies and the uprising are one."

"No!" Munna said firmly as she rose from her seat. "Chelle, I admire you greatly, but you think everything has to do with the revolution, and that is simply not the case. Hardly anything has to do with the revolution, least of all the prophecies."

Chelle looked at the old lady, bewildered. "But we *can* win. The prophecies can tell us how to win."

"The prophecies can tell a great many things," Munna said in her gravelly whisper. "They have for a thousand years, and they'll keep on telling. It isn't just for this little conflict of yours. Kings and queens have come and gone. Entire civilizations have risen and fallen. Do you know how many wars have been fought since the prophecies were first recorded?"

No one answered.

"Hundreds, perhaps thousands," Munna continued, pointing to Nelson, then to a knife on the table.

"If prophecies aren't meant to be used to help people, why were they recorded in the first place?" Chelle asked.

Nelson cut Munna a slice of apple. She smiled as he handed it to her without the peel, which was hard on her teeth.

"Oh, but they *are* meant to help. The prophecies warn us, that is how they help. They show us how to find our original path."

"That is the same thing the revolution is going to do."

"I know you believe that Chelle, but war is not a natural thing. And winning something that isn't natural isn't really possible."

"Have you read the prophecies?" Chelle asked, raising her voice. "Do you know how to find them? Or do you already have copies?" Chelle looked around the cabin as if the prophecies might have been hidden there somewhere, with a fleeting thought that Munna was going to present them with the keys to the universe and they'd finally discover how to do the impossible, how to beat the massive machine pitted against them. "Damn it Munna, what are the prophecies really?" Chelle's voice was shrill, her eyes pleading.

Nelson looked at Munna in great anticipation, but she looked at Grandyn. "The prophecies, *these* prophecies, as you might have guessed, are not mere predictions scribed by a sage in forgotten time. They are something captured and carved from time itself, back when such things were still possible, back when we still understood how to do so much. Far more than we do now."

CHAPTER TWENTY-SIX

In an isolated nine-story building, Blaze stood in a darkened empty room, the size of two tennis courts. The purposefully nondescript architecture and the structure's location, on the outskirts of Los Angeles, were specifically designed for his purposes. He had nearly identical buildings scattered around the globe. His space on the windowless fifth floor had four-meter high ceilings. The four floors above were filled with relay and blocking equipment designed by him, or trusted employees, to thwart any monitoring of his data. At the same time, the four floors below utilized the latest tracer, tracking, and siphoning machines to bring in intercepted information by gazilla-bytes.

He had his knights working on the matter of Cope Lipton. It was impossible that he could have missed such a crucial detail in the giant puzzle of the Aylantik world, but he'd already learned enough to know that Cope was Booker's secret son, making him Deuce's uncle, and an important advisor to the trillionaire. Because of his position, and the complete secrecy surrounding his life, Cope Lipton – Blaze was almost certain – could be the missing piece he had been searching for. A way to make the picture complete so that he could finally achieve total control over the situation.

Blaze appeared as something like a modern day wizard with his long dark hair flowing wildly as he spun in the glow of more than fifty AirViews. He danced and ran among their constantly changing displays, absorbing the images and texts, turning on and off sound with quick flicks of his pinkies. The data influx was frightening in both its scope and its content. The world, like a kettle steaming for seventy-five years, was about to boil over into what would surely be the ugliest and deadliest war ever. Some AirViews showed scenarios of casualties so numerous that it translated to the total extinction of the human race. War could be a profitable business, but only if controlled. A war after so long a peace could be very challenging to control.

The danger flew at speeds so high that even his genius found it difficult to assimilate, but he knew two things for sure: he had to find Grandyn Happerman, and he needed the books. From then on, everything he did would be filtered through that knowledge. He also knew that Deuce Lipton, Lance Miner, and the AOI Chief also wanted those same things, and "want" was not meant in the way that an average citizen *wants* a new LEV or an upgraded INU, not in the case of the most powerful people on earth. They wanted Grandyn and the books like a drug addict wants a fix – their life depended on it.

The books were obviously important because of the prophecies. Grandyn was important for many reasons. He might be able to find and even decode the prophecies, but Miner and the Chief were still under the false impression that Drast had destroyed half of the books. Therefore, keeping Grandyn out of the hands of the others was crucial. Whoever had the books could control the war, and Grandyn was likely be the key to actually winning it.

Blaze spoke out loud to his empty room as he let the AirViews run random excursions into the possibilities. "This world rides on the unpredictable nature of a troubled youth." He laughed. "Oh, the irony of it. The madness of fate and cruel destiny of a misused crime."

The AirViews showed aerial images of large swaths of forests blowing in the breeze, of real time AOI missions, the moon colony, bases on Mars, near constant population figures for decades, possible faces of Grandyn Happerman, tracked PAWN movements, images of Chelle, Nelson, and Polis Drast together during the first years of their alliance, and more trees.

"You're out there somewhere TreeRunner, running wild like a virus." He stared into the closest screen with a forest, and quickly resized it to nearly four meters high and seven wide. "In those trees! A twenty-one year-old storm . . . a single lighting strike and it could all go up in flames."

He moved more AirViews into place and the room lit up in greens and browns like forests going on forever. He had the wide views of most major wilderness areas on the planet. At his command, they organized by number of Grandyn sightings, likelihood of survival, cross-referenced with movements of AOI, BLAX-ERs, and the Enforcers. Wildlife data, temperature fluctuations, plant and tree growth rates were thrown into the mix. He watched as overlays appeared of captured PAWN facilities, locations of arrests and executions of TreeRunners, suspected PAWNs, Rejectionists, and Creatives. Finally the DesTIn system running the show added the variable that included the occasions the AOI thought they were pursuing Grandyn or the times they believed they had actually killed him.

Blaze stared and suddenly waved his arms out in a wide, sweeping, crossing motion above his head. All the lights and sound froze instantly. He paced and studied several AirViews closely.

"You crafty little devil, Grandyn. You aren't out there in the woods at all, are you?" he said, then after a silence in which it almost appeared as if Blaze was waiting for an answer, he laughed for half a minute before shaking his head in disbelief. After several fast hand gestures, the AirViews showed more data, but nothing he could use. "Perhaps you're in the Amazon, but why would you keep surfacing? Why would you show your face at all?" he asked, zooming in on pixilated close-ups of a blurry face purported to be Grandyn. He ran a system with other photographs alongside enhancement and correction apps, which suggested it was Grandyn in the Amazon. "But I don't believe you're there. Because if you really were hiding, why would you venture out of a well-stocked bunker buried beneath the impenetrable forest? Why expose yourself when you're safely tucked away in the safest place possible?"

Blaze stood silent as every AirView filled with hi-res images of the Amazon forest.

"You're not harvesting rubber, you're not shopping for groceries!" Blaze walked slowly among the AirViews, as if strolling through the largest jungle on earth. All that was missing were the humid air, rich soil, and thick vegetation under his feet. "I'll tell you what you're doing Grandyn. You're trying to distract us all. You're keeping us on our toes, just out of reach, dangling that carrot on a stick, and while we all chase you around the world from forest to forest, we're missing something else, aren't we?"

Again he waited for an answer that didn't come, so after a long pause, he provided it himself.

"We're missing something that you want more than your own safety, and what is that Grandyn? Do you want war? Yes, I think you do. Do you want the books? Your father's books? Of course you do. Do you want to destroy the AOI? The people who took your mother and father from you? I'm certain you do, and who can blame you? But what do you want most of all? You can't have it all . . . or can you?"

CHAPTER TWENTY-SEVEN

Nelson, Chelle, and Grandyn stood in the still air of the cabin, embraced by the fragrances of pine and organic earth, waiting for Munna's next words. She sat there in her straight-backed chair, also seeming to be waiting for something. Her thick gray hair resembled the mane of an aging lion, and the alert eyes of a cat gave her a regal appearance rather than that of a little old lady. Her presence, particularly if she were focused on you, gave the constant impression that something profound was about to be said, something important about to happen.

"No, I don't have the prophecies," Munna said. "I've never even read them, but . . . I have felt them. I've talked to people who *have* read them, and the power of those visions could be seen, even partially understood, in the eyes of those who have grappled with the words." She swept an arm out to the three of them. "You all want the prophecies, everyone wants them, but be careful what you wish for. You might not be ready when you finally get it." Munna looked down into her empty hands as if something might have been there a long time ago and she hoped it might have magically returned. "All this time spent searching, and not a moment to prepare."

"Cope Lipton had read the prophecies," Nelson said. "And his father, Booker."

Munna nodded.

"Is there anyone left alive who knows what they contain?"

"Me," Munna answered.

"But you said you hadn't read them," Chelle said.

"Reading them and knowing what they contain are two very different things." Munna looked sternly at Chelle. "It is not a simple matter. You all imagine it to be so casual to read these prophecies and suddenly know the future, but you cannot imagine, cannot begin to comprehend, what it is to actually *know* the future."

No one said anything. None of them had ever seen Munna so agitated. Finally Grandyn, realizing their time was running short, pressed her. "Are the prophecies dangerous?"

To his relief, she smiled at him. "All knowledge can be dangerous in the wrong hands, and this, being the most ultimate knowledge, is the *most* dangerous of all. Why do you think they have been hidden so well for so long? Why have only a handful of people read them?"

"The corrupt people in power have kept them from us," Chelle answered.

"Yes, yes. Of course we can always blame those corrupt leaders who always seem to lie their way into power and end up stealing all kinds of things from us, and to some extent, in this case, that is also true. But the corrupt leaders throughout history mostly share one common trait besides greed, they are not very smart. It doesn't take a genius to lie and cheat. It is easy work for cowards and empty men." She shook her head. "Booker Lipton was an enlightened man, a rebel in every sense of the word, who fought to bring down corrupt leaders and shed truth into the world, and yet . . . when given the chance to publish the prophecies, he decided instead to suppress them."

"What?" Nelson asked, stunned.

"They were not lost or stolen, the government did not find and destroy them," Munna said. "Booker Lipton buried them."

"Why?" Nelson asked.

"Because knowledge is dangerous in the wrong hands."

"But he helped to publish other works by Clastier."

"There are two kinds of knowledge, aren't there?" Munna asked.

"Apparently dangerous and *too* dangerous," Chelle said.

Munna nodded. "Something like that. Inner knowledge can be dangerous for those who deny their power as individuals, our place in the universe." She paused. "But external knowledge which comes from others can be dangerous to the innocent if wielded by tyrants. Clastier wrote about a great many things and his writings were divided into three sections. The *Attestations*, the *Inspirations*, and the *Divinations*. The former two were the bulk of the work and comprised his teachings and philosophies. The *Divinations* – a series of predictions for the future – were his direct understanding of what he saw in the prophecies. But what you must understand is that even though he had access to all the prophecies, even he chose to limit what he released, just as others had before him."

"How did he decide?" Grandyn asked.

"I don't know, but it appears, and Booker believed, that he selected key events around war and dark periods when significant loss of life and spiritual oblivion would occur . . . his predictions included the Banoff."

"But who was he to decide? Who made Booker king? Why not let it out and allow us all to know?" Chelle asked.

"The prophecies don't just say things like, on July 29th 2108, such-and-such will happen," Munna explained. "They change with the influence and pressure of all that has already happened and all that is yet to come. The only constant in the universe is change."

"That's exactly why we *should* know, so we can affect the

change. The very fact that the prophecies are *not* written in stone is why we must give them to everyone."

"Why?" Munna asked sharply. "So you can decide that war is what's needed to make change?"

"Sometimes war is the only way to stop injustice," Chelle said. "Look at what the Aylantik is doing. We're at peace, yet the AOI kills as if we're at war."

"War is never the way," Munna said. "Violence cannot stop violence any more than hate can stop hate."

"There are times in history when war did end violence."

"No!" Munna snapped. "It only rearranged the sufferings! Historians' slanted versions answering to hidden masters and propagandists' lies owed to the same corrupt group made it seem that it was about making things better. About honor and fairness. We redraw the borders and memorize dates, but the same war has been raging for thousands of years. It has *never* ended."

CHAPTER TWENTY-EIGHT

The deteriorating situation in the Amazon continued to distract Deuce. He had already ordered BLAXERs into the region, something that would horrify his son, Twain, if he'd known. Twain had followed his great-uncle Cope's path of non-violence and empowered-meditation, and long argued against sending armies into the forests. But Twain didn't know about the escalations in the Amazon because he was missing. Deuce preferred to believe his son had just gone into silent solitude to advance his spiritual practice.

As Billie Holiday sang, "I'll Never Be the Same," Deuce stood in his San Francisco office twisting AirViews, searching for clues to where Twain might be. He hadn't seen nor heard from him in months, and although his instinct told him his son was still safe somewhere in the redwoods, he wasn't sure. He shifted his screens and viewed aerial coverage of the Amazon and other forests closer to home. A zoom from his wife suddenly interrupted his concentration. As she had daily, for almost seven weeks, expressing concern for Twain, she urged Deuce to go looking for him.

"It's been too long without word. Twain would know we'd be worried and wouldn't do this to us," she said, and he agreed.

After the zoom he summoned Nolan, one of the BLAXERs traveling with him. "Get the team together," Deuce told him.

Nolan, an efficient man with chiseled features, understood that Deuce wanted the eleven elite BLAXERs trained for special assignments. He touched his Eysen INU, and after several keystrokes into the projected light, Nolan looked back up to his boss. "Set in twenty-eight minutes," he said. "Where are we going?"

"Redwoods."

Nolan nodded. "Twain?"

"Yeah," Deuce said. He'd spent so much time concerned with finding Grandyn and the books that he'd probably let a few more weeks go by, without going after Twain, than he should have. But Deuce knew Twain wanted solitude, and was willing to trust he'd be safe in the redwoods. He also knew that his wife saw things differently.

"How are we looking down there?" Nolan asked, pointing to an AirView showing satellite images of the Amazon covered in brightly colored lights. AOI agents had set up a base there as they closed in on Grandyn. Drawn to the area for the same reasons, Miner's Enforcers were also on hand. Miner was hoping to beat the AOI to the lost TreeRunner.

With so many fighters concentrated in such a remote part of the world, Deuce worried that it could be a precursor to the war. At any moment anything could spark the three powerful armies from a pursuit mission to the first open battle between major forces since the Banoff war. The lights showed positions of the troops.

"We're the blue ones," Deuce said. "AOI is Red, and Enforcers are yellow."

"What are the green ones?" Nolan asked.

"Rejectionists . . . there used to be more."

Nolan shook his head. "They can't really hide with that many AOI down there."

"Very few were caught," Deuce said. "We managed to warn them, and most escaped into the mountains before the build-up."

Nolan smiled, then pointed to a large section lit in yellow. "Miner has us outnumbered down there."

"Just recently. Miner is completely on edge and desperate to find Grandyn."

"Has he authorized the use of force?" Nolan asked.

"That would be my guess." Deuce had little doubt that Enforcers would engage his BLAXERs, but he'd suspected for quite a while that Miner had already made the unprecedented decision to authorize his Enforcers personnel to fire on AOI troops. Deuce brought up more AirViews, showing the many forested regions where the three armies were bumping into each other. The AirViews floated all around Nolan and him as both men silently studied the images.

Most major forests around the world were in varied states of chaos as multiple sightings of Grandyn, and the hunt for him, intensified. Scientists were working diligently in an effort to uncover the reasons behind lack of Field coverage, monitoring failures, and communications issues that had plagued heavy wilderness areas across the globe, and the AOI was now also pouring more troops into small forests.

Whether violence began in the Amazon, in Oregon, or in some other area, Deuce knew that when the real war broke out, the Enforcers would join with the AOI to fight PAWN, the TreeRunners, and whatever ragtag band of Rejectionist and Creatives could be pulled together. But there were two questions that the AOI couldn't answer.

If the List Keepers really existed, how big were they, and what capabilities did they have? Although most AOI analysts assumed that Deuce's BLAXERs would join PAWN and the other rebels, some speculated that Deuce might try to remain independent. Miner and the Chief believed there might be a chance to recruit him to their side. The thinking was that Deuce had too much to lose.

CHAPTER TWENTY-NINE

Munna pointed at Grandyn.

"What do you think Grandyn? Each of us is born with a death sentence. An unknown moment in our future when we'll be snatched from this human world, breath surrendered, lost to those who cared for us."

"All but you, it would seem."

"Grandyn, do you think I'll live forever?"

"I guess it's not possible."

"Anything is possible, but forever is a very long time . . . the way we view it, anyway. But I may live longer than I care to. You see, I have assumed a certain role in trying to mediate something between those who want change and those who want revenge." She looked at him carefully. "We've all done things."

Grandyn slowly looked at each of their faces. "Do any of you know what happened to my father?"

Chelle looked surprised and disturbed by the question. "Grandyn, you were there. You know what happened."

"He was alive when we left him . . . he could still be alive."

"Oh, Grandyn. I wish that were so," Chelle replied. "But he

was seconds from death. Maybe if we'd gotten him on the Flo-wing . . . "

Grandyn clenched his jaw, fighting emotions thinking back on that day. "But even if he didn't survive, what happened to him?"

"Do you mean his body?" Chelle asked.

Nelson looked at Munna. She closed her eyes.

"Yeah," Grandyn replied. "Where did they take him?"

"Who knows," Chelle said. "I used every contact I had and all the evidence said he was dead and the AOI would have just burned his body, with the other rebels. It was the start of the Doneharvest. They were killing thousands."

"Munna?" Nelson said.

"It is only rumors," she said with her eyes still shut. "There is no need for this."

"What rumors?" Grandyn asked.

"Munna thinks it's possible that Runit lived."

"What!" Grandyn snapped. "Is that true?"

Munna opened her eyes. "I would have told you if there was any proof."

Chelle's stunned expression, as she looked from Nelson to Munna, made it obvious she had no idea.

"There are so many wild bits of information, allegations, and speculation flying around these days," Munna said. "It must be remembered that revolutions breed lies and hope."

"But there is a chance?" Grandyn said.

"Where did you hear these things?" Chelle, recovering from her shock, asked.

"We have thousands of sources," Munna said impatiently, then turned to Grandyn, her tone softening. "There is always the possi-bility that your father could be alive. However, we have not been able to locate him or verify that he survived beyond that day."

"But do you believe that he did?" Grandyn asked.

Munna stared into his eyes for a long moment, before finally nodding slowly. "I do."

"And do you think he is alive still?"

"Yes," she said very quietly.

"That's a lot of hope you're giving him," Chelle said. Her tone short. "Giving all of us."

"Hope is a powerful thing," Munna replied.

"If Runit is alive," Chelle began, "that changes everything."

After Munna promised to get word to Grandyn as soon as any additional information came to light about his father, and they convinced Grandyn that there was nothing he could do until more was learned, they returned to the contentious topic of how to proceed with the revolution.

"We must come to some kind of agreement," Chelle pushed.

"Is *that* possible?" Munna asked.

"War is coming," Chelle began.

"Unless you can show us another way to unseat Aylantik and dismantle the AOI," Nelson added in a tone meant to calm his sister.

"The AOI must be more than dismantled," Grandyn said.

"See?" Munna said. "Three different, and quite rigid, positions."

"And *your* position?" Chelle asked.

"My position is illumination."

Chelle squinted at Munna in annoyance. She was tired of the old woman's philosophical responses and questions. Chelle needed practical and decisive answers. Sometimes she even wondered if Munna was as old as they said she was. How could it be possible? And to look like she was half that age… "What does that even mean?"

"Easy Chelle," Nelson chided his sister.

"Nelson, I understand you worship her," Chelle said.

"Respect is different from worship," he responded.

"Whatever. But Munna, with all due respect, you say illumination and yet you keep the prophecies from us. You say war is wrong and yet you have been a figurehead for the oldest revolutionary group in existence. We have waited long enough. We're ready. We can *win*. How can you stand in the way of this revolution when you know the atrocities the AOI has committed for decades and decades?"

"I do not have the power you imagine Chelle. If you can find the prophecies and understand them, I cannot stop you. If you have cause and a willingness for war, I cannot stop that either."

"But you can," Chelle said, rising from her seat and stomping toward Munna. "Why pretend you can't stop it? You know there are those in PAWN, the majority, in fact, who will not act without your blessing."

"I will never give my blessing to war, and I know of your plan to incite my followers. Your tricks are not new. Do you know how many wars in the pre-Banoff days were started under false flags? You'll allow the AOI to destroy an enclave of women and children somewhere and suddenly the outrage will be impossible to contain. You'll have your war."

"I don't need a false flag. The AOI gives us cause every single day. It is you allowing innocent lives to be lost by delaying the war, which is inevitable anyway!"

"It is the same war."

"If you had allowed war three years ago, before the Doneharvest cut our numbers and strategic advantages, we might have already won and the AOI would be history. Do you know what that time has cost us?"

"Time is a funny thing . . . do you know what that time has cost?"

"She's impossible Nelson!" Chelle slapped her hands together and stormed to the door.

CHAPTER THIRTY

Munna closed her eyes as if in meditation.

"I'm sorry," Nelson said to Munna as Chelle left the cabin. "She's so passionate. She's lost so many . . ."

"I know, Nelson. It's all right." She waved dismissively.

Nelson followed after Chelle.

Munna winked at Grandyn.

"I'm with Chelle," Grandyn said. "I want the prophecies so we can win the war."

"The prophecies are not the only answer," Munna said, smiling knowingly.

"Then why does everyone want them?" he asked.

"People want the short answer, but when you've lived as long as I have, and partly how I've lived this long, a kind of knowledge seeps into your mind." She looked at him as a parent does a child when trying to find a way to explain a complicated topic. "We accumulate experiences in life that people believe teach us things, that give us wisdom. But actually, those things only unlock, or awaken, the latent knowledge already within us. Do you see?"

"I think you're saying that we learn from within rather than through the material world," he said slowly.

"Yes, yes, you got it." She beamed.

"But how does that explain why people want the prophecies if they can get the answers elsewhere?"

"People don't trust the things they hear inside anymore, but if they see the same information written down, they have no trouble moving armies based on it."

"But the prophecies are remarkable," he said in a voice filled with awe. "I mean, hundreds of years ago someone wrote down these things that are happening today. They even knew about my parents, and me. That is nothing short of miraculous. Don't you see how anyone would take that as pure magic?"

"Yes, that is my point. But what if you could sit in meditation and learn far more than the prophecies could ever tell you? What would that seem like to you?"

"It would feel like *I* was magic, a wizard or something. Is that really possible Munna? Can you do that?"

"We have lost so much to the Aylantik. They promised a utopian society, something humans had always longed for, but we sold our souls for gadgets and fake food."

She stared at him. He noticed for the first time that her eyes were unlike any he'd ever seen. The depth of them astonished him. It was like looking into one of those mirrored booths at a carnival where the reflections seem infinite. A thousand eyes filled with trees, ocean waves, and stars stared back at him, a million, more. Looking at the impossibly old woman caused a warm sweep of serenity to envelop him. It was the gentlest experience of his life, and even without her answer, he knew Munna could do anything.

Grandyn wanted to ask her so many questions, but the first one to escape his lips seemed oddly simple. "I'm sorry to ask you this, but do you know? I mean, how long you're going to live?"

"I will live as long as is necessary to do what I've come to do."

"And that is?"

"To change the direction of our people."

Grandyn nodded, wanting to understand, thinking he did.

"Sometimes I think the prophecies are but another distraction," Munna continued. "It is hard to know who made such great decisions in the past and to what ends. There have been such great manipulations of so many . . . the masses can be swayed very easily, and those with power and wealth have learned the tricks well enough that they can perform them effortlessly, with little more thought than they would use to spray a nest full of bees to stop the buzzing."

"But they can help us, and they can show people what is possible."

"Yes, if anyone notices the root of it. Prophecies have come to light many times in the past, and parts of *these* prophecies have even been seen before. Does anyone care? Does anyone even remember? And when these that are sought now, when they appear, will people only marvel at the fact that *predictions* came true? Or will they wonder how they could have been made so accurately, so long ago?"

"You tell me," Grandyn said, smiling. "You can see the future. Can't you?"

"The future is a murky place, always moving, ever-changing." She rubbed her wrinkly fingers across his forehead. They felt like warm crepe paper. "This is why the final Clastier prophecies were so remarkable, so powerful. He figured out a way to leave prophecies that could change as the circumstances and forces of the world ebbed and flowed."

Munna moved her hands together in circular motions, seemingly delighted by this part of her talk.

"Nostradamus, Malachy, Cayce, and others have all made great prophecies, many of which have come true, but with the passage of time the accuracy of their furthest predictions fades. This is because each passing day exerts tremendous pressure on the one to follow. If someone predicts a happening, even one hundred years into the future, then the events of thirty-six thousand five hundred days are all pushing against the prediction. Surely that will move and gray what was once a very accurate forecast."

"Nelson told me they change. I didn't really believe it. I guess he got that from you."

"No, I suspect he learned that from Cope," she said. "But his sister has been told the same thing. She wants the power of the prophecies, so desperate to win her war, and yet she doesn't trust the power from which they originated. That mistake will cost her more than a look at the prophecies, it will deny her the very thing she wants most . . . victory."

CHAPTER THIRTY-ONE

Grandyn found Chelle and Nelson leaning against a large and twisted madrone tree about ten meters from the cabin. Nelson lit a fresh bac from one he just finished as Grandyn walked up.

"Munna said the meeting is over," Grandyn said.

"What meeting?" Chelle asked. "This was just a waste of time."

"What are you going to do?" Grandyn asked.

"I'm going to finish what your parents helped to start," Chelle said. "Thirty days from now we'll be at war, and the Nusun's population will finally learn that their history, their precious world of comfort, is all a lie."

"Then we still have time to convince her," Grandyn said.

"She will *never* change her mind," Nelson said. "I think you could tell her that the Aylantik was about to execute another billion people and she still wouldn't agree to use force against them."

"How can she be so resolute?" Grandyn asked.

"She has seen things none of the rest of us has," Nelson said.

"Please," Chelle said. "She's an old lady who has spent too

much time in the woods, just like you have Nelson. The AOI must be stopped."

Grandyn nodded.

Nelson took another drag and looked back to the cabin.

"Deuce is close to getting all the books back together," Chelle said. "If he does, do you think that between the two of you, you'll be able to find the prophecies?"

Nelson nodded.

"If we can find my dad . . . "

Chelle looked at Grandyn as if he'd screamed profanities. "Listen, to me. Runit may be out there somewhere, and next to you, I want that to be true more than anyone. But there has been nothing to suggest that he really might be alive. So cling to the hope if you must, but at least go on living as if he's gone. Understand what I'm saying?"

Grandyn shrugged. "We better get going. We've been here too long."

"You're going to vanish again, aren't you?" Chelle asked.

Grandyn pursed his lips and nodded, mostly with his eyes, as he looked at Chelle, anticipating her disapproval.

"We won't stop looking for you."

"I know."

"Please come with us," Chelle implored. "Once the action starts, it's going to get really ugly out there."

"It's pretty ugly right now."

"No, I mean the world is going to implode. You won't recognize it. Food could get scarce. Anything that was reliable before will be dangerous," Chelle said.

"I'll manage."

"Okay," she said, giving him a hug. "Just make sure you stay in touch with Deuce. When he gets the books, we'll need you to help with the prophecies."

"I won't be far," he said.

Nelson had said goodbye to Munna, but Chelle refused. It wasn't until the two of them were ten minutes away from the cabin that Chelle spoke.

"Do you think Grandyn will really help with the books?"

"How many Grandyn Happermans are there?" Nelson asked.

"What?" Chelle understood the question, but was having trouble putting it all together. "You mean the Grandyn we just met might not have been the real Grandyn?"

"That's what I'm saying."

"Oh, come on Nelson. That was Runit's son or you're not my brother."

"It very well may have been our Grandyn, but we don't know for sure."

"Then who in the hell was it?"

"It could be some kind of advanced android."

"There you go with that writer's mind again. I can tell an android from ten meters away."

"Not if there is a new generation of them."

"Has Deuce told you something? Has one of his companies developed these human-like androids?"

"He hasn't, but I'm planning on asking him about them as soon as I can."

"Then where is this coming from?"

"Just look. Over the past few years there have been four different and credible reports of Grandyn's death. Our spies have logged six more separate Grandyn-alerts within the AOI, while they have deployed extra manpower to move on verified sightings of our young friend."

"So the AOI isn't perfect . . . in fact, we're counting on that."

"No, they aren't perfect, but these sightings are sometimes simultaneous and thousands of kilometers apart."

"The List Keepers?"

"That's what I was thinking."

"As you're aware, we don't know a lot about them, but from what we do know, they could be capable of something like that. It would explain how they've kept him alive all this time. Put ten Grandyns out there and confuse the hell out of the AOI, especially if you put them all in the forests where their normal surveillance equipment doesn't work."

"Right. Either that or Grandyn has discovered some secret network of portals."

Chelle rolled her eyes. "You spent too much time in the woods with Cope Lipton."

"Maybe," he said tentatively.

"But could that technology really exist to make an android so human-like that it could fool people? Fool *us*?"

"I'd say yes."

"And you think the Grandyn who came here might not have been the real one?"

"What if the real Grandyn isn't even alive anymore? What if the AOI never let him out of custody?" The shadows of the trees seemed to close in around them.

"Polis was in charge then. He let him go."

"Was Drast *really* in charge?"

"Stop it! Stop right now! I don't need you laying all your paranoid conspiracy theory plots on me."

"Maybe there are advanced android Grandyns running around out there, but Polis let our Grandyn go and the Grandyn we spoke to today was the same one, the real one."

"If you're wrong, or even only half-right, we're in serious trouble. We talked an awful lot about our plans and the prophecies today."

"If you think that Grandyn was some kind of a robot spy, why didn't he kill us all?"

"Do you think if we died, the revolution would stop?"

"Of course not."

"Then why kill us when you can have access to all the inside information of your enemies?"

"I can't talk to you when you get like this. You'll make me crazy!"

"Like what? I'm sober. You know what the AOI is capable of. They could do this. And it doesn't have to be *them*. It could be Blaze Cortez, or Lance Miner. He's got his own army out there looking for Grandyn."

"If this is true, then it could be Deuce behind it, or the List Keepers, for that matter. Everyone has a stake in this revolution. Everyone wants something different. And everyone wants to find the lost TreeRunner."

"And no one can be trusted . . . not even Grandyn."

CHAPTER THIRTY-TWO

Chelle glanced at her brother as they approached the clearing where the Flo-wing would pick her up. *What he said might be true,* she thought. *What if Grandyn hasn't been lost all this time? What if he's been hiding within multiple copies of himself?* The variables and scenarios played out in her exhausted mind. *Maybe I should run back to the cabin and try one more time with Munna. I should have had a PAWN team ready to grab Grandyn. Maybe I could still get one to catch up to him, find out if he was real. We could hold him prisoner until we have all the books.*

Nelson lit a bac and looked back at the way they had come. "I'm not sure I should stay there any longer. It probably isn't safe."

"Munna is still there," Chelle said, looking nervous.

"Her people are coming soon, but she wants to talk with me before she leaves. She's been trying to convince me to take her to find Twain Lipton."

"Twain? What's going on with Deuce's son?" Chelle asked.

"He's missing."

"He is?" she asked, surprised and concerned. "We're all lost in the damned woods." She felt suddenly sad, as if she couldn't go on much longer.

"Maybe, but don't worry. In spite of what Munna says, we're going to find the prophecies, and they *will* show us how to win." He patted her shoulder

"What if she's right and we never do win the war?" Chelle asked. "That woman makes me crazy, but there is something about her."

"You have no idea. We're all arguing about who owns what, the price of peace, the cost of medicine, whether we want revenge or something more noble, and all the while Munna may have quietly discovered the greatest secret of all time."

"What's that?" Chelle asked, feeling queasy.

"Immortality. Munna may have figured out how to live forever."

Chelle laughed nervously. "As if such a thing were possible. And if it were, who the hell would want to live forever?"

Nelson shrugged. "Sure, write it off to my author's mind. She hasn't aged a day in more than fifty years. She outlived everyone else who lived pre-Banoff by decades, and aren't you amazed she can do all this travelling through the woods when it wears me out?" He took another drag from his bac.

Hearing the Flo-wing, she looked up. "Everything wears you out. I sometimes worry you won't live long enough to even see the revolution."

"Nice change of the subject, little sister." Nelson smiled. "Don't worry about me. I'm a writer. My books are out there making sure I'm going to live forever." Although the AOI had banned most of his earlier works, he'd released many others under pseudonyms.

"I hope so." Chelle hugged him and kissed his cheek. "When Deuce finally rounds up all the books, can't you find the prophecies in them without Grandyn?"

"I wish I could, but the truth is I'm not even sure we can find them *with* Grandyn." Nelson saw the concern flood her face. He worried about the strain on her. "Can we win without the prophecies?"

She forced a smile. "I'm not even sure we can win *with* the prophecies."

He watched the Flo-wing carrying his sister fly off until it disappeared far beyond the treetops. Still he waited until the sound of the engines faded completely. He always worried that the Flo-wing carrying her would explode into a fireball. His writer's mind again, he told himself, but these were the worst of times, and it felt as if danger had replaced the oxygen in the air.

By the time he reached the cabin, Grandyn was gone and Munna's people were waiting. He suspected they had never been far away in the first place. Even Chelle had a PAWN combat unit minutes away on standby. For all he knew, Grandyn had a forest full of TreeRunners camouflaged in the trees surrounding the cabin.

Danger, danger, they lived in a world of lies built upon fabrications atop a foundation of crimes and deceit too vast to acknowledge. Or, as Nelson had once written, "The unknowing masses don't realize they are trapped in a tangle of subterfuge and slowly suffocating inside a counterfeit paradise."

"I'm concerned about Twain," Munna said, greeting him.

"I'm concerned about a great number of things, and our dear friend Twain, I'm afraid, is far down on the list."

"Nelson, don't be like your sister. The state of the world is not everything. Twain is a rare soul. You've spent enough time with him to know that he is more like his uncle Cope than his father.

We need him and, I suppose, if you want to look at it in terms of the revolution, you need his father not to be distracted. Even now, Deuce is heading to the redwoods to look for his son, and you know he'll never find him. He may know those woods better than most, but you and I both know there's more to it than that. There's a reason no one can get a solid signal in the forests, and there's a reason no one ever found Cope Lipton, just like they're never going to find Twain."

"I know," Nelson said, still uncomfortable with the knowledge he'd obtained during his time spent in the redwoods with Cope and Twain. He took a swig of his favorite drink, a blackberry brandy moonshine made in Oregon. Munna shook her head disapprovingly.

"You were allowed that time with Cope in order to convince your sister to abandon the war, but you haven't even told her what you discovered there, have you?"

"No," he said, taking one last pull before screwing the cap on the flask and putting it away. "She's not ready. She'd have to have been there. Chelle hardly believes me when I tell her ordinary stuff that I truly believe. Something like this, something I'm not even sure about... she'd probably have me locked up."

Munna smiled. "The truth is the truth whether someone believes it or not. It will not change, but truth has an interesting way of working. It stays the same and waits patiently while everyone else changes."

"Chelle isn't ready for change."

"Then she's in for a big surprise, because the revolution is going to change things more than she can possibly imagine."

CHAPTER THIRTY-THREE

Chelle sat in an isolated room in the sprawling underground bunker buried deep in the mountains south of Eugene, in the Oregon Area, and read the message from Terik a third time. Just like the first two readings, she shivered and involuntarily looked over her shoulder.

How the torg did he get into my INU? "And how did he get to Drast?" she whispered to herself. "I don't know who you are Ander Terik, but I do know you're trouble."

She flicked her finger and Drast's message played again. It wasn't his voice, rather a computer-generated audio, but there was no doubt this message was from him.

"Jingles," it began, a name only he had ever called her, and not for almost twenty years, during the earliest days of their friendship. Upon their first meeting he had called her "Sea-Chelle," but after getting to know her radical, unstoppable personality, he changed it to "Jingles," after a silvery shell that resembled the handle of a lasershod, an advanced handgun, because Chelle was a fighter. *"You're, no doubt, surprised to hear from me after more than two years of silent absence, and I trust you're pleased at my survival. I hope you knew I had lived. Mr. Terik has agreed to help us communicate. In exchange*

I have done certain things for him, but neither what, nor why is open for discussion per our arrangement. Please respect that, as any investigation on your part as to his methods or motives could prove disastrous for our cause."

Chelle thought about that for a minute. If Drast trusted him, that would have been good enough for her prior to his arrest, but now that he resided in an AOI prison, anything was possible. He might have been tortured or coerced in any number of ways. But as the voice continued, it became more difficult to imagine that Drast himself had not sent the message freely and secretly.

He talked of a coordinated prison break across all AOI facilities and the importance of the books. Drast claimed that Runit's books, which the AOI had intercepted, were not destroyed, and that he could provide the location. But it was what he said next that made her desperate for Drast to be alive and well, for his words meant they had a real chance to win the revolution.

"Jingles, there are cracks in the system. The AOI is not unlike the rebels. There are factions, much smaller than what you deal with, but there are pockets. I'm not talking about low-level informants or spies. These are people near the top, people with a conscience."

When had he discovered them? she wondered. If it had been before his arrest, why hadn't he told her? Although it had been too risky for them to communicate much, they did manage occasionally to have a direct conversation. If it had been after his imprisonment, how had he accomplished that trick? Chelle decided that since she was listening to a recording made by the greatest traitor the Aylantik had ever known, originating from within the walls of one of the most secure facilities on the planet, run by the most intrusive and lethal organization in existence . . . there were two possibilities.

Either Drast was even more powerful than she imagined, or he was dead.

"Said-scans," she whispered to herself.

The AOI used Said-scans, which gave them the ability to read the brains of dead people. No one understood exactly how much information could be retrieved from a person's memory, but apparently it was extensive. Certainly it would have been easy enough to find out that Drast used to call her "Jingles." She needed to think of a test to determine if it was really him, or if it was just an elaborate AOI scheme to get inside the hierarchy of PAWN on the eve of revolution. Depending just how deep they could go, figuring out something that could prove, without a doubt, that it was Drast, presented a great challenge.

The experts within PAWN told her that the current thinking was that Said-scans could not detect emotions. Drast loved her. There must be a way to use that information to test if it was a trap. But what if they could detect the memory of emotions? Surely Drast's brain had thought about his feelings for her, and he would have remembered that, leaving a traceable imprint.

Chelle borrowed an INU from PAWN, no longer trusting her own, and zoomed the one person who might know how to beat a Said-scan, a person who might just be willing to help, and the last person she trusted.

"My stars, if it isn't Nelson's younger sister," Blaze said, as he answered her zoom.

"How do you know that?" she asked, shocked she'd been so quickly recognized and that he knew it was her when the zoom had been from an unidentified and unregistered INU.

"Your brother is a chubby, scruffy fellow. Where did your startling beauty come from?" he asked, as his holographic image bounded out of the INU and circled her body, inspecting it as if he were shopping for a prostitute.

"How did you know it was me?" she repeated, moving away, uncomfortable with his virtual presence.

"Darling . . . may I call you darling?"

"No."

"Lover then. Lover, I'm an intelligent man, I'm sure you've heard. And an intelligent man always knows when a beautiful woman is present. An extraordinarily intelligent man and an

extraordinarily beautiful woman, as in this case, even more so."
He smiled, brushed his long hair aside, and moved closer to her.
"Why did it take you so long to zoooom me?" he said,
pronouncing "zoom" as if it were two syllables, and the second
one was shifted into fifth gear.

"I'm sorry I didn't wait longer," she said.

"Of course you're joking, but you'd never admit that. Please,
play through."

"I have a problem, and I thought you might help."

Blaze laughed hard. It seemed a genuine laugh, almost friendly,
but Chelle couldn't tell and, not knowing, decided to be offended.

"I made a mistake."

More laughter. "Oh, lover, you've made many mistakes and you
have many problems. Let me guess which one prompted this
zoom." He stopped and stared at her. Then he gasped quietly,
catching himself. "Forgive me lover," he whispered close to her
face, "but your eyes... they are exquisite, *los que siempre he estado
buscando.*"

"What language is that?" she asked.

"I'm sorry, I spoke to you in the native tongue of my ancestors.
Spanish comes to me in moments of passion." His eyes never left
hers.

"And what was it you said?"

"Your eyes, I spoke of your eyes." His virtual hand reached to
touch her face. She stepped back, slower this time. "Your eyes are
the ones . . . the one I have always sought."

She nodded, smiling. "You are, I have always heard, a man of
extremes. Rude, yet charming. Helpful, yet dangerous."

"Yes, lover, that's me. My reputation is often a wall that
protects me, and sometimes it is one I must endeavor to climb
over in order to achieve my aims. Is this one of those times? I'm
afraid you think me disingenuous." He brought his hands to his
heart. "Must I climb the wall to prove my affection for you?"

Chelle laughed. "You're a caricature of a leading man in a romance novel."

Blaze made a sad face. "I am wounded."

"You want to please me?"

"Oh yes."

"Then help with my problem."

"Which one?" He paced and, before she could answer, began to rattle off a list. "The location of the books? No. The AOI closing in on Grandyn? I think not. The growing tensions in the Amazon, a place where you would least like war to break out? Perhaps, but what could I do? Deuce's missing son, ah, a personal situation, possibly tragic if the AOI has him, but that's not it either." He pulled AirViews through the light stream and presented them to her, each showing images of what he had already mentioned. He continued flipping them, and the next showed Nelson. "How can you get your brother to lose weight, quit drinking and smoking . . . it is more important than you think, but we don't have time for poor old Nelson at the moment." He made another sad face.

Chelle sighed.

"Weapons? You're so close to war, but you are ever so outgunned. Weapons should be what you're asking about, but it's not."

"I could just tell you and stop wasting all this time."

"Where is the fun in that?" he asked. "And how can I impress you with my amazing powers unless I guess exactly what's on your mind?"

She shook her head, now almost amused by his theatrics. "Go on."

"No for weapons . . . a shame. But don't worry lover. For you, I will let you come back to that one. Deuce, you know, cannot be counted on as you think."

"Really?" she asked, as if his statement were the silliest thing she'd ever heard.

"Oh yes. I would never lie to you. But again, we'll do that dance another time, perhaps naked." He raised an eyebrow.

"Oh, come on!"

"Okay, I know you have a world to conquer, so I will get to the end of something other than your patience." He stared again into her eyes. "Mmm, that blue."

She frowned.

"Your problem is with Ander Terik, and whether you're able to believe the message he has brought to you."

With all the cliché the moment called for, she stared open-mouthed, even a little dizzy.

Blaze bowed.

CHAPTER THIRTY-FOUR

Grandyn had left the meeting with Munna, Chelle, and Nelson feeling strangely optimistic. Could his father have really survived? There was a chance and even the slightest hope could make everything more possible than the absence of him.

The second breakthrough was the realization that the revolution might be upon them. Grandyn wanted war, and Munna was all that stood in the way. Even with all her supposed power and knowledge, it seemed she would be unable to stop it. Chelle had spent years forming alliances and laying the groundwork. What's more, even though Munna might have it within her power to stop the war by a pronouncement, she did not seem willing to try without Chelle's agreement. In fact, Munna wanted everyone to concur that violence was the wrong path to change, and she implied the importance of that during their conversations, but Grandyn was still trying to understand it.

Why would Munna, who so badly wants to avoid war, be willing to let it happen rather than insisting that it not?

Already a thousand kilometers away from Nelson's cabin, Grandyn sat, unafraid, in an ordinary house in an ordinary residential neighborhood. It reminded him of his father's place, his childhood home. He missed that life and the old librarian more with each passing day, as if each hour he grew closer to his father's age brought more understanding as to who his father really was, how great a man, and a further recognition on just how much he'd lost.

He thought back on their final night together. Runit, a Shakespearean scholar, had quoted Hamlet.

"To be, or not to be: that is the question:
Whether 'tis nobler in the mind to suffer
The slings and arrows of outrageous fortune,
Or to take arms against a sea of troubles,
And by opposing end them? To die: to sleep;
No more; and, by a sleep to say we end
The heartache and the thousand natural shocks
That flesh is heir to, 'tis a consummation
Devoutly to be wish'd. To die, to sleep;
To sleep: perchance to dream: ay, there's the rub;
For in that sleep of death what dreams may come . . ."

Grandyn had played the passage over in his mind hundreds of times over the past three years. They were lines that contained new meaning in each reading. They were, in fact, vital to everything because his father had told him they were the key to finding the eight books. The eight books which contained the prophecies, or at least, led to them somehow. A treasure map? A coded key? Something else entirely? No one seemed to know for sure. Yet in spite of all that was at stake, it was the words of Shakespeare that his father had whispered that final night to the darkness when he thought Grandyn had fallen asleep.

"Doubt thou the stars are fire;
Doubt that the sun doth move;
Doubt truth to be a liar;
But never doubt I love."

Those were the words that haunted Grandyn, that made him want to cry. Tears, though, were difficult to come by. They'd been used up on his mother, his father, his girlfriend Vida, and countless TreeRunners who had been taken from him by the darkness which shadowed his once sunny world. In these dark moments he believed his father must be dead . . . three years . . . if Runit had had even a single breath remaining, he would have found Grandyn by now.

Grandyn looked at the AOI logo. Its cold, sharp pyramid piecing the circle of earth, or was it the sun, the "I" for intelligence symbolically appearing to support the entire Aylantik structure, a subliminal arrow formed by another pyramid, the wealthy elite, and a third tiny pyramid set atop the "world," a secret for the power elite, the A-Council. Though they were not acknowledged or even known, Grandyn had studied this emblem, just as he'd studied everything about the AOI and their Aylantik government. He'd been taught always to look beyond the obvious.

I, like everyone, was born innocent, unaware that the world I'd arrived in, the paradise I'd been promised, was a lie, he wrote to Fye, punching the virtual keys with his fingers as if they could erase his turmoil. *The promise of Aylantik had been so great that it blinded me, and almost everyone else. The entire society has been created to keep us in our place, to feed the rich, but the old lady is right. There is something inherently wrong, more than just their greed.* He paused to listen as a LEV went by. One at a time was okay on the quiet street, more than that could mean an AOI raid. *They had a chance to fix everything that was wrong with the pre-Banoff world, and they did, but sadly, they fixed it only for themselves.*

He stopped writing as anger overtook his thought. His hands tensed and trembled. Too much had happened, too much that he took on his shoulders. His father had raised him to be brave and true, to face what came and rise to the occasion, but what does that mean when everything is at stake – the lives of millions, the future of the world, the truth in the remaining books – he did not know.

What am I supposed to do? How do we change something this big, fight something this big? Grandyn balled his hands into fists and pounded the table. *Too much.*

His anger quickly turned to depression. The knowledge of what had been done during the Banoff and in the present constantly droned in the background of his thoughts. The noise and vibration of it became too much to bear.

He looked at his lasershod and considered ending his life. It was not a new thought, and it didn't happen daily, but every week or two, after a heavy day of running, pretending, or both, he would contemplate his end. However, it was usually the days when he had time to think, when the pull to find his parents and friends tattooed another reaper onto his mind, erasing another smile, another patch of flowers left over from that long-lost innocence. He wanted so badly to cry.

The lasershod looked so easy, seemingly a way to peace. Instead, he wrote more in his letter to Fye. *My need for revenge is what keeps me going, but it is also killing me. There is a toxic seed in the force that drives me on to avenge. I wish I were like you, with your noble endeavor to right a wrong situation. But my fire comes from a desire to see them all bleed openly while leeches, maggots, and vultures eat them alive.*

He eyed the lasershod as if waiting for it to come to him, but went on writing.

Or to walk in Munna's footsteps, with her resolute call for peaceful change and nonviolence like Gandhi or Martin Luther King, or those other rebels of the past that we're forbidden to learn about, not allowed to even know their names. I'm so grateful I was raised in a library . . . it may be all that saves me. That, and you, of course. If I'm even to be saved at all.

Grandyn picked up the lasershod, gripped it tightly.

"Dad, help me!" he groaned, pointing the weapon at his face. He looked into its smooth black metal end, narrower and slightly shorter than an old-fashioned gun, precisely machined, one hundred percent accurate and highly lethal. It felt like strength, something that could solve problems, right wrongs, and perhaps transport a person to a different reality. Sweat dripped from his temples.

His trembling hand put the lasershod back on the table.

I have such guilt, he wrote, *and if I'm to be denied my revenge . . . living with that failure would do a better job of killing me than this laser-shod ever could.*

CHAPTER THIRTY-FIVE

Hilton Prison officials allowed inmate Evren outside solitary confinement for ninety minutes each day. Thirty of that was spent alone on a three-by-three-meter dirt pad enclosed by an old-fashioned, three-meter-high chain-link fence, his recreation time mandated by law. But it was the other hour, his mandated socialization time, that Evren made most use of. None of the inmates knew his true identity as Polis Drast, former head of the AOI for the Pacyfik region. If they'd known, he'd be dead.

The AOI had gone to some trouble to keep one of their former leaders alive. During the first few months of incarceration, a waiver had been issued and he spent twenty-four-seven in isolation until enough work had been done on his face as to make him unrecognizable. His transformation was complete when he, like all inmates, had his head shaved. He and his fellow convicts had all celebrated the news that Polis Drast had been killed, making his Evren cover story even more solid.

Safe in his new identity, instead of lying low, he used his knowledge of the AOI to his advantage. In his prior role he had read the files of most of the prisoners at Hilton, since he'd actually been responsible for getting a majority of them locked up.

"Mite" was an early conquest. The stubby Asian man had earned his nickname by being an explosives expert. Mite, short for Dynamite, didn't use the forgotten nitroglycerin-based explosive. Instead he used pulse, EMFs, laser, and nano-particle varieties. He'd been an AOI contractor, but was caught supplying materials and technical knowledge to a group of Rejectionists with links to PAWN. Normally, Mite would have been executed, but like almost all the other residents of AOI penal facilities, he'd been allowed to live because the AOI believed he might be useful at a later time. Additionally, in the case of Mite, he was one of the top scientists in the industrial, space, and munitions explosive field.

Evren, of course, knew this and wanted to be friends with Mite for the same reason the AOI did.

"What do you say today, Mite?" Evren asked as the most important sixty minutes of the day started.

"Evren," he said, holding out his two fingers in a "peace" sign and inserting them into Drast's, whose were arranged the same way. The modern equivalent of bumping fists stood for being plugged into the same program. "Good, man, I say good things today."

"Any news?" Evren asked, glancing up at the guard tower. News was supposed to be kept away from the inmates. They had no access to the Field, and their only entertainment came in the form of AOI-censored movies appearing on AirViews in their cells.

"Heating up out there," Mite said, watching an android guard patrolling fifteen meters away.

The android, and other nearby devices, were monitoring them constantly, including audio and visuals, but Evren had managed to get micro-Whistler-mimics for a number of his important inside "crew." The micro-Whistlers with "mimics" attachments were miraculous devices that fit into their mouths. The Whistler blocked their conversation from being monitored, and then broadcast a false audio prerecorded by DesTIn artificial intelligence systems to replicate small talk – weather, food complaints, etc.

As a college professor, Drast had said several times, "For each way to monitor, a way to defeat that monitoring will be invented." So far it had proven to be mostly true. The AOI had not yet detected mimics, and didn't appear even to know the technology existed.

Evren nodded. "It's close." But the recoding of their conversation would have that as, "It's cold."

"And the chamber-slot is installed." Even with the mimics, they still spoke in shorthand, as Drast had also said that there will always be a kind of arms race in the surveillance industry, and new ways to defeat the defeating systems would, inevitably, also come.

Evren eyed a fly and wondered if it was real or a drone. But Mite had just given him excellent news. The chamber slot was the plan to breach all AOI prisons at once, and installed meant the systems and people were all in place to carry out the action. It would happen as soon as PAWN struck. That part he was still trying to get a handle on, but he knew it would be soon, and, when the chamber slot occurred, he would be free.

"What're the numbers?"

Mite answered with a series of numbers which told Drast which guards were with them. They had four humans so far, and were hoping for one more, but the support would come from nine androids that would be remotely reprogrammed over the Field during the final hour. It was a bold plan that only a former AOI head could have organized. Drast had been working on it for years, long before he became inmate Evren. Back then he had not been expecting to be on the inside, but nonetheless, that possibility had always haunted him.

"What about Tiger?" Evren asked.

Mite raised an eyebrow. "Are you sure we need that crazy torg?"

Tiger was a seemingly crazy inmate who'd earned his nickname inside by killing two inmates at an AOI prison in Arizona. This was his third institution in just five months. "Torgon if I care!" Tiger screamed one day when a guard threatened to transfer him after he threatened to eat the guard's ear for not allowing him to make a zoom. "I'm gonna see 'em all sooner or later."

Tiger had originally been locked up for murder, but Drast didn't know the details, as he'd come from Australik, the region that contained the countries formerly known as Australia, New Zealand, and surrounding islands. Tiger, a volatile man well over two meters tall, intimidated even the toughest Hilton residents. Part descendent from aborigines, and the rest a mixed mutt of European blood, his dark skin and electric blue eyes gave him a haunting look. His appearance was further enhanced by concrete muscles and white and yellow tattoos depicting him slaying dragons.

"Here he comes," Evren said.

"I'll see you later," Mite replied.

"No, stay. You just think he doesn't like you."

"I guess I misunderstood the last three times he told me he hates me so much he wants to set fire to my soul and use the ashes to smother any relatives I might have."

"He didn't mean that. It's all part of his act," Evren said. "Hey, Tiger, how are we looking?" The mimics sent the audio. "Hey, Tiger, what's the movie tonight?"

"I'm set for this weekend," Tiger answered Evren, while scowling at Mite. "It'll be worth it just to get away from this piece of trash."

"Hey, leave Mite alone. He might start to think you really don't like him," Evren said, smiling.

"Don't like him, ha! Maybe I should kill him for the transfer."

"No, no more killing or they may just execute you instead of transferring you. You must have some damned glowing hot information for the AOI to have let you live this long."

"They like me killing inmates." He shot a look to Mite. "It saves them the trouble."

Evren laughed. Mite just sat there trying to look tough, which wasn't too hard since he hated Tiger right back.

"Just push the guard, don't kill him," Evren said. "According to our informants, Pacyfik is over-crowded with the Doneharvest and they can't kill everyone. With the revolution looming, they need all the intelligence they can get from us cons."

"Why not just kill us all and do brain scans?" Mite asked.

As Drast, Evren knew this answer precisely. The Said-scans didn't always work, the process of data retrieval was tedious, the information gleaned was often incomplete and "one-dimensional," and it went stale. A valuable subject was always better to have alive. They could be tortured if necessary and, most important, they could be questioned as needed.

"They must have their reasons," Evren answered.

In the short period before they would all be returned to their cells, they worked out more of the logistics. Tiger and twelve other inmates would be transferred in the next two weeks for various reasons: medical, security, proximity to family, conflicts, etc. They would carefully spread word of the chamber-slot to the other prisons so that when the time came, the inmates would be ready, their assistance assured.

Evren sat in his two-by-two-meter cell and stared at the stainless steel walls. For two years he'd been living inside a tin can, guarded by the lowest bottom-feeders the AOI had to offer.

Although the majority of the inmates were good, honest revolutionaries, he didn't like trusting people, especially when some of them were real-life dangerous criminals like Tiger. Word could leak too easily, but there was no choice. Enough of the guards were in on it, not just at Hilton, but everywhere, that they had a slight tinge of protection. Drast still had people on the outside as well. There were thousands working toward the revolution, but the key to it all might *not* be Grandyn Happerman. In his opinion, it was the AOI. And Drast, better than anyone, knew the AOI was not exactly built on the loyalty of its agents.

CHAPTER THIRTY-SIX

Grandyn got himself together. In the end, it had once again been Hamlet that stopped him from pulling the trigger this time. "I am very proud, revengeful, ambitious, with more offences at my beck than I have thoughts to put them in, imagination to give them shape, or time to act them in. What should such fellows as I do crawling between earth and heaven?" Perhaps a gift from his father, after all.

He tried to reach Deuce, but unbeknownst to him, Deuce was deep in the redwoods, and therefore unavailable. Grandyn left a frustrated message. "Where are the books? Why is it taking so long?"

Sitting there thinking about Nelson, Chelle, and Munna, Grandyn realized that the books were as important to him as the revolution itself, not just because they could possibly provide the road to victory, but also because they were his father's. A link, and something more, a message, a real message, from whom, he didn't know. It could be hidden words from his father, but it was more likely from some unimagined, long-dead prophet who found a way to see the future and figured out how to warn them – the inhabitants of that future – how to save themselves from all that the prophet had seen.

Nelson had confirmed that they believed the books, which disappeared around the time of the attack that took his father, had not been destroyed by the AOI. He looked again at the AOI emblem and could almost see the flames in the glint of gold. "But where are they?" Grandyn had asked Nelson. "And even if Drast did save them, they could easily have been discovered and destroyed since his arrest."

"Deuce is working on it," Nelson had told him. "PAWN has some of the original books, and Deuce has about half of them, but I understand he's split them up into as many as eight locations. We have a dedicated team trying to find the books the AOI took, and Deuce has even more people working on the same thing."

"Three years? That's too long."

"If it weren't for the Doneharvest we'd have found them already. But don't worry. We *will*, and when we do, you have to be ready Grandyn," Nelson had said pleadingly, talking to him the way only someone who'd known him his whole life could. "Infinite-encryption means we can stay in touch, and your location will be unknown."

Infinite-encryption had been invented by one of Deuce Lipton's companies, and although it wasn't available to the masses, PAWN, TreeRunners, and a few other rogue organizations had access to it. For the rest of the malcontents, a simpler Whistler still allowed some protection from the AOI's snooping. The tiny device scrambled voice, data, and image communications within twenty-five meters of the INU partnered with the device. Grandyn recalled the days when they'd relied on what now was considered primitive technology and was amazed that they hadn't been caught.

Grandyn wanted to know what the prophecies said about the Banoff and those who had done it. The whole thing, and all that had occurred in the seventy-five years since, were incomprehensible to him. Nelson had told him once not to think so much about the "nightmare," adding, "It'll just make it all the more real." But Grandyn had been raised by thinkers, and he'd received a double dose of the trait that makes one worry and wonder. Every day, hours were lost trying to fathom the insanity.

Those in power at the time prior to the Banoff, the super-wealthy, thought they had no choice but to do what they did. Terrorists everywhere had changed the landscape, claiming victories around the globe. Traditional problem areas, like the Middle East and northern Africa, became unbearable, and the unrest spread. It spilled out of Afghanistan and Pakistan into India and China, then to other marginal areas. Sections of Mexico fell to guerilla groups. Eastern Europe, and even South Korea and Australia, saw flare-ups. Violence and unrest became the norm. At some point, the elites saw no way out and concocted the Banoff. They orchestrated the virus. Then, through planning and strategic deployment, combined with the use of inoculations and medication, they controlled the spread.

Grandyn remembered the conversation he'd had with Fye after she'd explained the motivation for the Banoff.

"In other words, they killed whom they wanted?" he'd asked her.

"Yes," she'd answered as if discussing a minor car accident. "Most definitely, certain populations were targeted. Historians would tell us that the huge loss of life among Muslims, Asians, and blacks was due to mistrust of western medicine and or immune problems, but nothing about the Banoff was accidental."

"How could they pull it off? How many knew?"

"They'd had a few dry runs in the early 2000s. Controlled epidemics were used to kill tens of thousands, then hundreds of thousands. The elites tracked medical and media response," she said, scratching numbers and something that looked like symbols from an old Asian language into her pad. The pencil flew across the paper while she spoke as if she possessed two independent minds.

"Apparently they learned well. No one would believe the Banoff was planned. I know it was, and I absolutely can't fathom the fact that those people knowingly did it."

He could still recall the feeling, like the wind getting knocked out of his lungs, an ache in his chest. He could not find words, he could hardly breathe. She had continued, not noticing his state.

"They saw it as the ends justifying the means. A chance to start over without war, hunger, crime, over-population, all the ills of the world could be erased. And you must admit, they created a wonderful world, but the AOI, initially meant to keep order and protect the Banoff secret, grew too powerful. The elite became afraid of losing all that they had created, all they had taken, and lived in fear that the Banoff secret might be exposed. They put all that fear into the hands of the AOI. The AOI made an art form of that fear, so much so that those three letters now represent it worldwide—the very definition of fear."

CHAPTER THIRTY-SEVEN

Miner, looking at his reflection on an AirView, pointed at himself and winked. He had not heard back from Blaze since he'd brought up Cope Lipton. He was now convinced that Blaze had not known about Booker's missing son. The Imps had known, and the Imps said Cope was dead. Blaze might have been surpassed by his own creations.

With things ready to explode in the Amazon, Miner was unwilling to leave the region, and had moved to a recently acquired building in the city of Manaus in the former country of Brazil. It was the largest metropolis in the Amazon basin, essentially accessible only by plane or boat. Even with the super speed of modern jets, it took almost three hours to travel there from Buenos Aires, and with sparks igniting in the revolution, Miner wanted literally to be completely on top of things.

Built just outside of Manaus, a solar-powered tower of green glass and nano-tech-composite-metal mirrored the massive surrounding Amazon jungle. Its thirty-one floors, most of them occupied by his Enforcers, as they prepared for war in the Amazon to breakout at any moment, currently contained the most advanced technology on the entire continent.

Miner had sent Sarlo to Denver on a recruiting mission. He wanted five Imps to come to Manaus to join him and several top commanders to run his war council. Imps didn't like to travel, definitely didn't want to work for others, and they couldn't be bribed with huge paychecks, so Miner was counting on their interest in the revolution. Imps had addictions to information, tension, and transitions, and many of them seemed to enjoy the added thrill of danger. He'd been right. Sarlo reported that more than thirty had been willing to come. She chose Miner's two favorites, plus three new ones that those two had recommended.

The Imps entered the room, looking like a well-dressed army of vampires awoken from the dead. Each appeared thinner than the other. Miner recalled saying, during their first visit to an Imp enclave, that they looked like stick figures, but studying them now he thought that description would be accurate only if they ate a few good meals. But their impeccable clothes, obviously custom fit and of the most advanced fabrics, gave them the respectable look of scientists visiting from another planet, one inhabited by a species of higher intelligence.

His favorite, an Imp called Charlemagne, greeted him in typical Imp fashion, with an uncomfortably long eye-to-eye stare and a cold, weak wave, then introduced the others. Miner had previously worked with the one named Descartes, who looked like the rest, painfully skinny with thin, prematurely gray hair. The one called Sidis seemed to be their de facto leader, perhaps the smartest or the boldest. He reminded Miner of Blaze Cortez, so he disliked him quickly, but would soon learn to respect the arrogant Imp.

"Arrogant Imp is a redundant term," Sarlo said later when they were alone.

"Arrogance isn't necessarily a bad thing if it's earned. The Imps might be the secret weapon that allows us to win this thing," Miner replied.

"But PAWN has Munna, and maybe the prophecies."

"For now. I'm hoping the first order of business for the Imps will be to find her."

"I thought they were here for war strategy?"

"Munna is a military target. If we can get her, we will have taken the heart from the rebels."

"But I still don't understand how the Imps can help. There is no record of Munna even existing. How can the Imps, whose special talents rely on computers, find her?"

"You're still not convinced that their knowledge goes beyond any Field interface," Miner said, unsure of his own beliefs. "Based on Charlemagne's finding Cope Lipton, something Blaze didn't even know, and the fact that we're fighting for control of some mysterious legendary prophecies said to be coded inside antique books, I think we need to give the Imps the benefit of the doubt." He suddenly had a flash of one of his war nightmares, but he suppressed it. Even so, Sarlo hadn't missed his expression. She spotted the grimace and knew he'd been hit by his curse, but said nothing.

"We've been looking for Grandyn, Munna, the books, and the prophecies for three years," Sarlo said. "If the Imps can find even one of them, I'll be a believer."

Miner's INU lit up. "The Imps are ready for us," he said.

CHAPTER THIRTY-EIGHT

Miner and Sarlo walked off the elevator onto the twenty-ninth floor and thought they'd been transported to a futuristic space ship. The entire ten-thousand-square-meter area was filled with AirViews far too numerous to count, and there were five banks of INUs that may each have contained a thousand Information Navigation Units. The stacked INUs resembled piles of whirling marbles, basked in dripping kaleidoscopes of abstract images, projecting rainbows of colors beyond what was visible in nature. The AirViews, like a carnival, multiplying and inventing dreams, took their senses to teetering heights from which fear and excitement merged in a moment of nauseated desperation. Instantly, they both shielded their eyes.

Descartes rescued them. "It is a bit to take in all at once," he said. "Please follow me. We have a section prepared over here."

He led them to an area cordoned off with black Tekfabrik curtains. Charlemagne, Sidis, and the other two were waiting. Miner and Sarlo joined them before they all sat in Tru-chairs scattered around a manageable series of AirViews.

"The probabilities show war beginning in nine days," Sidis began.

"Where?" Miner asked, hiding his shock that it would be so soon. Nine days remaining to avoid a war, his hope for peace fading faster with each passing minute.

"Seventy-three percent it's the Amazon. We're working on exactly where. There is a thirteen percent chance it will begin in Oregon. However, Mexico and eastern Europe, or somewhere in southern California and Spain are also registering."

"Can we avoid it?"

The five Imps shared rapid looks with each other. "Why would you want to?" Sidis asked.

"Why would I want to?" Miner jumped up. "We've been at peace for seventy-five years. Peace is prosperity. We're exploring and colonizing space, our medical advances are unmatched in human history, people are happy—"

"And you are wealthy," Sidis finished.

"Hell yes, I'm wealthy! There's nothing wrong with wealth. Anyone can achieve it in our great economy."

"*Really?*" Sidis asked.

Miner glared at him. "Really."

"Choose your delusions wisely Mr. Miner. The waves tangle in lies," Sidis said.

Miner looked at Charlemagne. "Who is this torg?"

"Does the truth offend you?" Sidis asked.

"Yes, Mr. Miner is offended by the truth," Charlemagne said as if Miner weren't there. "He is also bothered by things which do not fit his world view and can be irreverently upset by anything that goes against what he desires."

"Clearly," Sidis replied indignantly. "There are flights back to Denver in the morning."

"What's your problem?" Miner asked Sidis with a hopeful glance to Sarlo, a signal he'd like some help.

"Charlemagne, you know Lance is reasonable," Sarlo said, smiling. "We've worked together before. You know us."

Charlemagne nodded. "You must forgive the abrupt nature in

which we operate. The fragile human ego and insecurities of personality issues are time wasters we don't indulge."

"Oh, a little civility is beneath you?" Miner shot back.

"No," Sidis said. "Frankly, it's your mental capacity that is beneath us."

"Is this necessary?" Descartes asked. "Let's get to work."

"Fine with me," Sidis said, "but we don't have much time, so let's not squander it."

Everyone else was suddenly agreeable, and Miner was left to swallow his anger. He needed the Imps, but if everything didn't go well, if they didn't help in impressive ways, he silently vowed that Sidis would receive a visit from Enforcers.

"Fine," Miner said, forcing a smile. "My question stands. Is there still a chance to avoid war?" He looked at Sidis and decided that even if the Imps were a big help, he might send Enforcers to have a "chat" with him anyway.

"War, while not inevitable," Charlemagne said, "is so likely that our time and resources are best spent in search of the things you need to win."

"Then we can win?" Sarlo asked.

"I speak in general terms," Charlemagne said. "No one wins a revolution exactly, yet there are ways Mr. Miner may keep his wealth, effectively destroy PAWN, and keep the Aylantik in power, but even that will not be pretty."

"And it is far from assured," Sidis added. "In fact, it is less than probable at the moment."

Sarlo reached out and touched Miner's hand. She hadn't done it many times over the years, but the message was clear. *Take a deep breath.*

"There were some books stolen from the Portland library three years ago. We need to locate them," Sarlo said. "We also would like to know the whereabouts of Grandyn Happerman, who is the son of the librarian who helped remove the books."

Charlemagne nodded.

"And Munna," Miner added. "We need to find the woman they call Munna."

"Munna is a witch," Descartes said.

"We can be of no help with Munna," Charlemagne quickly added.

"What are you talking about?" Miner asked, trying again to control his blood pressure, glad his health alerts were on silent mode.

"She lives forever, she controls energy, and we have no way to reach her waves. She is a witch," Descartes repeated.

"What do 'a witch' and 'reach her waves' mean?" Sarlo asked.

"Munna is like an Imp, except she has no implant. Where the average person's brain capacity is utilized by the biological functions necessary to live and navigate its environment, most people have no idea about something infinitely more powerful than our brains . . . consciousness. Humans generally run that aspect of themselves on autopilot, unaware of their potential. Munna, on the other hand, has discovered a way to access universal consciousness."

"And what exactly does that mean?" Miner asked.

"She can do almost anything," Sidis said. "She can actually control her own cells down to a molecular level. It is one of the reasons she has lived for so long."

"And how do you know so much about Munna if there are no records on her?" Sarlo asked.

"We wander in the same realms," Descartes answered.

"You've tapped into universal consciousness too?" Miner asked.

Sidis smiled at Miner and then looked at the other four Imps.

One of the Imps that had remained silent up until then simply whispered, "Yes."

Suddenly, a dark AirView came to life in an explosion of stars, nebula, quasars, galaxies, and conjured blends of streaming light. The demonstration lasted less than a minute and ended with a burst, and then the face of an old lady appeared.

"Hell, is that Munna?" Miner asked, shocked.

"Yes, Lance. I am Munna," she said, smiling.

CHAPTER THIRTY-NINE

Chelle was stunned by Blaze's "guess," and assumed he must somehow have faked the message from Drast. There was still the underlying hope that Drast was really alive, but she didn't know what to think. The only thing she absolutely knew for sure was that Blaze Cortez could not be trusted.

"Is Drast alive or not?"

"Didn't you just receive word from him?" Blaze asked. "Do dead men contact you often? If not, then I think Drast himself has answered your silly question."

"If you didn't send it, how do you know about this *secret* message?"

"Do you know so little of me lover?" He stared into her eyes seductively. "We're the same, you and I. Made mostly of secrets . . . our desires are things we want nobody to know. Our methods, though often harsh and made from broken things that fill the saddest parts of us, are, in the end, something beautiful."

The sincerity in his voice, the disarmingly haunted expression he wore, and the accuracy of the words captured her momentarily. And he saw it. His holographic image reached for her hand, she allowed hers to linger in the digital-colored air. Then, telling herself that Blaze was nothing more than a character like those in Nelson's books, she pulled away. *He's invented this illusion of himself, knowing me, knowing he might reach me, knowing I might trust someone like that.*

"Don't go," he said. "This is real Chelle."

"Using my name rather than 'lover' was a nice touch, but I'm not quite as easily manipulated as you might have guessed." She stared at his hurt expression, eyes filled with sadness and loss so deep that she thought that part of the façade must be genuine. "If Drast is alive, you must prove it to me."

"Why should I do that? It makes little difference if you believe it or not."

"That's not true. If you didn't care, you wouldn't know about it. You must realize that if Drast is alive and able to communicate from an AOI prison, then the rebel alliance is strengthened, and regardless of which way you want the war to go, this is a matter of great consequence to either side."

"Suppose I want the Aylantik to win?"

"I was under the impression you didn't care who won, so long as you profited."

"That could change if you and I were on the same side lover."

"Damn it, we're talking about the fate of the world, millions of lives in the balance, and you're flirting like a college kid, like a jerk."

"Yes, you're right. Why enjoy life when we can take it sickeningly serious?" Blaze shook his head. "But have it your way. Instead of showing you the bridges to the stars and creating light from the aching darkness, we can discuss prisoners, death, and war. Where would you like to begin?"

She looked at him regrettably for a moment, then repeated her question. "Is Drast alive?"

"He is. If you want proof, think of a test only he could pass and give it back to the courier, what's his name? Terik."

"But if they are using a Said-scan on him then they would be able to answer anything I ask."

"If that's all you're worried about I have a contact inside Hilton Prison. I'll arrange for a zoom."

"A zoom! With Polis?"

"Sure, something as simple as a zoom is not a problem."

"From inside an AOI *prison?*"

"Haven't you heard? I'm a wizard!"

"Seeing him only works if they haven't made some kind of look-alike android out of him."

Blaze laughed. "You're a challenge, aren't you? Impossible to ever satisfy. Do you know what wizards do? We do the impossible all the time."

"What's that mean?"

"Answer your old friend Polis Drast. Please don't mention my name. He never cared for me. I'll arrange a zoom, and then you decide if you think it's really him."

Chelle realized there wasn't much to lose at that point. Whoever sent the message already knew how to get into her computer. There were infinite encryption codes with the reply instructions, and she could respond without talking about the revolution or any other sensitive material. "Okay. But I want to know how you profit from this?"

"Oh, lover, sometimes a man does things for a beautiful woman only because she is so beautiful." He smiled. "There are rewards more valuable than money, even more important than power. The thing that I speak of . . . is pleasure. It gives me pleasure to assist so lovely a woman, so brave a warrior. You do not have to trust me, but I'll give no reason to do otherwise."

In spite of her best efforts not to fall for his lines, she smiled.

And so did he. "I'll contact you when it's arranged. Farewell until then."

Chelle composed her reply to Drast and read it over twice before she followed the instructions to get it to Terik.

Polis, I never dared imagine you had survived your unfortunate arrest. This is incredible news. I'm sure you understand that I must be certain it is actually you I am communicating with, so I have a question that will need to be answered before we continue. There was a piece of information I gave to Beale the night before his death. I meant to provide the same data to Runit. Now, in light of all that has happened, with time running out, if you're in a position to take the necessary action, the secret should be given to you. It is critical, if it is actually you who receives this message, that you respond. And please tell me if you already know that to which I refer.

Chelle felt confident that the message would get past any AOI screening, and only hoped that Drast would be able to decipher her meaning. That is, if it really was Drast receiving it.

CHAPTER FORTY

Inside the bunker, Zaverly stomped into the weapons room and found Grandyn. She couldn't believe the orders. "Grandyn, we're going back out there."

He shook his head. The disappointment in her face upset him, and the feeling was a surprise. "This has to stop. I'm going to the supervisor."

"I've just left him. We have no choice." Ten knuckles cracked at once like firecrackers.

"I'll tell him I'm sick, that my ribs aren't healed, something."

"We *have* to go."

"Why? The AOI is all over the place. We should just evacuate and relocate to somewhere safer."

"They want us to engage them," Zaverly said.

He read her eyes, saw devastation mixed with determination that tore at emotions he didn't know he had. They both understood that intentionally engaging the AOI, in the open jungle where they were vastly outnumbered, was suicide.

"Why?" he repeated.

"I thought you were so important that we had to do anything

to protect you," Zaverly said with a shaky voice. "But suddenly it looks as if they're sacrificing you."

"Maybe they have a higher opinion of my abilities than you do." He smiled, trying to make light of their desperate situation.

"I don't think that's possible," she said, not amused. "They haven't been out there with you."

"Maybe it's you. Everyone knows you're superhuman. Maybe they finally realized you're our secret weapon. Maybe you're invincible."

"Shut up Grandyn!" She stopped just short of shoving him again. "Don't you get it? We're going out there, and we're probably not coming back. The AOI *knows* you're down here. They've put three years into this, into tracking the lost TreeRunner, and now they have you cornered in a patch of the Amazon." Zaverly paused as if something had clicked in her mind. "That's what they're doing... They're sending us out there because if you don't get caught soon, the AOI will probably just obliterate five square kilometers of the rainforest. The Aylantik has plenty of weapons that can do that, you know."

He nodded. "The order probably came down from Parker. She's not my biggest fan."

"Even if she was," Zaverly began, "twenty-six dead TreeRunners might be something they can tolerate to protect you, but hundreds? In one swoop? How many do we have down here, and the whole installation, all the bunkers? It's too much to give up for you. They need you right now to pay back the TreeRunners, to give your life to save the rest."

"But what about you? Why send you with me?"

"I volunteered."

"What?"

"They were going to send Lloyd," she said, not looking at him. "I couldn't let that happen."

"Well, you can't go."

"You'll stop me?" She smiled quickly. "I don't think so."

"Lloyd is a good guy."

"Lloyd is definitely nice, but you'd last about ten minutes with him. It's not just a unit of grunges . . . half the torgon AOI is going to be out there."

"Zaverly," he said, putting his hands on her shoulders, silently staring into her eyes for a moment before continuing. "You are not going to die for me."

"Not if I can help it," she said, never losing his eyes.

"You know this is a suicide run. I'm being used as bait, a sacrificial lamb."

"That's what's so crazy," Zaverly said, stepping back so his hands fell away. If his hands had stayed on her shoulders any longer, she would have pulled him into an embrace, and that couldn't happen. She wanted it to, just not before they were going into battle. They couldn't afford to be soft and mushy. They couldn't afford much in what was probably going to be the final hours of their lives. "How long until the AOI annihilates the rest of them anyway? Until they crater this whole area?"

"Maybe it'll give them time to get out."

"Something isn't right. I don't know what it is, but I don't buy it that they've saved you for three years only to toss you to the wolves now."

"It's a timing thing," he said. "The war is about to start."

"Too bad," she said, grabbing her gear. "We're just going to have to surprise them and survive this. I plan to be in that war. I plan to help win it."

CHAPTER FORTY-ONE

Munna looked into the room, smiling. "Lance Miner, how interesting to meet you."

Miner, still stunned, looked at the five Imps.

Sidis shook his head as if to say, *We didn't do this.*

Charlemagne shrugged, as baffled as the rest.

Sarlo couldn't help but smile back at the old lady.

"How did you do that?" he asked, referring to the explosion of stars, nebula, quasars, galaxies, and light in which she arrived.

"I heard you talking about me. I understand you've been wanting to meet for years, just thought it was time to pay you a visit."

Miner looked around for a weapon. This woman was his enemy. He wanted to take her into custody, and if that wasn't possible, killing her was fine with him. But of course, she wasn't really there, just a type of hologram. "Where are you?"

"I'm near some lovely trees," she said. "And you're in a lovely spot yourself. The Amazon is one of my favorite places. Let's not scar it all up with a war."

"I don't want war."

"Yes, I know. We share that in common."

"You don't want war, but PAWN—"

"PAWN is not me. They have their own ideas about how change should come."

"Change?"

"Yes, Lance, change. I may not want war, but a change is gonna come." She smiled again. "You still have time to be on the right side of that change."

Miner laughed. "Oh really, is that why you're here? To get the sinner to repent before judgment day?"

"Lance, do you know how old I am?"

"I've heard rumors, but you look younger than I thought you would."

"You think power comes from money, from controlling people . . . You have no idea. I have no possessions, no money, I control no one with rules, laws, or manipulation, and yet for years you have sought to destroy me, because you fear my what?" She stared at him intensely. "You fear my *power*."

"Fear is not in my vocabulary, Munna. You're mistaken. I don't want to destroy you because of your power, I want to destroy you to add to my power."

She smiled. "Perhaps Sarlo will explain it to you later."

Sarlo burst out laughing.

Miner glared at her.

"Where do you think my power comes from Lance?" Munna asked.

"My advisors here tell me it comes from your alleged ability to access universal consciousness."

"Do you believe in universal consciousness?"

"I have a vague notion of something," he said, waving his hands to the heavens.

"And do you believe I can access it?"

"I think if you could do what my advisors say you can, then you wouldn't be wasting time with me, and you would have already won this war."

"You have forgotten, I do not want war. And you clearly don't understand how the universe works. May I suggest you read some books? And Lance, please leave me to my work. Don't waste *your* time looking for me or trying to stop me. I'm the best chance you have to stop the war that you so dearly wish to avoid."

Her image faded, replaced by a three-dimensional book, which was now on his INU. *"Observations of the Universe, a Conversation with Cope Lipton,"* by Nelson Wright.

Munna stopped and waited for Nelson to catch up. Somehow she seemed to get younger in the redwoods. Nelson had a harder time accepting he was fifty-four than believing she was one-hundred-thirty-three. He vowed once again to give up smoking, drinking, and eating. That was it, he decided, that's what was killing him. He'd never seen Munna eat, maybe some nuts and seeds once or twice, and he'd peeled an apple for her a while back, but he couldn't think of much else. And she certainly never touched alcohol or bacs.

"Okay," he said to himself. "I'll give up drinking and eating, except for nuts, seeds, and berries. And I'll limit my bacs to no more than seventeen a day – one every hour I'm awake." He always enjoyed his own sense of humor.

"Here we are again!" Munna said as she reached him. "It's been three years since I brought you here to meet Cope."

Nelson nodded, too winded to answer. He checked the time on his INU and reached for his bacs. *Surely it's been an hour since my last one. We've been walking forever,* he thought.

"Why do you insist on killing yourself Nelson? You're such a talented man."

"Last time I was here, Cope was still alive," he said, lighting a bac and ignoring her criticism.

She smiled. "We need minds like yours. You can sway people . . . but that is significantly more difficult to do if you're dead."

"The year I spent with Cope was the most important time of my life. He changed how I view everything." He sat on a nearby fallen tree. "Why did you arrange it so I could stay with Cope? Why me?"

"Because you have the power to get the message out." She looked at him, her eyes glowing in the muted light of the late morning sun, filtered by thousands of centuries of old trees. "Those things you discovered are more important than the revolution. The prophecies are part of the proof of what is possible. They aren't meant to be used to win a war, they are meant to end war."

In spite of his sister fighting so hard to start the revolution, he believed Munna. Because of his experiences with Cope, he knew she was right, but he lacked her deep references that formed the core of her beliefs. It was as if he had not completed something, like reading a book with the last chapter torn out. "Perhaps if I read the prophecies. Maybe if I live to be as old as you . . . I know in principle we should avoid war, but I lack the faith you have."

"For what?"

"That we could remove Aylantik and end the AOI without bloodshed."

"Perhaps you cannot." They stood in the shade of a huge tree.

"But we can't allow them to remain. Even another day is too long."

"There are other ways to find change . . . there are always other ways."

"Then, by all means, please tell them to me."

"Come," Munna said, walking again.

"Are you going to answer me?"

"Oh, Nelson, didn't your time with Cope teach you anything? The answers are always here." She waved her arm in a circular motion above her head. "The answers are all around us."

He followed her silently for a while. Every so often he squinted into the space between some of the particularly more massive trees, hoping to discover an answer. Cope had been easier to understand, more direct. Sometimes he and Cope would play cards, and in between hands and draws their conversation would be as if two old friends were hanging out. But at the end of the evening, Nelson would realize he'd learned something. Sometimes it was big, like the time they'd been discussing their favorite foods – Nelson claiming pizza and Cope craving apples. "The real ones," he would say, "the ones right off the tree, never sprayed, just some tree forgotten in an overgrown corner of somewhere."

Still unsure how it happened out of that conversation, Nelson first considered the power in simple things. Real power, as if a single thought could change the world. *A pebble rippling in a pond*, he recalled, looking up through the branches of a mighty tree he remembered from his time in the forest with Cope.

"Answers all around," Munna echoed her earlier words.

Nelson wondered if it might be possible somehow to overthrow Aylantik with words. After all, words were at the center of the revolution . . . the books, the prophecies, his own writings, the history of the Banoff, and the rules of the Doneharvest and all the names lost in between. Words. A pebble rippling in a pond.

"Twain was here with you and Cope. You know that young man fairly well, I suppose," Munna said. "Where would he go?"

"You mean if he didn't want to be found?"

"Yes."

"Don't you think if he doesn't want to be found we should allow him that?"

"I thought we'd already settled that. Deuce is out here looking, and that brings many complications. Twain will have other times to seek his meaning and understanding. Right now we need him to be with his father."

"But I still don't get your concern. Deuce doesn't agree with your anti-war stance. What does it matter if he misses his son? We know Twain is safe."

"It is more than a 'stance,' and it is not about him missing his son. Deuce must be convinced that war is not the correct road, and only Twain can do that. You should know, from the perils of Grandyn and the other TreeRunners, that being in the forest, even the redwoods, does not ensure one's safety."

CHAPTER FORTY-TWO

Standing in a small wooden shed on the edge of the forest, Grandyn, with hungry eyes, stared at the holograph of Fye. His desire went beyond wanting to touch her real flesh instead of the digital apparition standing next to him in the pale evening light. It exceeded every measure of what he knew as a man of lust. Fye had not only saved him, she filled the missing parts that had been ravaged by AOI plots and schemes. Grandyn may have seemed lost to everyone else, but without her, he'd be lost to himself. Fye, in a real sense, was his entire world.

She returned the stare, kissing him with her eyes, imagining their shared passion changing the hue of the surrounding air to some shade of magenta. "When do I see you again?"

"I don't know," he replied. "The torgon AOI has me running around the clock. We're so close to this thing erupting that they're throwing everything at any Grandyn sighting."

"It's so dangerous now. The systems show the probability of them catching you at eighty-eight percent. It's never been that high."

"They won't catch me."

"You don't know that." Her voice was strained. "Twelve

percent. That's all you have. Can you escape in such a small amount of space? If things ignite in the Amazon, your survival chances drop to less than seven percent."

"What do you want me to do?" It killed him to hurt her, to scare her.

"Come to me. This is the only place you'll be safe."

"You know I can't do that. Everything I've worked for in the last three years will be for nothing. My mother's death, my dad—"

"You don't carry this whole thing on your shoulders, Grandyn. You're one man, you're twenty-one, you—"

"I'm a Happerman. This is my fight. I know there are others fighting, but everyone has their own agenda, and this cause is mine. I've got to find the books and unravel the prophecies."

"Grandyn, you don't even know if the prophecies are real."

"They are."

"I know you believe that, but how do you know?" She scribbled letters on her pad, not even looking at the paper.

"I know because Munna is real, and she says they are. And Nelson, I've known him longer than anyone else in my life, and he says they're real. And, because . . . I just know it."

"But what if they aren't?"

"They are."

"But if they *aren't*?"

"Then I'll still have the books. The real books."

"But they're just books. We have all that data preserved."

"They aren't just books, they're my dad's books. He would expect me to keep them safe."

"I know. I just don't want you to." She flipped a page in her pad and kept writing. He was so used to her strange habit of sketching words and symbols that he hardly noticed it anymore.

"We're almost there," he said.

"Where? The books? War?"

"Everything. Can't you feel it?" His voice rose. "The whole

world is about to explode, and we can't stop it . . . but we do have the power to change it."

"The List Keepers look at it differently. Without war, the List Keepers go on. Revolution, the List Keepers go on. The books, the prophecies, Munna . . . whatever happens, we go on."

"I understand that. But the rest of us, the two point nine billion survivors of the AOI who don't even know the List Keepers exist, let alone who they are or what they do, we have to go on regardless of what you do."

"You're a List Keeper," she said quietly.

"To you I am . . . but . . ." He looked at her softly, wanting to take her hands. "But to me, I'm a TreeRunner, I'm a Happerman, and I have to stop the AOI."

"You have to save the world." She smiled, remembering when they first met, before she loved him, before events had spun even more out of control and Fye had said the same thing to him.

He nodded, but barely smiled. He remembered too. "I got a message from Deuce, sent before he headed into the redwoods. I'd asked him, not too politely, how much longer until he had all the books together. He gave a complete accounting. The problem is that right after we got the books out of the library and hid them in a barn, Chelle let Deuce take what turned out to be about one-third of them. Munna ordered the others split up and moved, but the Doneharvest created chaos. As you know, the AOI intercepted several shipments and moved them to a warehouse where they were supposed to be destroyed."

"But Drast saved those."

"Right, we know that now. But the AOI didn't get them all, as we originally thought. Several of the shipments got through, but the people in charge were killed in AOI raids just hours after they had safely hidden the books."

"But surely Munna would know where they are?"

"She would if they had reached their final destination, but they didn't. Remember, the Doneharvest exploded with a shocking show of force. In all that confusion, the PAWN agents who were moving the books were forced to drop them at temporary locations. Those agents were killed that same day."

"You mean everyone who knew where they were is dead?"

"So it would seem. But Deuce has had a team working on it for three years and they just uncovered a hidden cache. Once we get Drast's books, Deuce estimates we'll have about ninety percent. That's enough to give us a good chance to find the missing eight works that contain the prophecies."

"Progress."

"Still a needle in a haystack, but you've shown me repeatedly that nothing is impossible."

"I don't have any doubt that you can find them, but then what? Lance Miner, Deuce, Blaze, Chelle, they all want the prophecies. Are they really going to let you keep them?"

"I haven't figured out that part yet, and I know Nelson will be there, but right now I'm the only one who knows about Hamlet. I'm counting on Shakespeare to save me. After all, I'm the only son of the Last Librarian."

CHAPTER FORTY-THREE

Inside the AOI Hilton super-max prison, Evren had only an hour a day in which to recruit and conspire with inmates, but he had the remaining twenty-three to work the guards. This was even easier since all the senior officers knew his real identity as Drast. He was too important, and still held secrets the AOI needed. Even prior to his arrival, a deputy to the Chief had briefed the top guards. Deaths at Hilton, like most AOI lock-up facilities, were not unusual, and the Chief needed Drast protected. Drast was the highest-ranking PAWN arrest they'd ever made. He was a deep probe into whatever the AOI was up against. If war were to be avoided, his information would help her do it, and if war came, his information could help her win it quickly.

The directive to "keep an extra watch" on Evren/Drast had unintended results. Most of the guards resented their low-level assignments with pay to match. They were easy targets for the once powerful former AOI Regional Head, and, remarkably, Drast somehow still had access to a seemingly untraceable and significant pool of money. More than that, he could see into all their personnel files. He knew how to get to each one, and he knew how to cover his tracks.

Even the most intelligent of the guards weren't sure what Drast was doing. They brought him encrypted messages and smuggled out his responses. They brought him in good food and helped him avoid the mandatory booster shots, but Drast remained a mystery to them. Whenever they discussed him among themselves, words like "complicated" and "confusing" were almost always used to describe the inmate known as Evren.

As Drast was escorted to the visitors' room, he slipped a thread to a passing guard. A thread, the length of a wooden match and the diameter of angel hair pasta, could contain the equivalent of a terabyte of data. Osc, right beside him, didn't even notice the exchange. Drast preferred to keep his minions as separate as possible.

Terik sat in an old-fashioned brown folding chair made from plantik. He nodded to Osc as Drast sat down. Osc took the cue and left the room. Knowing time was short, Terik sent a small AirView from his INU toward Drast before he even said hello.

A generic female digital voice read the message. *"Polis, I never dared imagine you had survived your unfortunate arrest. This is incredible news. I'm sure you understand that I must be certain it is actually you I am communicating with, so I have a question that will need to be answered before we continue."*

Terik spun his AOI pin while they listened. He didn't know he was doing it, but Drast, a man who missed nothing, did. *It could be an annoying habit, or it could be something else*, he thought. Either way, the former AOI regional head didn't like it.

The voice reading Chelle's message continued, *"There was a piece of information I gave to Beale the night before his death. I meant to provide the same data to Runit. Now, in light of all that has happened, with time running out, if you're in a position to take the necessary action, the secret should be given to you. It is critical, if it is actually you who receives this message, that you respond. And please tell me if you already know that to which I refer."*

Drast smiled broadly, almost giggled. "Good work Ander, absolutely wonderful work." He slapped the table as if to punctuate his enthusiasm for the message.

Terik was satisfied that Drast was so pleased. "Apparently you know to which she refers?"

"Oh yes," he said, still smiling. "I most certainly do. Does she know who you are?"

"I gave her my name and AOI credentials."

"Brave . . . aren't you concerned she'll try to blackmail you?"

"I don't think she'll risk losing the conduit to you, and I think she's more worried about how the AOI got into her INU. In fact, I think she's terrified. That's one reason I'd like your response as quickly as possible. If she knows it's really you, I think she'll relax and not do anything crazy."

"Chelle never does anything crazy," he said, laughing again, giddy from her words.

"I've done my part. Are you going to give me the rest of what I need?"

"The books?"

"Of course, but I want everything."

"Everything? You can't handle everything."

"Why?"

"Because you're twenty-something, you're already in far over your head, and I can't believe you haven't been caught."

"I'm smarter than you think."

"No, you're not." Drast finally stopped smiling. "You think a career in the AOI, rising through the ranks by any means necessary, will somehow bring you the power you crave?"

"It worked for you."

"Did it?" Drast widened his eyes and looked around. "You're playing a dangerous game, and my files would only make it more dangerous for you."

"What if you die?"

"You mean what if they execute me?"

"One of the two is going to happen sooner or later. You're not getting out of here except in a box."

"Don't have much faith in the rebels, do you?"

"Are they going to save you? Bust you out of here?"

"Maybe . . . The thing about being young is you think you know everything, but I've been working on this since before you were born, so imagine for a minute that I might have a few more bases covered than you give me credit for." His scowl slowly formed back into a smile. "I'm the biggest traitor in the history of the Aylantik, yet I'm not dead. I'm not even doing time in the worst AOI prison in the world. They locked me up in my own damned region. They've gone to an awful lot of trouble to make sure I'm comfortable, and I wouldn't be surprised if I outlive you. Why don't you run those variables in your INU sometime? You might be shocked at the results."

"What about the books?"

"Deliver my response to Chelle, and I'll give you that information."

"I want the books now."

"I'm sure you do, but that's not going to happen."

Terik looked at Drast and realized he really was way out of his league. "Fine. What's the message?"

"It's a simple one. Three words. I love you."

CHAPTER FORTY-FOUR

Blaze sat with his knights around the clear, round table filled with electronics that gave the piece of "furniture" the power of one hundred thousand INUs. Each of his twenty-four lieutenants studied AirViews floating in front of them. The mix of CHRUDEs and Imps processed a staggering array of information, including up-to-the-second AOI troop movements, thermal readings of forests around the world, and Mood-monitors.

The latter were massive programs that compiled each communication from every citizen of the world, and combined it with Seeker footage which tracked public movements of the population to create a Mood-monitor showing, with alarming accuracy, the exact mood of an individual, segment of the population, or the entire world at any given minute.

Although the coming conflict had been largely hidden from the populace by strict Aylantik control of the media and the entire Field, there were clear indications in the moving wave presented by the Mood-monitor that people were "sensing" trouble. As the brilliant collection of intelligence gathered at the round table continued to grapple with what that revelation might mean to the outcome of the war, Blaze called the meeting to order with ominous words, "If we don't begin the revolution soon, we will no longer be able to control the outcome."

Morholt, one of the CHRUDEs, spoke first, as usual. "You can see by the Mood-monitor that in a matter of days, a small percentage of the population will begin to fear war. Within a few more days, that fear will spread into a firestorm until, in less than two weeks from now, preparations will be made with demands upon the government that will make it unstoppable."

"The AOI doesn't have enough troops to canvass all the areas where Grandyn has been sighted. They may burn the forests if they don't find him soon," Lucan the Butler, a particularly wiry Imp who never smiled, said, displaying an AirView showing a simulation of out-of-control forest fires around the globe and the resulting destructive impact. "The damage to the environment would be devastating."

"We have detected substantial buildups of AOI troops around the Amazon, Russia, and China Areas, and smaller, but still sizable ones, in Canada, India, and Australia Areas," Galahad, another Imp, added. "They are spreading their forces very thin."

"They aren't just looking for Grandyn, but clearly he is their biggest fear. The AOI must know about the prophecies," Blaze said.

"They could simply wait for PAWN or the Rejectionists to come out for a fight and take them out from the air, but sending in vast amounts of troops or burning forests are desperate measures in order to keep peace."

"Yes," Blaze answered.

"Why are they so afraid of war when they are so clearly superior to the rebels in every measure and capability?" Galahad asked.

"Because they know something," Blaze said. "Lance Miner may not know what the prophecies say, but he knows enough of the Banoff secrets to be worried that they say too much. The population may be unarmed, but give two point nine billion people a reason, and they will force change. That is what the Aylantik fears. It doesn't matter how powerful the AOI is. If the masses turn on the government, it's over."

"The Aylantik has shown, since its inception, that they are not afraid to exterminate huge numbers of people who do not fit into their world view," Bors, a CHRUDE, said. "Let's not forget the strength the Health Circle wields. In many ways they are far more powerful than the AOI."

"Excellent point, Bors," Blaze said. "And if I were a betting man . . . wait, I am a betting man. Well then, I would bet that it all comes down to the Health Circle and the List Keepers. Any luck Galahad?"

Galahad had been as obsessed as an Imp could be in finding a way to infiltrate the List Keepers shields, or "black holes," as they were known, which were legendary among the Imp community. Imps had long been in a race to find a way in, and Blaze had offered a large bounty to any Imp who could gain access to the List Keeper's system. Galahad and Percival, another of Blaze's Imp knights, had a personal competition, and worked constantly on the project. They didn't do it for the money, or even for the vast strategic advantage it would give Blaze. They did it because it was labeled impossible, and they believed otherwise.

Galahad shook his head in response to Blaze.

"I'll find them," Percival said. He worked on the theory that the List Keepers, who were long thought to be masters of the digital realm, were, in fact, using some other kind of quantum network to do their business – whatever that might be.

Blaze smiled. Percival was his favorite. "I believe you will. Now, I have another matter to deal with."

He gazed around the room at his brain trust, the knights all linked into the massive INU table. He knew information was power, but that intelligence was supreme power – and he had both. But there were some missing pieces: the List Keepers, the prophecies, and Cope Lipton.

"When we next meet, I need two things. No more blank screens with Cope Lipton. Something must exist on him or Lance couldn't have discovered him. I believe it came from an Imp. No one else could have cracked a secret like that. Find the Imp, find me Cope, or find enough data on him to make me think I slept with his wife."

He moved a few fingers and the AirViews around the table filled with Grandyn's face.

"We don't need to find Grandyn to use him. Eight hours from now, I need to see every contingency, every simulation, and every scenario for how best to *use* the TreeRunner. Dead or alive, books, prophecies, or not, Grandyn is the key. But as you know, there are many locks that a key can open. Locating the correct lock, that is our quest."

Once the room cleared, Blaze remained, studying the troop buildups around the globe. INU generated estimates for all those involved in the conflict. Unlike the AOI, PAWN, Miner, and Deuce, Blaze had no army. He believed they were an outdated relic of the pre-Banoff world. In reality, the others weren't traditional armies in the regimented sense.

The AOI was more like a giant SWAT team, Deuce and Miner's were more in the guerilla warfare class, and PAWN had a combination of the "farmers with muskets" model: high-tech cyber warriors and modern weapons accumulated in all manner of begging, borrowing, and stealing. Deuce had provided the majority of PAWN's advanced weapons stash, either through funding or direct shipments. It was the reason PAWN believed Blaze would be on their side in a conflict, but Blaze knew better. He was an expert at playing all sides so that even those working for him might not know where his loyalties were, and, in Blaze's case, did he even have any loyalties?

"Lover," Blaze said as soon as he saw Chelle's face projecting from his INU. "I was hoping to catch you in the shower or somewhere interesting, but you seem to be loading equipment into a truck."

"Yeah, Blaze, some of us work for a living. I, for one, do what ever is necessary for the cause."

"Do you?" He flashed a devilish grin. "I should try to think of something for your cause that you'd be willing to do *anything* for."

Chelle moved away from the crated weapons she'd been readying for shipment to a potential battle zone and took off a pair of gloves. "Did you zoom to harass me, or as you call it 'flirting', or do you have something worth talking about?"

"Cranky today? Too bad, and I'm afraid my news might not improve your mood. It seems that I'm not the wizard I claimed to be. I'm unable to get a zoom arranged with Drast, but it would not have done much to allay your concerns since you would not have recognized him."

"Did they hurt him?"

"No. Nothing like that. But his appearance has been completely altered. They are serious about wanting people to believe he is dead. They even altered his retina and facial patterns."

"I would know his voice," Chelle said, trying to imagine what he would look like now.

"Not possible. They did a procedure there as well. Seems they were concerned someone might recognize his voice from all his speeches in the media."

"Then I'll have to wait for his response. I was hoping to have some sort of verification without having to wait for this AOI agent, but now I'm not sure if I trust you or the AOI less."

"Really? You might want to give that some thought, lover. When the war starts, the eight sides will quickly merge into two sides and, at least while the fighting rages, there will be only one person who can help you. The man standing in the middle of it all . . . and then you will trust Blaze Cortez whether you like it or not. The question is, will *I* trust *you*?"

CHAPTER FORTY-FIVE

Another Grandyn sighting. This time, by AOI agents on a routine patrol in the endless Russian forests. It had been a brazen attempt to steal food from an AOI vehicle, left while the agents went on a four-hour sweep of the area on foot. "It was almost as if he wanted to get spotted," they told their commander in the initial report. "How he's avoided capture all these years is baffling." But they had verifiable data, including the clearest images taken since his disappearance.

The face went through the FRIDG system and matched every point with the computer scans, down to the millimeter. The chain of command sent the news flying to the top, and within half an hour of the sighting the AOI Chief had been pulled out of a meeting. By then the Ruskan region head had alerted all area units and hundreds of agents were arriving.

Within hours, at the orders of the Chief, thousands were streaming in. She was now convinced that the TreeRunners had been more sophisticated than previously imagined and most of the earlier sightings had been look-alikes. "But this one is no decoy. We finally starved him out," the Chief said triumphantly to her gathered top advisers. It had been her idea to beef up patrols in those northern forests of the Russia Area. "He has to be somewhere so remote that we can't see him," she'd said. "It's the only way. He's been playing the odds for three years, hiding where the forest is largest and our presence is smallest." But even she had been stunned by his mistake. "He must be hungry. There's probably almost no support for him up there. Perhaps they missed his last supply drop. Never mind. He has nowhere to hide now." But even as she said the words, the Chief worried that this might be another Shasta, where a Grandyn sighting they'd been all over – whether it had been him or not didn't matter – came up empty.

AOI had specifically trained on Grandyn drills for more than two years. They all knew forest procedures, where technology was limited. No eyes in the sky, no trackers, tracers, or grid sweeps. But they did have Collins-HG3s, the autonomous flying weapon, and thirty-four were deployed. Agents fanned out and released thousands of swarm drones. Suddenly, a unit of grunges hit Alert-99. It meant they had a visual on the target.

"This is team leader eight-eight. Target has just dropped into a manmade hole."

"Confirm. Target is Grandyn?" the on-sight commander answered.

"Affirmative. Target is Grandyn!" A strange static interrupted the transmission for a moment. "We have light in the hole." The team leader set a relay, trying to get images out, but the static returned. "There's a ladder. It appears to be an entrance to a tunnel."

"Pursue! Pursue!"

The Chief, monitoring the live feed, was more than tempted to take over, but her agents were far better trained than she. The commander directed ground-penetrating scanners to the sight of team eight-eight and also ordered explosives, which could crater the earth to a depth of thirty meters. At that point, the Chief contacted the commander.

"Do *not* use explosives. I need a body. Not only do I want his brain scan, but I have to be damned sure this is Grandyn."

"But he could escape."

"I'd rather that than to mistakenly think we got him. If we lose him, which you won't, we can catch him another day. The intel he holds is too valuable. Am I clear?"

"Yes, ma'am." The commander didn't agree, his mission was to stop a dangerous revolutionary, but he knew he could not argue.

"This is team leader eight-eight. We're inside the tunnel. Are you getting visuals?"

The Chief and the commander both watched live images on their respective AirViews. The Chief sat in a darkened room halfway around the planet. Her AirView, fifteen meters across and ten tall, showed the dimensions of the tunnel as everything was instantly analyzed. Height: two-point-two meters. Width: one-point-two meters. Depth: four-point-three meters. The tunnel shocked her in its sophisticated construction. Located in an extremely remote location, the floor and walls were smoothed concrete, the ceiling tiled and lit with some kind of illuminating bricks, plus ventilation.

Lance Miner received a zoom, and an AOI agent secretly linked the feed to him. He manipulated several AirViews while watching the images come in and out. Within minutes an Enforcers team was en route, ETA – one hundred and ten minutes. They would be outnumbered and might be too late but Miner had to try. He needed Grandyn.

He flipped his coin and was so outraged when he got another tails that he turned it over to make sure there was, in fact, a heads side.

Chelle got word shortly after Miner, but she didn't have the luxury of sending anyone to help. PAWN had nobody within a thousand kilometers. All she could do was hope there were enough Tree-Runners there. Unable to reach Parker, that group's leader, she zoomed Nelson, who had gone to the redwoods to help Munna find Twain. She knew it was almost impossible to get a zoom, but she tried anyway.

"We found Twain!" Nelson shouted, as her image came through. "He's barely alive."

"What?"

His voice was trembling. "The beach was our closest extraction point."

"Where are you?"

"We hiked out of the redwoods. We're on the coast some-where." He panted. "Munna got a zoom out and her people are on the way."

"What about Deuce?"

"No sign of him."

"What happened to Twain?"

"I don't know. Shallow breathing, very thin. He may have been starving. I don't know," Nelson repeated. "I carried him out."

"Are you okay?"

"Fine. Maybe. I don't know."

Chelle didn't like any of it; Grandyn on the verge of being killed or captured, Deuce's son near death. Twain was a person Munna deemed important enough for her to go personally into the wilderness to find him, and now Deuce might be missing. She watched Nelson light a bac and figured he could handle more news. His reaction was not what she expected.

"It's not him."

"What?"

"Grandyn has been sighted in the Amazon, India, Germany, and California Areas, not to mention all over the Pacific North-west, and now Russia. How is he getting to all those places?"

"Jet, Flo-wing? I have no idea, but it's more than possible. Why wouldn't he keep moving? Maybe Deuce is funding him, or who knows?"

"I don't think it's him."

"What if it is?"

"Then we can't do anything about it anyway."

"Don't you care?"

"Of course I care. I love him like a son—"

"And he can find the books, unlock the prophecies."

"That too." Nelson found his flask and held it up to Munna. She shook her head and continued to watch over Twain, lying motionless and unresponsive in the sand. Nelson checked the sky for any signs of a Flo-wing as he took a swig. "Grandyn is not a kid. He's become a sophisticated strategist and has as much, or more, reason as any of us to want the Aylantik ousted. He's too smart to get trapped in the Russian wilderness."

"You're awfully sure."

"That's because I know we're going to win, and we need Grandyn to do it."

"The AOI is convinced it's him."

"They've been convinced before."

"Polis is alive," she said, unable to suppress a smile. "At least I think he is."

"Wow, you're full of surprises today."

"He's in Hilton Prison. He sent me a message and I sent him a test."

"Amazing. See? Good news. We found Twain and Polis is alive. It can't be Grandyn."

"That is not logical reasoning, but I hope you're right."

"Here comes the Flo-wing. I'll be in touch. Try to reach Deuce, or his wife, or someone in his organization. I hope Twain will live long enough to see his father again."

CHAPTER FORTY-SIX

Team leader eight-eight followed the tunnel. The images he beamed up became more sporadic, the smoothed concrete walls and tiled ceiling seemed to snake on forever. Each of the team of nine agents held a lasershod, an infrared night vision, and various virtual shields – sonic, atom, and light-based – but they were nervous. Anything could be in this tunnel. It didn't belong here and it spoke of an advanced, organized foe, not some starving TreeRunner.

The on-site commander's voice came through the team leader's earpiece. "We're sending in a mini-Collins-HG3."

"Down," he ordered. The team dropped to the concrete floor ten seconds before the mini- Collins-HG3 flew above their heads, navigating the tunnel like a bat in a cave. The flying weapon relayed back images only as far as the team leader, as its signal could not penetrate the ground. The unit was flying autonomously and had been programmed to detain or injure the target. The team was back on their feet and jogging now in an effort to catch up to the HG3. They were feeling much safer and more confident with the mechanized back-up.

The team leader watched the images on a tiny AirView floating in front of his eyes. It responded to his retina, and would darken or become translucent as needed. "HG3 now nine hundred meters ahead of us," he reported, but most of his signal was lost to those above. "Nothing but empty tunnel." He didn't understand how Grandyn could have disappeared or gotten so far ahead. After another five hundred meters he stopped his team. A sick feeling filled his stomach.

"How long is this torgon tunnel?" one of his men asked.

The team leader shook his head, but gave no verbal response. They kept running. Then, suddenly, the AirView showed something in the tunnel ahead – a small object, maybe a brick. He stopped his team again, concerned it might be a bomb. Four meters beyond the object, the tunnel just ended in what appeared to be a solid wall. "What the hell?"

"Trouble receiving," the Commander's voice crackled in his ear.

"HG3 has found an object."

The Commander and the Chief only heard "object."

"Target, do you have a visual on target?" the commander asked.

"Negative, HG3 is at the end."

"End?" the Chief asked, astonished.

"There is only an object."

Again they only heard "object."

"What is the object?" the Commander asked, exasperated.

The HG3, now one-point-six kilometers from the tunnel entrance, hovered over the object. The team leader waited. It took a couple of seconds for the HG3 to zoom in on the object.

The sick feeling in his stomach worsened. "It's a book . . . It's a printed copy of *War and Peace*, by Leo Tolstoy."

The Chief heard that part of the transmission, but stared at the images of the trees above the tunnel in disbelief. "Grandyn is just screwing with us now," she said to herself. "Where is he?" she asked the commander.

Before he could answer, an explosion ripped through the tunnel, sending a surge of flame and debris into the team like a shotgun blast. There were no survivors, and no sign of Grandyn. It would take weeks to excavate the site. The Commander believed there was no way Grandyn could have escaped the tunnel. "Grandyn's body is down there. We'll find it," he told his superior.

The Chief laughed derisively. "He's probably up in a tree watching your people make fools of themselves."

She didn't care about the team of dead agents down in the hole, and that infuriated the Commander. "I'll take the people we have left and scour the area. If he's alive, he can't be far. We'll find him."

"You do that Commander!"

Miner, surrounded by Imps, could not believe the events in Russia. "They let him get away again!" Part of him was pleased that Enforcers might be able to get in there and find the fugitive, but mostly he was just outraged that a single twenty-one-year-old "kid" could embarrass the AOI like that. He checked an AirView. His crew was still seventy minutes out.

"You won't find Grandyn in Russia," Sidis said.

"How do you know?"

"Same way Munna found you . . . all the information is out there. Why don't you understand this concept?"

Miner looked to Sarlo, hoping she would calm him with a glance. She did. "Explain it to me," Miner said.

"I don't have the practice, nor the discipline that Munna does, but everything we want or need is already connected to us."

"We're all one, 'Krishna-Sidis?'" Miner asked with a sarcastic sneer.

"Do you imagine *we* are accidental? That life arose on this planet in the middle of the vastness of space? Have you been out

there and looked back at this little blue sphere floating in an infinite sea of blackness?"

"What's your point?"

"I guess my point is that you probably won't grasp this until
you die."

"Are you threatening me?" Miner rose, and as if they'd been
monitoring the room, two Enforcers brutes burst in and walked
quickly to Sidis.

Sarlo shook her head.

"You are too nervous Miner," Sidis said. "If you could see what
I see, you would know that you've already lost," the Imp
continued in a tone Miner didn't understand and certainly didn't
like.

"Get him out of here!" Miner yelled.

The Enforcers guys stepped toward Sidis.

Suddenly, all the lights went out. Alarms sounded. Flashes of
bright pulsating light colored the room in a frantic strobe effect.
Loud music blared distorted Bach and Wagner. All the INUs in the
room, including the ones on the Enforcersrs' necks, projected
hundreds of AirViews. No one could see anything. Lance felt as if
he'd been dropped into a horror movie funhouse as images of
dying soldiers and diseased civilians blinked on and off.

For several nightmarish minutes it went on, and then it
suddenly ended, as if it had never happened. The Imps were gone,
all but Charlemagne, the original Imp from Denver. He stared at
Miner disapprovingly.

"We were your last chance," he said, standing to leave.

"Please, Charlemagne, don't go. Sidis is the only one I had a
problem with, he's just so . . . you know . . ."

"Honest," Charlemagne finished.

CHAPTER FORTY-SEVEN

Chelle smile, having received the update that Grandyn had escaped yet again. "How does he do it?" she asked herself out loud. Her INU lit up at the same moment and she eyed it suspiciously. When she saw it was Terik, she opened the feed and read his message.

"Polis really is alive!" she sang. She had asked him a question that he could answer emotionally but which would confuse the memory probes of a Said-scan. The night Beale had died, the information was that she loved him. She had told him every single day. Drast would have known that, and also would have known that she would have liked to tell Runit she loved him prior to that fateful predawn attack. And, finally, she wanted Drast to know that after all these years, she loved him too.

"Drast's response," Terik had said, "is simply three words, 'I love you.'" Chelle had already prepared her message back to him, hopeful he'd pass the test. She quickly sent it to Terik. It told of vague plans and asked, in an old code they used to use when he was Regional AOI Head, to establish a new code based on that one so that Terik and others could not read their correspondence.

Terik, still in the prison parking lot when he received Chelle's response, contacted Osc. Although, they would not be able to get Drast to the visitor's room again without raising suspicions, Osc agreed to take it to Drast's cell while Terik waited.

Drast was delighted to hear back so quickly, and spent the next fifteen minutes drafting his response. He told her he would send a new code by another method. When Osc brought the message back out, Terik was furious that it did not include the location of the books. "You tell Drast not another message goes out unless he gives me what we agreed upon!"

"Ander, look at his message. He says he'll get her the code in *another* way. That means he has another method to get to her."

"Then why did he use me in the first place?"

"Maybe you were the only one who could make the first contact for some reason. How did you do it anyway?"

"Long story."

"Okay. It's probably best I don't know." Osc winked. "Listen, Drast did say that he has to give you the information you want in person."

Terik nodded. "I guess that makes sense. Can you get me in to see him tomorrow?"

"I think so."

Drast walked out onto the three-by-three-meter dirt pad and stared at the guard tower in the distance. *Soon*, he thought, *soon*. He swatted a fly, or a mosquito, always wondering if they were micro-drones. This one he slapped on his arm and saw the organic smear. He liked killing bugs, but he'd prefer to smash a drone.

A human guard opened a gate in the old-fashioned, three-meter-high, chain-link fence that surrounded his patch of open air. Drast slipped him a "thread" as he passed, on his way to his mandated one–hour of socialization. Mite, the short, stocky Asian man who had become one of Drast's closest lieutenants, marched up, smiling. He held out his two fingers in a "peace" sign, inserting them into Drast's.

The android guards were patrolling close by, and keeping a constant watch on Drast/Evren. The two inmates were using micro-Whistler- mimics, so their monitored conversation would be picked up as one about food, weather, and sports. But Mite had real news, and Drast was anxious to hear it.

"One of my old clients spotted Tiger at Vegas."

Drast smiled. It had worked. Tiger, the crazy aborigine with dragon tattoos and wild, icy blue eyes, had faked a fight with a guard several days earlier.

"Then we're on the way. Once the revolution begins, the prisons will be ready."

Drast's plan relied on getting word to specific inmates at other AOI facilities like the prison in Vegas. He had other methods to get strategies to them, but first contact had to be personal. If all went well, Tiger would be transferred two more times before the end of the month. Drast had others on the move too.

"My project is progressing," Mite added. "Another few days and we should be able to roll it out."

"What about testing?"

"An incident in the kitchen should do it." Mite's genius for explosives and logistics was an integral part of Drast's grand scheme. Mite had a method of creating nano devices that could use the electrical systems in the prison to detonate charges, strategically placed, to cause havoc and allow all gates to be forced open. The system, if it worked correctly, would liberate all AOI prisons around the world at precisely the same time. The AOI was efficient: everything was linked. If Drast's inmate operatives could reach enough facilities before the deadline, they would get them all.

Drast was pleased. He had access to so many AOI files that he'd been able to hand-pick the inmates most likely to cooperate with his plan. One thing he knew for sure was that all the convicts held by the AOI would do just about anything not only escape, but also to work at bringing down the evil empire. He had long counted on that miscalculation by the AOI. They were so centered around information and intelligence gathering that they had inadvertently created a dissident army that should have been executed upon arrest. Instead, they kept the brightest opposition minds alive in case they could glean more data from them or use them to catch others. It was a major mistake, one on which Drast planned to continue to capitalize.

The AOI might have been expecting to fight the PAWN army, but they would be surprised to discover another powerful force to reckon with: the dissident army freshly liberated from dozens of AOI prisons, led by a fierce general. Drast.

CHAPTER FORTY-EIGHT

Two days after the Russian tunnel debacle, the AOI got another chance. This time they had plenty of resources available. In the dense forests of Washington Area, Grandyn had been spotted by a patrol of specially-equipped forest drones. They weren't able to send data from the deepest parts of the rainforest, but returned twice a day for a data dump. Thirty-nine minutes earlier, one of the units showed up with four images that were immediately confirmed through AOI INUs to be Grandyn Happerman.

The geography fit better than the Amazon or Russia. It had always bothered the Chief that the Grandyn sightings in distant locations were so far from where he'd been raised in Oregon Area. AOI profilers had all shown that on a personal level it would be unlikely the twenty-one year-old would venture away from his home territory. However, on the strategic side, there were two indications. First, that he would stay within the forests, terrain and climate for which he was best trained and most accustomed. Second, as predicted by other models, his best strategy would be to seek the most remote regions with a greater concentration of anti-government populace, such as the Amazon.

Her instinct told her he was, and always had been, in the old Pacific Northwest. She had sometimes fallen into the excitement and drama of a close encounter or a false alarm, but she had always believed he'd be found close to the Oregon Area.

The Chief also thought the same of the books. It would make sense to send them far away to some obscure, out of the way place, but they were difficult to move, and were probably still within a few hundred kilometers of where they were when the librarian took them three years earlier. So, when word came of the latest Grandyn sighting in the rainforest of Olympic Earth Park in what used to be Washington State Area, she became more excited than usual. Although, almost afraid to believe it, she had a good feeling that this time they would get Grandyn.

It wasn't as if the AOI had been unsuccessful. Much focus went to the thus-far unsuccessful Grandyn hunt, but in the three years of the Doneharvest, thousands of TreeRunners had been killed or imprisoned, and more than one hundred thousand Creatives, Rejectionists, and PAWN members had been executed.

What the Chief was most worried about though were the sixteen hundred and twenty-two corrupt AOI agents that had been discovered. There must be more, and she was determined to find them all. She *had* to find them. Another thirty-nine thousand "ordinary" citizens had also been arrested for having negative thoughts or conversations counter to the Aylantik. But, most important of all, a once imminent war had so far been averted.

The Chief waited for the latest update. She'd ordered three thousand troops into the forest to assist the six hundred already there. Another two thousand were preparing to go, if necessary.

Less than three meters away, the man pointed a laser-trained pulse-enabled assault rifle at his target's head. "What's your name?" the man shouted, his cap blazoned with five-centimeter-high white reflective letters all TreeRunners had grown to fear, "AOI."

The target raised his hands, hoping not to be shot. He didn't immediately answer, his eyes darting in search of an escape he knew didn't exist.

"What's your name?" the AOI agent yelled again, this time with more urgency.

The target hesitated.

Two more agents arrived from the brush. "Take him, take him!" one screamed, about to fire his own weapon to punctuate his words. "It's him. He'll burn us." The agents knew the stories: Grandyn always seemed to escape, disappearing like a ghost in the forest.

"My name is Grandyn Happerman," the target said.

The agents didn't take their eyes off him. "On your knees," the first one commanded. "Slow-leee. Nice and slooow."

Grandyn took a breath, measured the distance in his mind and did calculations. *How long will it take for them to reach me, to gag me, to kill me? Do they have brain scan equipment? Can my friends get here in time? Was the assignment worth this?*

"Knees!" the second one yelled, breaking him from his rapid thoughts.

Grandyn, in sluggish, stilted movements, slowly took a knee, a position that would still allow him to spring up into a roll, or an arching backflip landing in the thick foliage.

There's an old dry creek bed back there that in less than four meters drops off to a sudden deep ravine. If I could only get there, he thought. *I've come too far for it to end this way, for these three AOI grunges to be the ones to bring down Grandyn Happerman.*

"Shoot him!" the second one barked. "He's scheming something. He's got backup."

"Only if it's necessary," the third one responded.

"How about it, Happerman? Are there more of your tree running rebel trash on the way?"

Grandyn knew there were only mere moments left to decide on a course of action. His thoughts were coming in split second flashes. *If I spring back and don't make the creek bed, will I still be able to bite the neuro-cap? Will I have time to make the ravine? Or, will their lasers tear apart every bit of cover before I make it?*

He looked from man to man. The second one was the most likely to shoot first. It was amazing he hadn't already taken a shot yet, but fortunately he was also in the worst position to stop his escape.

Grandyn prepared to jump. It would be almost impossible to make it, but he knew that those coming to help him would never get there in time. *I'm dead either way.* The AOI would discover his secrets and then kill him quickly.

His muscles tensed, and he held eye contact with the second grunge, waiting for him to blink, or turn, or start to speak again, any distraction. And he did.

The second man turned to the first agent. "He's going to bolt!"

Before the second man even finished the "e" in "he," Grandyn was in motion. Pushing up with his bent leg, swinging his other knee until they aligned and he could spring off in a soaring backward flip. The shots came slicing through the air. The colored lights of the lasers shredding the leaves and splintering the bark were the last things he saw.

The stinging lasers cut into his chest. It felt like being cooked from the inside, the agony increasing with each heartbeat. He tried to focus in those fractions of a second, but even in his final breath, he couldn't be sure if he'd bit the neuro-cap in time.

The body of Grandyn Happerman hit the ground almost softly as whipping twigs and giant ferns broke his fall, cradling the Tree-Runner one last time. The forest bid farewell to one of its own as the three AOI agents untangled him and roughly hauled his carcass into a clearing. They would have to drag and carry the traitor's remains for more than three kilometers before they reached a pull-out zone. One of them knew enough to check his mouth and found the neuro-cap still intact. He smiled at his comrades as he held it up.

"Gentlemen, we all just got promoted."

CHAPTER FORTY-NINE

Deuce and his crew were deep in the redwoods, still canvassing for Twain, when a fresh unit of BLAXERs finally tracked them down.

"Sir, Twain has been found," one of them told Deuce.

"Is he okay?" Deuce asked.

"He's alive, but barely," the man said. "Sir, I don't know much. He's in some type of coma."

"Who found him?"

"Nelson Wright and Munna. They're still with him."

"Let's go."

It took almost twenty minutes of hard, steady jogging until they reached the clearing where a Flo-wing waited. Once in the air, Deuce got on his INU and zoomed his wife. She had just made it to the hospital in Portland and promised to zoom as soon as she saw Twain and talked with the doctors.

Deuce had more to worry about than just Twain's health. He knew word had already reached the AOI that his son was in the Portland Hospital. Knowing Deuce and his wife were on their way to the hospital, the Chief could be planning anything. Then there was the Health Circle--what injections had they already given

Twain? Since the AOI knew, then Lance Miner knew, meaning more trouble. And what about Munna and Nelson Wright? The AOI or the Enforcers had been searching for them and suddenly everyone knew where they were. Seventy-five years of building a revolution could crumble in the coming minutes.

His INU told him that the situation in the Amazon had escalated, and that tensions were ninety-eight-point-two percent likely to lead to open combat between the opposing forces within nine days. The next flash that appeared took his breath.

"Damn! *Damn!*" he said.

"What is it?" Logan, a top BLAXER who sat across from him, asked.

"Grandyn Happerman has been killed."

"Are you sure?"

"I'm not sure of anything with Grandyn, but the AOI has a positive ID."

"Where was he?"

"Olympic Rainforest."

"That could be right."

"I know," Deuce said, sliding AirViews around until he got the one he was looking for and waited to see if Nelson would accept contact.

"I can't talk now," Nelson whispered from a voice-only mode. "Twain is still alive, but critical. Your wife is with him now. I waited until she came. Now I need to get out of the city."

"A crazy risky thing you did for Twain," Deuce said. "I'll never forget it,"

"He'd have done the same for me . . . and I was able to hold off HC . . . out."

The contact went dead, but Deuce was relieved. Nelson had somehow been able to stop the Health Circle from giving Twain injections. He hoped to learn how he'd managed that. He'd wanted to tell Nelson about Grandyn, but there hadn't been time. Nelson was going to have difficulty getting out of the city.

"Logan, get everyone you can to Portland now. Find Nelson, help him get out of there. At the same time, I want Twain and my wife evacuated in the next fifteen minutes."

"To where?"

"I'll let you know." Deuce went to work getting a full medical staff and hospital set up on an island he had off the coast of Vancouver. After he had all the right people working on that, he tried to zoom Chelle, but before contact could be made he got a report that Enforcers and AOI had teams moving into Portland. "Are you seeing this?" he asked Logan.

"We're on it," the BLAXER commander answered. "How far can we push this?"

"You start the torgon war in Portland if you have to. They are not taking Twain or my wife!" Deuce created more AirViews and zoomed his commander in the Amazon. "I need some noise down there, some big distractions for AOI and Enforcers. Grandyn's dead, so it'll take some doing to keep their attention in the Amazon."

"Sir, am I understanding? You are authorizing engagement?"

"I'm authorizing anything and everything you need to do to get the attention of our adversaries." Deuce signed off. There were other contingency plans to put into play.

As the wealthiest man in the world, his ability to get things done was almost limitless except when up against an extreme superpower like the Aylantik and their vicious AOI. He'd always thought of them as a pre-Banoff mixture of the Nazi SS, the Soviet KGB, and the US NSA, CIA, and Special Forces all rolled into one. But now that they were going after his family, he considered them to be more like thug rapists, and he planned to stop them.

BLAXERs in plainclothes entered the hospital less than two minutes behind the six AOI agents sent to secure Twain's room. More were on the way, but the massive deployment to the Olympic Rainforest, two-hundred-sixty kilometers to the north, had delayed a larger presence. The BLAXERs caught the AOI still in the lobby, and with the element of surprise took out the entire team while suffering only two injuries. The team went on to secure the floor where Twain and his mother were. Immediately, his bed and the attached monitors were wheeled to the Q-lift. Enforcers units were only six minutes away.

Portland suddenly erupted into a series of fires, break-ins, and accidents. Seventy-two hostages were taken in a building half a block down from the hospital. Outside the city, "rebels" attacked an AOI weapons depot. Within a forty-five-minute window, there were more emergencies and crime than the entire Pacyfik region normally saw in a decade. The AOI was overwhelmed. During the chaos, a Flo-wing landed on the rooftop pad of the hospital and picked up Twain, his mother, and the two injured BLAXERs.

The remaining mercenaries would keep the AOI and approaching Enforcers soldiers busy at the hospital until Twain was a safe distance away. Then, they hoped to vanish into the confusion of the city. The Flo-wing carrying Deuce was still fourteen minutes away, and now that his family was safe, his flight plan would follow them to the island where doctors would be waiting.

The bulk of the diversions in and around Portland weren't to aid Twain's escape, but rather to give Munna and Nelson the necessary cover to get away. With Twain taken care of, Deuce zoomed Chelle.

"Have you heard?" he asked as soon as he saw her face.

"Just," she said, looking exhausted. "Was it really Grandyn this time?"

"All their internal communications still say it was a positive ID, and moments ago I found out he didn't get his neuro-cap open."

Chelle's eyes filled, and she dug her top teeth into her bottom lip, hoping the pain would stop her emotions. Deuce recognized her efforts, but he still wasn't sure about her, and couldn't make up his mind if she was upset about Grandyn's death or the fact that the TreeRunner had not destroyed his brain before dying.

"I've authorized action in the Amazon."

"Why?" she asked, suddenly snapping back. "If Grandyn's dead—"

"That's exactly why we need to act now. Without the threat of Grandyn being in the Amazon, Enforcers and the AOI will pull their troops. The numbers are significant. We need them to stay down there if PAWN is going to have a chance to beat back the AOI in the southern California, Florida, and Michigan Areas."

"How are you able to monitor us?" she asked, visibly upset that he knew their plans.

"Never mind. And you're welcome for keeping your enemies in the Amazon," Deuce answered, annoyed. "Try to trust me just a little bit, okay?"

"We'll talk about that when this is all over."

"Your brother saved my son."

"Twain's okay?"

"I don't know."

"I'm sorry. Nelson told me, and I tried to reach you. I should have asked about him, but I just got so distracted with the news of Grandyn."

"I understand," Deuce said, but he didn't really. "I'm not sure where he and Munna are. They stayed in Portland a bit too long."

"What? They went to Portland? That's crazy!"

"They were afraid to leave Twain, and there was nowhere else to go. He's barely hanging on." Deuce's voice broke. He turned away from the INU.

Chelle saw his back shaking.

"I'll check in later." Deuce choked out the words and then killed the connection. Logan looked over at his boss, and then moved to another seat, giving him privacy.

Deuce stared out the clear side of the Flo-wing and fought a losing battle with tears. "Please let him live... please, please, please don't take my boy!"

CHAPTER FIFTY

Nelson saw his INU light up but didn't dare respond, as AOI agents were less than fifteen meters away. He and Munna were sitting in a LEV, and even if they were willing to risk going through a checkpoint, they had no way to start the vehicle.

At least the agents hadn't seen them yet. They were busy patrolling a street opposite them. He assumed they were looking for him, until a gang of men ran from a building on the other end of the street. The agents pursued, but a few seconds into their chase an explosion obliterated all but one of them. The surviving AOI agent, in what would be his dying gesture, opened an AirView and zoomed the details of the incident.

"We've got to get out of here," Nelson said to Munna. "A hundred AOI agents will probably be here any minute."

She nodded, surprisingly calm. As they got out of the LEV, he scanned the area. Portland was a town he knew well. Memories had been seeping into his mind ever since they had left the hospital. But there was no time for reminiscing. All his concentration would be required to navigate the maze of Seeker cameras and AOI agents who were systematically tracking and hemming them in. Nelson was surprised they'd made it out of the hospital since hospitals were known to have one of the highest concentrations of Seeker cameras.

Nelson had learned quite a bit about Seeker since Deuce had sent him the first diagram detailing the camera locations in the library, three years earlier. He'd studied with the help of PAWN experts and additional information from Deuce, and had taught new recruits techniques to avoid detection. But knowledge of the system also brought an awareness that unless you had every location, going completely unseen was nearly impossible, especially in a hospital.

"I'm afraid the AOI might have let us slip through just so they could follow us," Nelson said to Munna, as they hurried across a small park.

"Where do you think they hope we'll lead them?" Munna asked in an amused tone. "There are only a few they want more than us. Grandyn, Chelle, some others perhaps, but they would not pass up a chance to finally get me. No, Nelson, we are being helped."

"I'm sure Deuce would normally be doing everything he could, but with Twain fighting for his life—"

"I was thinking of another Lipton."

"Cope?"

She smiled.

Nelson didn't have time to think about that or debate her esoteric nature or the philosophical ramifications that a man he'd come to know as a mystic, and one he'd watched die, could help them right now. Nelson looked ahead and saw more AOI agents at the far end of the next intersection. Help or no, they needed to get off the streets.

After checking the time, he realized they might be able to catch a Transit-LEV to the interstate in about seven minutes, if they could travel the three and a half blocks in that time. Munna was one hundred thirty-three, but it was his own lungs and stamina that worried him most.

As they moved along the sidewalks, Nelson reminded Munna to walk on the curb as much as possible since it was the only part of the sidewalk without sensors. He continued to dodge Seeker locations, but knew they were being picked up on some of them. He'd found a baby blanket at the hospital, which Munna was now wearing as a scarf, in an effort to thwart the FRIDG facial recognition system, but on the late June day, it might get flagged as suspicious. Fortunately the streets were crowded, which made blending in easier while creating a challenge for Seeker to get good views.

"Look over there," Nelson said, pointing to several columns of thick, gray smoke rising from a row of buildings to the east that seemed to be constructed entirely of green and blue glass.

"And there," Munna said, waving her arm to the west where the sky filled with black smoke behind the massive and well known silver "three rain drops" buildings, named for their interlocking tear-drop shaped design, with one structure supporting the other two, giving them the appearance of falling rain. Today, the engulfing dark haze made them seem to be a storm for giants.

Portland, normally one with very little noise pollution, was suddenly blaring with sirens, alarms, bullhorns, and shouts. Nelson welcomed the confusion, and looked again at his aged companion. *Perhaps we are getting help. But some of this must be from Deuce*, he thought.

They made it two blocks before too many AOI vehicles and troops crowded into the roads ahead. Nelson didn't know what to do, and then, as a flashing light of a low flying AOI Flo-wing caught his eye, he knew just where to go. They cut through an alley and there before him, with moments to spare before a squadron of AOI blocked their passage, was the beautiful Portland Library building. It stood as it had for two hundred years, looking like a guard, a messenger from another time among the gleaming modern city of solar roads, lights, and rotating composite and glass structures which constantly transformed the skyline.

"We can hide in there," Nelson said, leading her to a back

door. "If we're lucky, they didn't change the codes." The building had remained vacant for three years. He tried the code, but nothing happened. "That's okay, there's a window around that side which I remember never latched properly."

They found themselves in the basement with only a hint of light from the below-grade windows, which were dimmer than usual after three years of accumulated dirt.

"I could navigate this old place blindfolded," Nelson said, leading her up to the main floor.

The building seemed a ghostly realm, a distorted copy of its former grandness. A lingering, stale, chemical odor permeated everything. Much of the main floor had been cleared, but then whatever plans the Aylantik had for the antique structure must have been interrupted. Perhaps resources were required for the Grandyn hunt, or maybe the Polis Drast arrest had something to do with it. In any case, it was a terrible scene.

Row after row of shelves were coated with black and red film, so much red it was as if the air itself were tinted with blood. The blood of books, the bleeding brilliance of all of humanity's collected knowledge and history. Books were no longer physical artifacts to be studied, but rather digital facsimiles that could be manipulated, controlled, and . . . erased.

"We can see what's happening out there from the windows on the upper floor," Nelson said, but that was just an excuse. He wanted to see, had to see, like a grieving parent going to the scene of the accident where his child died.

"Tragic," Munna said quietly, as they reached the top of the steps. A layer of dust, ash, or chemical residue coated everything. The color red had never looked so evil.

"Runit used to brag that there were thirty-three kilometers of shelves filled with books in this library. And there were thousands more they didn't have room to display." Nelson took a deep breath of the toxic air and coughed. He wanted a bac but, was afraid if he lit one in the building the whole place might go up like the explosion they'd seen ten minutes earlier that wiped out the AOI agents. He stood silently, staring, his face wrinkled up as if watching the execution of a loved one, his eyes haunted with a look of devastation.

"We can't stay here," Munna said. "If they've tracked us anywhere nearby, they'll surely check here." She could almost see the past consuming him. "Can we get out the other side?"

"Yeah, I know, yeah," Nelson whispered, barely coherent.

"Come," she said forcefully, her gravelly voice not allowing for argument or delay.

He managed to uproot his legs and moved towards the stairs.

CHAPTER FIFTY-ONE

Just as Nelson and Munna reached the front entrance of the library, his INU lit again.

"Where are you?" Chelle asked as he opened the connection. Before he could answer, she saw the familiar twin staircases, once so magnificent, behind him. "Whoa, talk about full circle! But it's the first damned place they'll look. Listen, Deuce has half of Portland in chaos trying to give you a diversion."

Nelson looked at Munna as if to say it had been Deuce, not Cope, helping them after all.

She just smiled.

"Okay, you're about ten blocks from the Willamette River," Chelle continued. "We can't get a Flo-wing to you. They've shut down air traffic, but I can have a boat at the river. Once we get you far enough out of the city, a Flo-wing can grab you, or we can go all the way to the ocean if needed."

"Can you give us some help with the best route?" Nelson asked.

With hacked access to Seeker, she reverse-tracked AOI movements and sent details to Nelson's INU. "I'll update it as much as

I can," she said working an array of AirViews. Chelle gave him the boat's description and wished him luck.

She wanted to say, *"Don't get yourself killed, big brother. Grandyn is dead, and you're our only hope to find the books and decode the prophecies,"* but she knew he'd fall apart. It already seemed as if the war had started in Portland and the Amazon at least a week before they were ready . . . the timing couldn't be worse, and if they lost Munna and Nelson, it would be the shortest war in history.

As they walked out the front door, Munna turned to him and said, "You may not believe it, but Cope *is* helping us for the same reason we helped Twain. The future depends on it."

AOI Prisoner 1018 woke up and looked around. The fogginess in his head felt insurmountable. Some days were like that. Then, slowly like ice melting on a cloudy winter day, it began to come back to him.

"The cyborgs," he whispered to himself. "I'm in the custody of cyborgs." They had been extraordinarily decent to him, inasmuch as jailers could be decent. It seemed strange to describe a cybernetic organism as being nice, but that is exactly what he would do if asked. If he ever got out of there, which they had told him on numerous occasions would not ever be permitted.

He'd spent considerable time—something he had an endless supply of—trying to figure out a way to beat them, to escape. He knew these "created beings" had some living part to them, but for all he knew they could possess monkey brains. He'd read about advances that were almost impossible to believe. Even androids were incredibly life like and they were nothing but machines. Even so, he considered himself lucky to be in the custody of cyborgs, an entity in the middle of the scale that had humans on one side and androids on the other. He believed they would be the easiest to defeat, if that time ever came. Time is a funny thing, he thought.

Had he really been there for three years? That's what to cyborgs told him. There were just two of them. They had numbers for names, but long ago he'd taken to calling them Cause and Effect. The two "advanced" beings were kind enough to answer to the nicknames he'd given them.

For nearly thirteen months, he'd apparently been in a coma of some sort. No one believed he would ever wake up. Yet they kept him alive. Their orders were clear—Prisoner 1018 was important. Do all that can be done to keep his heart beating, his mind with enough oxygen, do not surrender. And the medically trained cyborgs had many techniques at their disposal. In the years 2098-2101 death was a thing that could be manipulated if the tools and timing were right. And at this isolated, secret, and incredibly advanced facility they had the tools and the time.

When 1018 finally woke from the comma, it took another fifteen months of physical therapy to get him back to "normal" and during all that time he had no idea who he was. Only once he was physically healthy and able to handle rigorous endurance tests and active in exercise and mental challenges did they attempt the dangerous and complicated memory inducements.

Prisoner 1018 could still recall the day, only a few months earlier when he first realized he had a son. It took several more weeks until he could remember his son's name. And then, less than thirty days ago, it all came flooding back, and he understood everything, how he got there, who he'd lost, what they were trying to do, and most of all, that he was the last librarian.

CHAPTER FIFTY-TWO

Zaverly, hidden in the upper branches of a tree, surveyed the surrounding Amazon jungle. A relay report broke the silence. The message brought confusion and despair. "Grandyn Happerman killed by AOI in Olympic Earth Park, Washington State Area, Pacyfik Region." She looked four meters below and clearly saw Grandyn's head among the leaves, definitely alive.

"Grandyn, the AOI just killed you in the Olympic forest!" she shouted.

He looked up. "I didn't feel a thing."

"It's not funny! Who was that who died in your name?"

"I'm sorry, sometimes humor is the only way through pain . . . I have no idea who it was."

"Don't you want to know?" she asked, watching the smoke gather in the distance.

"Yes. I would. The way things look down here, I may be meeting him soon."

"Don't say that."

"Sorry," he said again.

She didn't answer. Her relayer, used to communicate in the dense jungle, relied on old-fashioned radio waves. It beeped, distracting her as another update came in. The fire was spreading. Communications had been spotty. The whole area was in turmoil.

For the past few hours, reports had been pouring in about battles breaking out all over the Amazon. It wasn't just PAWN and AOI, in fact PAWN was so far the least involved. Two private armies, believed to be controlled by the super-wealthy pharmaceutical titan Lance Miner, and his trillionaire rival Deuce Lipton, were engaging each other and AOI forces. But they had bigger problems.

Someone, Zaverly suspected the AOI, had ignited huge areas of the forest. Fires were spreading all over, and every fifteen minutes they'd been getting word of new outbreaks. She had a bad feeling about the day.

It's a bad omen that the AOI is claiming to have killed Grandyn in Washington, she thought. She was about to call in backup to see if someone could help them get to the other side of the fires when communications went out completely.

The flames tore through a stand of palm trees deep in the Amazon. Zaverly watched through digital binoculars that automatically estimated the distance at just over seventy-one-hundred meters. With wind speed, humidity, and numerous other variables factored in, the device calculated they had two hours until the flames reached them.

"Grandyn, the flames are traveling faster than we can," she said. "If we don't start moving now we'll be trapped."

"But there're reports of fighting that way," he said. "All we can do is head north for the river."

It had only been weeks since the rainy season ended, and the way to the river would be a mucky, near impossible, trek. The recent moisture was helping to slow the fire's progress, but it was still moving faster than anything she'd ever seen in the rainforest.

"We can go west," she suggested.

"It's too dense. We'd have to move too slowly, and if the winds pick up we'd be trapped there, too."

She checked her binoculars again. In only a few minutes the flames had grown larger and closer. The device recalculated and showed the fire catching them in one hour and thirty-six minutes. Sixteen thousand different tree species made up the more than five hundred billion trees that populated the earth's largest jungle. The AOI, or whoever was starting the fires, was risking a far greater calamity than just allowing some rebels to remain hidden.

After the Banoff, scientists had discovered just how important the forests were to keeping the balance, and ultimately life, on the planet. It wasn't just oxygen, although that was a critical role they'd long understood. It seemed that trees helped to maintain healthy oceans and to regulate the earth's climate. Aylantik had created a university with campuses near the three largest forests in the world to do nothing but study trees.

One of the main reasons the rebels hid in the forests was that the AOI was forbidden to destroy them. They could not risk mass deforestation even to prevent a revolution. The other benefit was that the forests were the only place on the planet where the Field, and all the systems of communications, monitoring, and weapons which relied on it, were completely blacked out. Even satellites could not penetrate the thick canopies. Scientists had been struggling unsuccessfully for years to discover the reason. The more the trees were studied, the more mysteries were uncovered.

Grandyn yelled up to Zaverly, "There's another fire out to the west!"

"We're running out of choices!"

"There's only one choice . . . I'm going to the river!"

The river, aside from being more difficult to reach, also meant more encounters with the AOI because they clung to the areas around the river for access, mobility, and supplies. More importantly, the river was wide enough in parts to allow for the Field and its vital communications and weapons management. Zaverly believed it was a death trap, but the other routes were closing in on them, and they couldn't stay where they were.

"I'm coming!" she shouted.

If fortunate, they might connect with other TreeRunners and PAWN teams. With the evacuations, the jungle should be teeming with allies, including Creatives and Rejectionists.

Zaverly swung and flipped her way out of the treetops and caught up to him on the ground. "I thought they'd tell us when the revolution started," she said.

"I guess this is their way of informing us," he said as a missile ripped through the trees six hundred meters ahead of them.

"That's too close," Zaverly said. "What are they after? That's not going to start another fire and there isn't a PAWN base there."

"A little Creatives camp is near that strike, but if they're going after stuff that small then we aren't going to make it to the river."

Zaverly grabbed him from behind. "I'm sorry," she said as he turned around.

"For what?"

"For being so mad all the time. It's not at you . . . well, maybe some of it was, but I've just lost so much. My family, our way of life. I mean, I know we all have, but I feel it personally."

"I know," he said. "I just never wanted to let you down."

"Really?" Her eyes filled, and she looked at him for a long time until he finally smiled self-consciously.

"What?" he asked, almost laughing at her seriousness.

"That's not really what I was sorry for." She put a hand behind his neck and another on the small of his back and pulled him into an embrace, a kiss that felt as lush and vibrant as the tropical forest surrounding them. She pulled back a few centimeters so that he could still feel her hot breath on his lips as she spoke. "I'm sorry I never told you I love you." Her eyes fell into his, like a drug he couldn't escape. "Because I do . . . I love you, Grandyn."

CHAPTER FIFTY-THREE

Drast, sitting in the sterile visitors' room of Hilton Prison, smiled when he saw Terik. "I didn't think you were coming. Thought you might still be angry."

"Angry?"

"That I haven't given you the location of the books yet. Didn't think you could trust me, did you?"

"There are checkpoints and surveillance everywhere. It's crazy out there right now. That's why I'm late," Terik said ignoring the "Mr. Nice-guy" routine, which actually worried him more than Drast's typically clipped demeanor.

"What's going on?"

"You mean you don't know?" Terik asked sarcastically. "I was beginning to think you knew when the World Premier took a leak and that you controlled the weather."

"No, that's ACE's department," he said, referring to the Aylantik Commission on the Environment. "Please, tell me the news."

"Someone is making a lot of noise in Portland. Security is being tightened across the region. Officially it's a crime spree of unknown origin, but it's mostly Deuce Lipton trying to save his son and keep Nelson Wright and Munna from being arrested by the AOI."

"What on earth are they doing in Portland?"

Terik, picking at the edges of his AOI lapel pin, told Drast what he knew. Drast paced the small room and then asked if he could get a quick message to Chelle. Terik agreed and recorded Drast speaking for two minutes in a form of code that sounded like a cross between one of the dead languages, maybe German, and a gibberish of numbers and letters. Once it was done, he pleaded with Terik to get it to Chelle as quickly as possible.

"Please apologize to her for my appearance. She remembers me quite differently," he said. It was a vain request and confirmed what Terik had come to believe. Drast had feelings for Chelle.

"I'll get it to her as soon as I leave. But don't you have other means of contacting her?"

"Yes. Once you made the initial contact, I was able to establish another way. You understand that I had to do this in case you became unavailable."

"You mean if my superiors find out what I'm doing and throw me in here with you?"

"Something like that . . . it's a dangerous world." He stared at Terik with the concerned look of a father. "Anyway, my other method is much, much slower and less reliable. And this is urgent."

"I'll take care of it."

"Thank you," he said, looking relieved. "Now, here's something you've been waiting for." He handed Terik a thread. "I went to a lot of trouble to save those books, probably part of the reason I'm in here, but also part of the reason I'm still alive. I do hope they prove to be worth all the effort."

"So do I," Terik said, smiling for the first time in many days. He thought of one of his father's favorite quotes: *Books cannot be killed by fire. People die, but books never die. No man and no force can abolish memory," Franklin Roosevelt.* Then he recalled another line from the same speech: *"In this war, we know books are weapons."*

Miner watched the AirViews come back to life. The Imps were gone. "You'll need to go back to Denver and collect another gaggle of Imps," he said to Sarlo.

"There may be thousands of them, but it's a small community," Sarlo said, frowning as if he'd told her to go find Santa Claus. "I doubt I could round up one Imp, let alone a 'gaggle.'" She made a face at his word choice. "You're done with Imps unless you can somehow make up with Sidis."

"Screw Sidis!" Miner scooped up some cherries from a bowl. They were specially grown without pits, which he hated. "I'll give Charlemagne a day to cool off. He'll get us back in." He popped a cherry into his mouth, holding out the dish to Sarlo, even though he knew she wouldn't take it.

"Without the Imps, you're going to have to pay Blaze a lot of digis for information."

"I don't give a damn about the money. I just don't trust the torg." He ate another cherry. "But we might not need him if we can get to Munna and Nelson Wright before the AOI."

"Before Deuce you mean," Sarlo said. "He has to be the one behind the Portland flare-up. The rebels aren't going to start the war in a city with no strategic advantage."

"There is a large Creatives population there, and PAWN may have no choice but to start the fight in order to save Munna and the writer."

"It's Deuce. PAWN isn't ready."

"You might be right, but in either case, it must be stopped or this may go down in history as the day the end of humanity began . . . a history no one will be left to read."

"Or write," Sarlo added softly.

CHAPTER FIFTY-FOUR

Chelle watched a series of AirViews as the situation steadily worsened. She had open zooms with Parker, the head of the TreeRunners, as well as the elected representative of the diverse Creatives community, and the three-member council of the Rejectionists. The twelve highest-ranking PAWN officials were also present across infinite encrypted connections. These important leaders were never physically in the same place, and even a joint conference like this one had occurred only once before, at the start of the Doneharvest.

"This crisis is forcing us into action," Chelle began.

"We're not ready!" one of the PAWN generals barked. "Years of planning, and mere weeks from our ready date, your brother and Munna go off half-cocked."

"They had no choice but to save Twain Lipton," Chelle said.

"One life," the general retorted. "Is the entire revolution worth one life? Maybe, if it is the life of a trillionaire's son—"

"One of the class of individuals we're fighting," the Creatives' representative interjected.

"Need I remind you that a major portion of our funding and a large percentage of our weapons have been provided by that trillionaire?" Chelle said. "And Munna made the choice. Are you going to question Munna?"

"Munna does not want war," the general said. "I think she would happily sacrifice our plans to save a stray kitten."

Images of roadblocks, checkpoints, and river patrols filled AirViews as the group of holograms mingled in disagreement and the discussions raged on. PAWN didn't have enough resources, and the generals were reluctantly following Chelle's orders to save Munna and Nelson. For hours they had continued expanding the chaos by all available methods in order to distract the AOI and spread their agents thin enough that Munna and Nelson could slip away.

"Look at this," one of the Rejectionists councilors said, pointing to the AirViews. Primitive weapons such as bricks smashing through windows and Molotov cocktails tossed at LEVs and AOI stations looked like pre-Banoff riot footage. "We've had to deploy some of our pre-planted explosives. That will cost us when the real fighting begins."

"This sure looks like real fighting to me," the general said, pointing to images of the Amazon. "And just as when the Portland Library theft prematurely brought us into the open three years ago and the AOI answered with the brutal Doneharvest, they will respond and crush us again, only this time we may not be able to recover."

"We're so close to being ready. Surely we can scramble and use this as a springboard for the Exchange," Chelle said.

"We've lost the element of surprise," the general snapped.

"Maybe not," another general argued. "They would not suspect a full counter from us in every city."

"We're definitely not ready for that," the first general repeated.

Chelle noticed a message from Terik come through her INU. She adjusted an AirView to private mode and flicked her fingers so that it would display text rather than audio. After a written warning from Terik about Drast's appearance, his face, or rather the face of inmate Evren, came on the screen.

It took her a moment to get used to him, but she recognized his eyes, and as she watched his lips move, she knew it was Drast. His words filled the screen, and there were translation issues that made it difficult for her to interpret the already complicated code, but once she got past that, his message was simple and clear.

"Do not start the war today. We need three more weeks. Do not let it begin now, or our war, and all our work will be lost for sure."

CHAPTER FIFTY-FIVE

Deuce, sitting next to Twain as he regained consciousness, felt as if he'd been holding his breath for hours. He might never know what had worked, the doctors, the healers, the prayers, a last piece of mystical magic from Cope. It really didn't matter. He could speak with his son again.

"Dad?"

"I'm here, Twain."

"Where...?" At first Deuce was afraid Twain couldn't see since he was right in front of him, but then Twain finished. "Where's Mom?"

"She's talking to one of the doctors," Deuce said. He called his wife. For the next five minutes she held Twain's hand and answered his quiet questions. They were on Ryder Island. His prognosis was good.

"You'll be fine," his mother said. "Dehydration, malnutrition, and some minor abrasions and contusions. You must have fallen out of a tree and knocked yourself out or something. Do you remember what happened?"

Twain remembered, but he wasn't going to talk to his mother about it. He wasn't going to tell anyone. Some of it was still fuzzy, but he knew two things for sure. He hadn't fallen out of a tree, and he needed to get back there as soon as possible.

Deuce watched his son very carefully while he and his mother spoke. There was a look in his eyes, a knowing that had not been there when he went to the redwoods. He wondered what Twain had seen and experienced during all that time. Had he found whatever it was that had held Cope to those trees for so long?

In a way, the entire family had become slaves to Booker Lipton's vision. His grandfather had somehow known what the world was going to become, and had prepared not only for his family's safety but for his family to be able to save themselves from the future he saw. Booker knew three things would be needed to shape or reverse what the world would be in 2100: financial dominance, technological power, and quantum knowledge. His two sons, his grandson, and great-grandchildren had been bred into that determination, that cause.

Deuce stared at his injured son and wondered how it could have been different. He didn't know another way because this was all he had ever known. *All that I am, and all that I ever was, was for this,* he thought. *Forgive me, my son. You were sacrificed to this fight long before I knew you. If I could have undone that, if there were any way to save you from this pain, any pain, this suffering, this war . . . I would do anything to stop it.*

Twain turned his eyes away from his mother and met his father's as if he'd heard his thoughts. The two men conveyed much in that glance, their mutual love, respect, trust, and an urgency that the last hundred years of their family's struggle, a thousand years of muddy history . . . it was all intersecting at this moment.

There is no time! Twain screamed with his look.

Deuce nodded, as if understanding everything. "Excuse me," he said to his wife. "I have to check on the people who saved Twain."

Down the hall, Deuce moved his hand quickly over a nano

scanner that verified his identity. Almost instantly, a heavy door slid open and he walked into a darkened room already filled with dozens of AirViews. As with most of his offices, the ceiling was covered with stars, this one showing the night sky as it would appear from a planet in the Canis Major Overdensity Galaxy. Sometimes he would stare at this close "neighborhood," a mere thirty thousand light years from our solar system, but today he didn't even glance up as the AirViews immediately stole all of his attention.

He jumped among the screens like a battle commander and took control of multiple skirmishes, redirected troops, drones, weapons and other resources. At the same time, he tried to raise Chelle.

It took longer than usual to get a connection with her. The infinite encryption system, contrary to its name, was limited in how much data it could protect at once. Efforts were underway to expand capacity, but a day like today was showing the limitations of the current system. As he tried to locate Munna and Nelson through the Seeker cameras and other means, he continued to create diversions wherever large concentrations of AOI agents were detected.

The most disturbing thing he witnessed was the amount of Enforcers personnel in play, both in Portland and in the Amazon. He had numerous ways to deal with the AOI, due to years of providing the agency with equipment through his secret subsidiaries and even with that, the AOI was a formidable foe. But Enforcers, with its mercenary mentality and guerilla tactics, was going to be extremely challenging.

Then, his warning maps began flashing red and yellow points of light. Yellow showed potential threats of conflicts within twenty-four hours, red indicated something much sooner, possibly in the next eight hours. What tightened his stomach was that these lights were blinking in more than sixty areas around the world.

"It's beginning, damn it," he whispered to the room.

He tried to think back on all he knew of the prophecies, the letter from his grandfather, everything Cope had ever told him, the strategies he'd studied for years, and any other stray thought that could tell him what to do next. He'd never imagined that the war would start this way. The act of kindness by Nelson and Munna to save his son had been the final spark to ignite the world war that would change everything and everyone.

Just then, his zoom to Chelle went through. "Are they safe?" he asked as she appeared.

Chelle had stepped into a side room to take the zoom while the other members of the revolutionary committee, known as the Exchange Board, continued their debate.

"Not yet, but they are outside of Portland." She further explained the details and their efforts to escape down the Willamette River. Deuce was able to bring up a detailed satellite view of their location. He immediately used the data to move more BLAXERs toward Munna and Nelson.

"How's Twain?"

"Improving. It was touch and go there for a while," Deuce said, while shuffling AirViews, trying to get more help to them on the river.

"I'm glad. Any idea what happened?"

"None," he lied. "I haven't had a chance to dig deeper into Grandyn's death. Have you picked up any intel?"

"I'm afraid all of our sources indicate that this time it *was* him. If it wasn't, he should have contacted someone by now." She worked an AirView, trying to pinpoint areas where she could safely pull PAWN units back to minimize the escalation.

"There's still a chance. I'll look right now." His finger moved though the air as if he were playing an invisible piano and more AirViews of various sizes, some three-sided and some filled with holograms and 3D images, appeared. "If he *is* alive, he might be lying low with all the action right now. The people he would most likely have contacted, Munna, Nelson, or me, have all been out-Field."

"Maybe," she said, doubtful. "How close are you to having the books?" Chelle wanted to get back to the Exchange Board before she talked to Deuce about Drast's recommendation to hold off the start of the revolution.

"We have all the books accounted for, other than what Drast hid. Do you think you can help with those?"

"Me?"

"I have a feeling he'd tell you," he said, watching more yellow and red lights fill his screens.

"Even if we get them all, without Grandyn it could be pointless."

"We still have Nelson . . . and we could employ an Imp."

"I don't work with vampires," she said.

Deuce ignored her comment, distracted by what he saw on one of the swirling AirViews. "The AOI is convinced they killed Grandyn. An unbroken Neuro-cap was found in his mouth. An on-site FRIDG verified his identity. He's being taken to Seattle AOI for a Said-scan. Once those results are in we'll know for sure, but it looks like we may have lost our TreeRunner."

CHAPTER FIFTY-SIX

Miner sat alone with Sarlo, the smoke from the Amazon clearly visible from the rooftop suite of the PharmaForce building in Manaus. Below them, the solar-powered tower of green glass and nano-tech-composite metal was a beehive of activity. Enforcers had already secured the airport, and were in air combat with StarFly jets, Flo-wings, and drones, but Deuce's BLAXERs weren't their only concern.

PAWN had proven unexpectedly resilient. They were engaging the AOI and Enforcers in the air, on the river, and, of course, deep in the jungle. Reports were still infrequent and vague, but it seemed obvious to Miner that Deuce had not been the only one supplying the rebels. They had weapons not manufactured or possessed by Deuce's many companies.

"This is not war," Miner said, watching two drones dogfight in the far distance.

"What would you call it then?" Sarlo asked. "A tennis match?"

"It is not war until Aylantik declares it, which they will never do. But more importantly, it is not a war until the people know about it!"

"There are more than a million people living in Manaus, who

may not have quite the same nice view that we have, but they can certainly see there is fighting in the forest. And what about the trouble in Portland? Another million people up there are going to be gossiping about the explosions and general mayhem."

"Rumors may leak out, but we're conveniently isolated down here, and the media will make no mention of so much as a traffic accident in Portland, at least to the rest of the world. As for the residents there who have obviously seen the violence, it will all be blamed on terrorists and the hunt for them," Miner said, looking at her as if she should know all this, but he reminded her again. "When people are afraid, they will believe anything the government tells them."

"You're inviting distrust of the media. You know what comes next . . . talk of corruption in the government will increase," Sarlo said. "I think we'd be better off leveling with the populace, telling them there are rebels threatening stability, wanting to take away their way of life. If people think their utopia is about to be destroyed by a bunch of selfish nonconformists with weapons, they'll stand with Aylantik."

"I wish that were true, but the AOI is not particularly loved."

Sarlo laughed. "That's for sure."

"And anyway, the opposition will not be." Miner spun his silver dollar on the desk in front of him and watched it surprisingly fall on heads. He stifled a laugh. "It's okay for them to be afraid of a small wild band of terrorists, but talk of war, *real* war, that is too much."

Visuals began streaming in on two large AirViews. Live audio feeds tracked three Enforcers units canvassing Portland. "We're outnumbered by AOI agents," a Enforcers leader announced. "We've just received word that the city is about to be put under martial law."

The smoke-filled streets, burning cars, and brigades of AOI in full riot gear punctuated the earlier reports of deteriorating conditions. Miner shuddered. The scene looked more like a pre-Banoff urban war zone than a shining city in his beloved Nusun, the single nation utopian earth his family had helped to found and that he'd nurtured his entire life.

"This war cannot happen," he fumed.

"It looks bad," Sarlo said, "but we can still stop it."

He swept an arm around to include the AirViews showing Portland and the windows overlooking the burning Amazon. "If we do something in the next five minutes, maybe."

"Stop. Why did this all suddenly erupt?"

He looked at her and slowly smiled. "Sometimes I forget how smart you are," he said. "This is all a smokescreen to make sure Munna and Nelson Wright escape."

"Exactly. So let them go."

"As if I have a choice. They seem to have slipped through anyway."

"Zoom the Chief and tell her that if the AOI stands down in Portland and in the Amazon, we may be able to put this genie back in the bottle."

Miner nodded and quickly got hold of the AOI Chief. Her face filled an AirView, and Miner noticed the dark circles under her eyes. Her always-rigid expression seemed to have a few more creases. Although sixty-two, her dusty brown hair, kept in a military crop, made her look younger, and Miner had heard she still did one hundred push-ups and fifty sit-ups every day. He'd also been told many times that she didn't like him much, and on at least one occasion she was the one who had told him.

"What is it, Lance? I've got half a world on fire and the other half running from me," she snapped.

"You're searching for Munna and Nelson Wright."

"Look Lance, I know you've got boots on the ground in the two hot zones right now, and you're racing for the same prize. So far your Enforcers AOI-wannabes haven't gotten in my way, but if they do, they will be removed." She glared at him. "So why don't you just tell me why you're bothering me."

"I'm proposing we stand down and allow Munna and Wright to get away."

"I'll bet you are." She did a double take and both glances were incredulous. "Do you think I'm an idiot? I'd end this conversation right now, but maybe you're going to say something else even funnier, and I could use a laugh today."

"Hear me out Chief. One thing you and I completely agree on is the need to avoid an open war with the rebels," he said.

She nodded.

"Things have escalated rapidly, but the rebels obviously weren't planning to start their uprising today. They are just trying to protect Deuce's son, Munna, and Wright. But we're about to see the accidental start of the first war in seventy-five years . . . a war we may *lose*."

She stared silently.

"Once the peace is broken, once blood is tasted, a cycle of war will begin that may never end."

She knew the warning. It had been made by Axel Doneharvest, the first head of the AOI, and the man the current crackdown had been named for.

"We're on the brink," she said, mulling over his words.

"But we can walk away. If we stop pursuing, they will collect their heroes and retreat into the woods to live to fight another day."

"They may see it as a sign of weakness."

"But it is not, and if they take it as one, it will be at their peril."

That made her smile. "It might just confuse the torg out of them."

The screen went black.

Miner, confused, looked at Sarlo. She shook her head and shrugged.

The Chief reappeared a few seconds later. "I've given the order. But so help me Lance, if I get wind of any advancement by

Enforcers in the next few hours, I will wipe them off the face of the earth."

"You'll have no trouble from me Chief."

With the zoom ended, Miner and Sarlo watched the AirViews and the windows. Within half an hour, there was a noticeable change. Most of the fires in Portland were brought under control. The Amazon would be another matter. It might be weeks or months until the burning stopped there, but at least the large scale fighting had subsided.

"We've got to stop the forest burns," Sarlo said. "Can you get the weathermakers to move in some rain?"

He eyed her as if she'd suggested murder. "That, as you know, brings in a whole other mess."

CHAPTER FIFTY-SEVEN

Munna and Nelson sat inside the small cabin of a solar-powered pleasure boat, slowly moving northwest up the Columbia River toward the ocean, toward freedom. They just missed a checkpoint at the confluence as they came off the Willamette, but the Columbia still had plenty of AOI vessels to contend with, any of which could seize or board their tiny craft.

"By saving Twain, we may have inadvertently begun the war," Nelson said. "Was his life worth trading for all the others that will be lost?"

"This day will end quietly," the old woman said, smiling.

"How do you do it Munna? I spent a year with Cope, and all that I saw and learned amazes me. It's better than any fiction I ever wrote. As you know, I've compiled many of Cope's views, and now I'm writing about my experiences with him and Twain, but even with all that, I don't have that blind faith that Cope did and that you and Twain have. What am I missing?"

"Your problem is bacs, and alcohol, and sugar, and—"

"I get it," Nelson said.

Munna smiled. "Knowing the truth is never about faith. It is about remembering, accepting, and, most importantly, it is about living. If we live as if we know there is more, then there will be more."

"Maybe if I ever—" Nelson was interrupted by Chelle coming through on his INU.

She told him Deuce's BLAXERs were going to meet them at a small town along the river called Prescott. An AOI island check-point was set up around the next bend beyond Prescott. The BLAXERs would escort them along the road until they could connect with a Flo-wing at the coast. But that didn't worry him nearly as much as what else she told him. They kept the zoom short, and afterwards Nelson filled Munna in on the new plan and then told her the rest of Chelle's news.

"The AOI thinks they have killed Grandyn," he said with a shaky voice, reaching for his now empty flask.

"Death is not always the end."

"Listen Munna, I appreciate your belief in the afterlife, but Grandyn was like a son to me. I loved his parents, and I've known him his whole life. So if you don't mind, I don't need to hear your rainbow and unicorn story about seeing him in the next incarna-tion or whatever."

Munna smiled. "That's not what I meant."

He looked at her, confused, and lit a bac.

Munna motioned to the window, which he opened to exhale his smoke. "I think we should not believe everything we fear," she said, but before he could launch into another protest of her philo-sophical reaction, she continued. "The prophecies talk of Grandyn beyond this time."

"But you said you haven't read them, and you also said they change."

"One does not have to read the prophecies to understand them."

Nelson laughed out a cloud of smoke. "Sorry," he said, as Munna brushed the air clear.

"When you find the prophecies, you will know what I mean."

"So we're going to find them?"

"I certainly hope so, or we may all die in a terrible war." She stared at him sternly. "Would you mind putting that thing out? There are no trees here to clean your polluted air."

He nodded, took a last drag, and crushed it under his heel.

"Thank you." She smiled. "I spoke with Lance Miner, and he—"

"Wait, you talked with PharmaForce-Miner?"

She smoothed the front of her soft, hemp dress. "He shares my goal."

"What goal? Lance Miner is the devil!" Nelson said.

"Lance Miner is certainly misunderstood, by himself most of all, and his methods are deplorable, but he is not the devil." She patted Nelson's arm. "More than anything he wants to avoid war."

"Because he knows he'll lose!"

"With war we all lose."

"Munna, we can win this war, and—"

"And what? You and your sister, Grandyn, and so many of the others seem to think if the revolution somehow succeeds in ending Aylantik rule and the AOI is dismantled, that all the wrongs of the past will be undone . . . but they won't."

"Of course not, but at least we'll know that the wrongs won't be repeated. The repression and the AOI reign of terror will end."

"To be replaced by what?"

"Maybe by Cope's vision of the world, or yours. Wouldn't you like that? Do you think it could ever happen with the Aylantik left in charge?"

"Perhaps . . . anything is possible."

"But you've seen, you've glimpsed, something of the future, or you feel it, or someone told you enough that you know what the prophecies might say." Nelson stood, his arms flailing. "You don't *want* us to find the prophecies, do you? Because they show that we can win, that we do win. Or, as Chelle believes, they show us *how* to win. Don't they?"

"They may show all of that, but what good will that do?"

"What good?" Nelson shook his head in disbelief and lit another bac. "Why are you so opposed to war? How can you say it is wrong to stop such atrocities as the AOI carries out by whatever means necessary?"

"Our society is on the wrong track, we have been for millennia, and we cannot get back on the right path if we keep walking in the wrong direction. Violence, in any form, for any reason, always takes us in the wrong direction." She frowned. "Put that thing out."

"But this is the real world," he said, absently extinguishing his bac.

"How can you say that after your time in the forest with Cope?"

"How could you talk with Lance Miner? What did you discuss?"

"I told him that I was his best chance to avoid war."

"But Munna . . . this war has been coming for a hundred years. Didn't you see what was going on in Portland? The war has already begun."

"No wonder you're so determined for a revolution." Munna shook her head, as if ashamed of a child. "If you think what we saw in Portland is the beginning of a war, you obviously have no idea what war really is."

Their argument was interrupted by their captain docking. "Prescott," was all he said.

Two tough looking men in tight Tekfabrik suits, which, if you didn't focus hard enough, made them seem almost invisible from the neck down, awaited them. They each carried lasershods and continuously scanned the area. A small AirView floated near their heads, but its contents were not visible to Nelson and Munna.

"Ma'am, Mr. Wright, you're to come with us for a rendezvous with PAWN at the beachhead."

"And who sent you?" Nelson asked, trying to sound like he might have a choice as to whether or not they would go with the men.

"We're BLAXERs," one of the men said, assuming that would be enough. And it was.

CHAPTER FIFTY-EIGHT

In the steamy jungles of the southern Pacyfik Region, the explosions and flyovers had decreased substantially during the past hour, but the Amazon still burned out of control.

"Grandyn," Zaverly said quietly, grabbing his arm and pulling him down.

They were each wearing sensors which picked up on human activity or mechanized actions. Hers had gone off first, as she was a step ahead, but as they hit the damp ground and sank into vegetation more than half a meter deep, his was blinking.

"It doesn't look like grunges," she said.

"Probably not, since we haven't been shot yet. Their sensors would have picked us up at least at the same time," he said.

"They've stopped," Zaverly said, noting what he could see on his own AirView. "Eight of them."

"What do you want to do?"

"They could be friendlies. They know we're here and we're outnumbered." Her INU lit up before she could finish. She smiled, popping her thumbs. "TreeRunners."

They verified with each other, and five minutes later the newly formed band of ten TreeRunners was moving in the only direction not in flames. "It's probably why the fighting has died down," one of them suggested. "How can anyone do anything in all that smoke and fire?"

Less than one thousand meters later, mosquitoes forced out by the suffocating smoke suddenly grew thicker. They braced for the bites of one of their natural enemies, a price of living in the tropical jungle.

"They're not mosquitoes!" someone yelled. "They're torgon swarm drones!"

They'd all been pursued before by the camera-equipped, bug-sized drones, but not like this. There were at least five swarms, each with hundreds of the flying terrors.

"They have lasers!" one of the TreeRunners yelled, as at least sixty of the airborne weapons attacked him. Zaverly shot a pulse above, trying to disperse the drones, but they'd already focused enough of their beams. A second later, the pain of cutting flesh and bone overwhelmed him as his severed arm dropped off, and the TreeRunner crashed to the ground, screaming.

A second wave flew over, using concentrating beams to slice open his head in a grotesque scene of modern warfare. Absolute horror and wrenching agony, then he was gone. Hundreds of new swarm drones appeared from the treetops.

"I've never seen so many!" Zaverly yelled.

"There are thousands!" another TreeRunner added as they fled, shooting pulses into the air.

"It must be the fire that's forcing them all into one area."

"The fire!" Zaverly shouted. "We can use that."

Another TreeRunner went down as they fled.

"Run toward the burning trees!" she yelled. The others quickly figured out her plan and headed closer to the fire line.

For the next fifteen minutes they ran at full speed, years of training put to the test. The swarm drones couldn't navigate the close trees and tangled vegetation as expertly as the TreeRunners did, and the remaining eight were able to keep the swarming micro-winged army at bay by spreading out, firing pulses, and weaving in and out of the trees.

Soon the smoke was so thick that breathing became difficult and the TreeRunners had to slow. The swarm drones had problems with navigating and began dropping off. Some crashed into trees or other drones.

"Shoot them!" one of the TreeRunners yelled.

With their lasershods set to pulse, they were able to pick off up to a hundred at a time as the confused drones were unable to deal with the combination of flames, heat, smoke, and pulses. The TreeRunners also couldn't take the increasing heat and stifling smoke and had to move away. The remnants of the "insects" were able to kill another TreeRunner before the battered team brought down the last of the drones and stumbled out of the smoke zone. The river and any hope of escape were still hours away.

CHAPTER FIFTY-NINE

Ander Terik watched the live feeds coming through his INU of another skirmish in the Amazon. The AOI had more than two hundred fifty Collins-HG3s in the Amazon basin, and hundreds more in forests around the world. The Chief may have been confident that they had killed Grandyn in the Olympic forest, but she was keeping the drones and other mechanized autonomous weapons deployed. In fact, Terik's high-level AOI clearances showed him that the Chief wasn't slowing down at all since Grandyn's death. She still had Chelle Andreas, Nelson Wright, and Munna to find, but it wasn't just that. The Chief didn't need the massive number of units she had sent into the forests to capture three revolutionary leaders.

She was preparing for war.

He moved several AirViews into position so they could be linked and watched at once. In spite of her rhetoric to the contrary, he believed the Chief had resigned herself to being unable to stop the revolution from turning into a large scale, potentially worldwide uprising. She had strained the AOI with all the wilderness occupations. Terik could tell that her strategy was to keep the war where the rebels were hiding.

Smart, he thought; *if the rebels get into the cities, they might find more sympathy from the populace than the Aylantik would care to admit. At the very least, violence in the streets would make life uncomfortable for the overly comfortable and complacent masses.*

The images on the AirViews changed to current Seeker-camera compilations, and even though Terik hadn't been trained in the Drone Tactics Division, he could tell that the sheer numbers of drones over most cities had to be almost twice the normal traffic. There was also a noticeable increase of AOI agents donning light-jetpacks and flying the skies around the smaller towns. The Chief was doing everything right. She was maintaining the peace by preparing for war.

Pulling up several more AirViews, he could see that the AOI was monitoring the movements of BLAXERs and Enforcers. Both groups, heavy in the Amazon, were listed as allies, but he was certain the Chief had contingencies for either or both of them going the other way. Unfortunately, his clearances didn't allow him access to that data.

Still, the size of their forces continued to surprise him as he expected the war would rely on technology-based weapons. But all the sides, including the rebels, seemed to be anticipating something like pre-Banoff style battles when people were used as weapons. There hadn't been a war in the modern era, and it had only been in the two decades prior to the Banoff that weapons became sophisticated enough that large numbers of soldiers were no longer required. But it had been the brutal Banoff war which had brought the Aylantik to power and showed just how dominating tech-weapons were.

So why the troop build-up? he wondered. *Perhaps the Chief and the other leaders are worried about something, or someone, else. Maybe they know more about the List Keepers than they're admitting.*

He scanned the profiles of Deuce Lipton and Lance Miner. It was part of his daily ritual, as the AOI constantly updated files and

Terik wanted to be sure he knew every detail and each change concerning all the key players.

There were dozens of new entries for the two moneyed men, but nothing of importance. If he made it to his next promotion before the war broke out, he'd have more clearances, which could help him in his rise to power. Prison officials, top Aylantik leaders, all AOI personnel, the Chief herself, and even the identities of the Council members were all in there somewhere, he just needed the right access. But that would come. In the meantime, there was dirty work to do.

He moved the AirViews to the side.

Terik looked again over the list of purported Grandyn Happerman sightings over the past three years, then he reviewed the reports of Grandyn's death – seven, including the one in the Olympic forest. He knew none of it was true.

A marvelous distraction, he thought.

Sitting in the parking area of Hilton Prison, Terik took his most drastic step in achieving his goals. He'd thought about it enough. He'd calculated every possible ramification. It was time.

He took the contents of the thread he'd received from Drast with the location of the AOI "burned" books and transferred the data to Grandyn's INU. Then he sent Drast's message to Chelle.

"Not a bad day's work," he whispered to no one. He spoke the address and his LEV instantly charted a course to his destination. "Now things are about to get *very* interesting."

CHAPTER SIXTY

As they continued toward the Amazon River, Zaverly and Grandyn had merged with two units of PAWN fighters and a group of Tree-Runners.

They ran between trees, as they'd been trained, but another wave of swarm drones found them and these had improved. The DesTIn-enabled autonomous mechanical trackers no longer crashed into trees, and, as they dove into a ravine, they found out something worse. This new generation could fire death lasers with extreme accuracy.

The neon-blue heat-beam hit him on his side while he was jumping one meter off the ground. Another purple heat-beam struck his waist area before he landed. As he went somersaulting down the steep bank, Zaverly was convinced the strikes had been fatal. She hit the medic button on her communicator, but knew they couldn't come in the middle of a firefight. It would be too late.

A Collins-HG3 flew in from above and she feared it was over for her as well. There was nowhere to hide. But then the large metal monster started picking off swarm drones. It shot an elec-tro-pulse that wiped out a group of at least twenty. She spotted a fellow TreeRunner concealed nearby, working controls. Somehow they had commandeered a Collins-HG3 and they were using it to kill swarm drones.

Zaverly slid down the ravine. Deep below thick vegetation of giant green leaves, she found him. "Oh, Grandyn." She panted and tried to slow her breathing. "Are you . . ." She saw life in his eyes. "You're still alive."

"I'm going . . ." he whispered.

"Don't talk, baby. We're going to get you out of here. Dorey got a Collins and turned it on them. We've stopped the swarmers!"

" . . . to die," he finished.

"Grandyn, you can't die! You're too important to the cause. We need you, damn it!" she cried.

He looked at her and tried to smile.

"You're too important to me. I love you! Don't go, baby, please." She cradled his head and pounded her medic button again.

"I have . . . "

"Don't talk, save your energy. Someone will be here any minute." Zaverly looked up the ravine and saw nothing. It was too steep to take him back out, but she had to try. "Come on Grandyn. I'm going to carry you."

"Not . . ."

"Yes, I am, and you're in no position to stop me." Her voice trembled as she saw the burned and bloody flesh where the strikes had hit, both on his torso.

"I'm not Grandyn," he said faintly.

"What? I'm getting you out of here."

"Not Grandyn," he repeated, a little stronger.

"What are you talking about?"

"Wan-ted to tell . . . you."

"Tell me what?"

"I'm bait, to pro-tect real . . . Gran-dyn."

She had heard him, but couldn't believe it. All this time she'd resented that he was getting everyone around him killed because he was Grandyn, and now he was saying he was never Grandyn at all. She looked into his eyes and shook her head.

"It's true," he moaned.

"Why?"

"Pro-tect."

"No. Why would you take such a suicide assignment?" She cried as she said suicide.

"I didn't know I'd meet the love of my life." His eyes closed

Her tears came harder. "Please, baby, don't die. Don't leave me."

"Love."

"Tell me your real name. I want to know who I love." She kissed his lips, and then screamed. "I hate you Grandyn Happerman!"

More than two hours later, when she arrived back at the bunker with his body, she found her supervisor.

"Did you know?" Zaverly demanded.

"Know what?"

"He's not Grandyn!"

"What? Who said that?"

"He did . . . just before he died because they thought he was Grandyn, because they've been hunting Grandyn, because he was just bait!"

"I don't know anything about this Zaverly. I'll see what I can find out . . . but if he really isn't Grandyn, then the real Grandyn is still alive somewhere."

"I don't care about the real Grandyn, I only care about the man I've fought beside and loved all this time. I want to know who he was, his name, where he was from, his family . . . I deserve to know who I loved."

The supervisor nodded and left the room.

It would be three weeks before she got her answer and his name. "It wasn't easy," the supervisor said. "It's all very classified. They've been using stand-ins for years in order to protect the real Grandyn. I don't even know if the real one is alive anymore, or if he's just a big piece of propaganda."

"How dare they!" Zaverly said, still bitter. "Asking innocent young men to sacrifice themselves for the coward Grandyn Happerman. Where is this famous TreeRunner? I'd like to tell him what a real man is, a man who died for him." She could not hold back the tears. "It was *not* a fair trade!"

CHAPTER SIXTY-ONE

The following day, Grandyn sat by the window. The view of the Cascades across the verdant rolling valley could not compete with what he saw inside the former restaurant. He really didn't ever expect to see them again, especially not these. It took a few minutes for it all to register in his brain.

His father's books had really survived. The day he lost his father, PAWN had tried to move the more than fifty thousand books still in their possession to a safer place, but most of those had been intercepted by the AOI. They were burned two days later, or so the reports had said. In fact, there had even been eyewitnesses, but somehow, Drast had saved them.

Grandyn had no idea how he'd done it, but they'd eventually been secretly parked in the old log building where he now sat. Apparently the place had once been a fancy restaurant. The structure must have been a hundred years old, maybe older. Who owned it, or why it remained empty, was unknown, but it was an ideal location to hide something.

Perched high on a cliff, surrounded by forest for many kilometers, it seemed an odd place for a restaurant to have ever been. The unbreakable, solar glass windows, keycode entry locks, and remote setting explained the lack of security. He'd also seen some serious fencing a couple of kilometers back.

He walked among the piles – many were still bundled – and rubbed his fingers on the straps. Grandyn recalled carrying and loading many of those same volumes after Nelson had wrapped them with the strapping machines. His father seemed present in the room, guarding the books, wanting them in order. *Are you still out there somewhere, Dad, hunting for these books . . . for me?*

There must have been fifty tables and hundreds of chairs stacked against the walls. It had been a busy place once upon a time. Grandyn pulled down a chair and picked up a random book, *The Seat of the Soul,* by Gary Zukav.

Why would a book like this be on the dangerous list? he wondered.

Savoring the old book smell, so much a part of his childhood, rubbing the paper between his fingers, fanning the pages, Grandyn saw the tear drop on the book's cover before he even realized he was crying.

"Dad, what do I do?" he cried. "Open up my eyes, show me, please." His hands were trembling.

The beam of sun from one of the windows landed directly on a stack of books across the room. He hoped it was a sign, but that batch turned out to be post-Banoff titles, which might be interesting, but certainly wouldn't contain prophecies. Then he recalled what his father had told him on that final night and started searching for titles.

Deuce had a letter from his grandfather, Booker, which discussed the prophecies. The letter, written more than fifty years ago, mentioned Grandyn's father, Runit, and a son he would have. Deuce's son was also apparently mentioned, although neither Grandyn nor Twain were identified by name. In the days around the library's closing, Deuce had shared a single clue with Runit. "I. II. Possess it, next . . ."

Runit, a Shakespeare fanatic, thought in Shakespeare plays and quotes, so when Deuce told him the clue, he almost instantly translated it to: Act one, scene two, of Hamlet, where the line appears, "Possess it merely. That it should come to this." Runit didn't tell Deuce, but instead discussed it with Grandyn the night before the brutal attack.

They had both agreed the line from Hamlet was apropos for the situation. Grandyn had suggested to his father that since they had the Hamlet clue, it was possible that the Shakespeare play contained the list of books. But in a final insight that had given Grandyn hope all these years, Runit didn't think a priest in the American Southwest, three hundred years earlier, would bother putting the titles of the books in code.

"The prophecies are coded into the texts of books. That seems hard enough," his father had said.

"Then how would anyone ever know which books?" Grandyn had asked.

"Perhaps there was a list of them that was lost to time, or his followers were entrusted with the titles, but the chain was broken after so long. According to Deuce, there were regular prophecies, and then these special ones. Maybe they were mixed up over the centuries, I don't know."

"But how will we find the right books?"

"Because we're experts on books." He would never forget how his father had smiled when he had said that. It had been what friends called the Happerman smile, the kind that made you feel like a party had started. Smiles had been so rare in those final weeks. Grandyn also remembered how good he had felt at being included as one of the experts. His father had taught him so much, raising him in a library, and he only hoped he was up to the task.

His first mission was to locate all the books published prior to 1847, when Clastier was still in Taos, New Mexico. After that, his story faded to legend and his death was more likely than his escape. Grandyn briefly considered the fact that Clastier, having knowledge of the future, may have included books published after his lifetime. But if that were the case, then the task would be impossible.

After several hours, he had seventeen books pulled and decided to contact Fye to test his theory.

"Where are you?" she asked, confident in the infinite-encryption.

"I'm sitting in a room filled with my father's missing books."

"You found them?" she asked excitedly.

"Thank Ander Terik and Polis Drast. His instructions led me straight to the books."

"How many?" she asked, neatly printing lines of numbers in her pad with a short but sharp pencil.

"I don't know, but a lot . . . twenty or thirty thousand, maybe more."

"Wow. I don't know how he did it. I've sent you the AOI reports of the burning. There was even footage showing tons of smoke. I'd love to know what he actually did burn in that warehouse."

"I need you to pull up the original list Nelson gave me."

"You mean the one Blaze Cortez's program created?"

"Yeah. It's all the books we took from the library, but I think you can use it to get to the source files. The digital copies were made from original publisher source files, or from older scans, so they won't match the physical editions."

"Okay, I'm with you. You can find the added words in the real books by finding it omitted in the ebooks, so you want to match the source file to the physical books?"

"Yeah, but how can I?"

"Give me the first line and the last line on a page from the actual printed book and I'll calibrate the e-book to it."

"You make being a genius look easy," Grandyn said.

"It is," she replied, smiling.

After they'd done that, she sent the results to his INU and an AirView opened displaying each page. She cross-checked more

titles while he started checking pages. He began with the seventeen titles he'd pulled already. The laborious effort paid off after
fifteen minutes when he hit a page that didn't match.

"I've got one!" he said, feeling his heart race.

Fye took a bit longer to confirm that it wasn't simply the result
of changes the AOI had made during their censoring program.
While she did that, Grandyn sent her the first and last line of the
next sixteen books. By nightfall, he'd confirmed that three of the
books contained code.

"Do you think they're part of the prophecies?" she asked him.

"What else could they be?"

"With the age of these books and the history of the world since
they were published, it could be anything."

"But it's not," he said confidently.

"No, it's not. I think you've found the treasure," she said.

"But we need five more . . . and then we need to decode them."

CHAPTER SIXTY-TWO

As the Flo-wing lifted from the hard packed sand of the Oregon beach, one of the BLAXERS moved an AirView between Munna and Nelson.

"You're safe now," Deuce said, in holographic form, as he stepped out of the AirView. "I've just notified Chelle. She's waiting to hear from you, Nelson."

"Thank you," Munna and Nelson said at the same time.

"You risked everything for my boy," Deuce replied. "I'll never forget that."

Nelson nodded.

Munna smiled.

"Of course, you're both free to go anywhere you choose. I'll have you flown to your destination of choice immediately, but I'd like to extend my invitation for you to join us."

"Us?" Nelson asked.

"Grandyn is on his way," Deuce said. "The reports of his death have been greatly exaggerated."

Munna looked at Nelson and smiled. "Death is not always true."

Nelson pumped his fist and whispered, "Thank you," to the sky.

"And I have all the books, or will as soon as Grandyn arrives."

"You have the books? The AOI books? The PAWN stash?" Nelson asked, looking from Deuce to Munna.

"A few days back, I gave Deuce the location of the remaining books in our possession," Munna said, "in exchange for his promise that they would not be used for war."

"How can you make a promise like that?" Nelson asked, scowling at Deuce.

"You originally wanted the books to preserve the truth they contain, but now you understand that they keep other secrets," Deuce said. "The prophecies that are hidden within the pages of certain titles make up a special book known as the *Justar Journal*, an ancient word meaning, simply, 'adjust.' Whoever gets the *Justar Journal* first may alter the future of mankind."

Nelson stared at Deuce, allowing the weight of his statement to sink in. However, he couldn't dwell on the magnitude of the situation because he wanted to avoid another debate with Munna. "That's a discussion for another time," he said, "but without the AOI books that Drast claimed to have burned, any prophecies will be incomplete."

"I have those as well."

"Excellent." Nelson nodded, reaching for his flask which he'd forgotten was still empty. "And Grandyn's coming? Then take me to the books."

Grandyn couldn't wait to get to Deuce's island. With all of his father's books finally reassembled for the first time since they'd left the library more than three years earlier, his hopes were high that Fye's program could find the secrets that Booker and Uncle Cope had promised that the books contained.

He wondered what his father would have thought about it all. Runit had always said, "People have no idea the secrets that are hidden in books." Grandyn also thought of what UC had told Nelson: "Everything humans have ever known is contained in books, but the true excitement is that within their pages is the path to all we have yet to walk, the things we have yet to learn." His father would have quoted that at least once a week, especially because Cope was now officially an author, since Nelson had secretly published his work.

As he watched the BLAXERS load the books into the fourth Flo-wing, his excitement grew. He'd received word that the flare-ups in the Amazon and Portland had ended. Aylantik spokes-people had been issuing spin all day, attributing the violence to accidents, petty criminals, and the resulting confusion. Full investigations and reforms were promised in order to avoid an unlikely repeat of the unfortunate events.

Grandyn believed it was a triumph for the rebels. He imagined that if they could decode the books, they might be able to defeat Aylantik. By taking the proof of the Banoff to the people, they could get the masses behind them, and the prophecies could show them the way through the Doneharvest to complete the Exchange.

There would be challenges, but they had overcome challenges every day of the past three years. If they could hold the coalition together and stay alive, the tools were now in their possession to destroy the Aylantik. He looked forward to the trials of the AOI leadership and the redistribution of the world's wealth, but what about UC's promise? The future could be more than he'd ever imagined. The future could be as long as forever.

If Deuce had succeeded, then Nelson and Munna would be at the island before he arrived. He walked back into the abandoned restaurant, which had kept so many books safe for so long. They had gotten them all, only the tables and chairs remained. He wondered whether this place, like the library in Portland, Nelson's cabin in the woods, and so many POPs, the PAWN Operational

Pods, would one day be museums to the revolution. He boarded the fifth and final Flo-wing and wondered where the AOI would be looking for him today.

He missed Fye, and wished she could go to the island, but it would be too dangerous. Still, it would be good to see Nelson again, to get his help with the books. But he was most interested in continuing his conversation with Munna. With all he'd learned, he had hundreds of questions for her. With her wisdom spanning a world of change, from the pre-Banoff years to all that had happened since, she could answer questions no one else could: the truth about his mother's death, Chelle and Drast's relationship, the A-Council, and Lance Miner. Munna might not want war, but she knew enough to help them win it.

Grandyn worked his INU as the Flo-wing soared over the mountains and the ocean came into view. He sent Nelson the list of what he'd discovered so far. There weren't that many pre-1847 books, so if they could find them all, there was a good chance to fill in the remaining titles. Thus far he had identified Homer's *Iliad*, and Milton's *Paradise Lost*. Those along with Shakespeare's *Hamlet*, and *Clastier's Papers*, which he knew were part of the eight but still hadn't been located, meant there were only four left to find. But he wasn't so sure *Clastier's Papers* were part of the eight works. It didn't make sense that someone would go to so much trouble to hide the prophecies and risk putting clues in his own writings. If the *Clastier Papers* didn't count, that meant there were still five to go.

Based on the complexities of the code and what Deuce and Nelson told me, Grandyn thought, *it sounds like these are somehow interactive prophecies. If that's true, just imagine the power.*

CHAPTER SIXTY-THREE

The Munna-Grandyn-Nelson reunion was an extremely happy moment. In spite of their philosophical differences, they truly liked each other. When Deuce entered the room, a noticeable shift in the chemistry could be felt, much the same way as a classroom of only students changes when the teacher arrives. No one was quite sure if Deuce could be trusted entirely, but they needed to trust him, and often the most clarity comes from a lack of choices.

"Thank you all for coming. Please, follow me." He led them to a small dock where they boarded a boat.

"Where are we going?" Grandyn asked.

"I'm glad you asked. We're on Ryder Island, but the books are located on a smaller island less than a kilometer away, called Runit Island."

Grandyn smiled. "You named an island after my father?"

"No. My grandfather did," Deuce said. "He collected islands and was fond of naming them after people he admired."

"But Booker Lipton didn't know my father."

"My grandfather knew a great many things," Deuce replied, "and some of them are just now coming to light."

They docked at a long wooden pier as the shoreline was rocky and shallow. Several other boats were already tied up. A worn, stone path led toward the center of the island. Twenty meters up the trail, an old carved sign, which could have been a hundred years old, confirmed Deuce's story. "Welcome to Runit Island." Grandyn couldn't resist taking a photo with his INU.

Ten meters beyond that, they found a covered area containing several old-fashioned golf carts. From there, Deuce drove them to a large stone building that seemed like it could withstand an aerial bombing. "It can't be seen from the sea or the air," Deuce said proudly. A combination of real and artificial vegetation, Tekfabrik, and the natural rocky terrain of the tiny island, it was an ideal place to conceal a treasure.

"Before we go in," Grandyn began. "Has there been anything at all on my dad?"

Nelson and Deuce exchanged a glance, but said nothing.

Munna shook her head slowly. "I'm sorry, Grandyn, there is not anything new."

Grandyn nodded. "A part of me, kind of thought he might be here waiting with the books."

"I wish that were true," Deuce said, knowing he was dashing the innocent hopes of a child longing for his father.

"Don't give up," Munna said quietly. "Anything is possible. Just look where we are, about to walk into a library of books many times thought lost forever."

Grandyn clung to the wise old woman's words, knowing she did not say "pretty things" without a foundation of truth. He felt guilty for the times he doubted Runit might be alive somewhere. Yet he'd lived a lifetime of death and turmoil since he'd last seen him and wondered if they ever found each other again, would his father even recognize him.

They walked into the building and found more than one hundred thousand books lined up on more than four hundred long tables. Around the exterior walls were enough shelves to hold the volumes.

"Shoot Deuce, you really did it," Nelson said. "Makes me want to cry."

"Wow," Grandyn said. "Let's go!" He jogged into the gymnasium-sized room.

Munna asked Deuce if there was a place where she could lie down. He took her through a doorway, not far from the entrance, which opened into a hall.

"There are ten rooms, all with ocean views. Choose anyone you like," Deuce said. "Are you all right?"

After assuring her host that she was merely tired after the harrowing events beginning in the redwoods, extending into the Portland fiasco, and then the long trip to the island, she took the first room and excused herself. The rooms were fully furnished with anything a guest would need, but Deuce assigned an assistant to be on standby should any of them need something more. He spoke briefly with Nelson and Grandyn, telling them a dozen of his most trusted people stood ready to help search for titles or do whatever they required.

"Please give me updates whenever you have anything to report. Even the smallest bit of news will be welcome." After they agreed, he headed back to Ryder Island to check on his son.

Grandyn and Nelson divided the room in half. Each would work a side. Lists of all pre-1847 titles were sent to the twelve assistants. The library didn't have a large collection of antique books, so very few were expected to be first editions, but the classic works would have been reprinted countless times over the centuries.

"I only hope the original text was kept intact. Even a minor change like bringing the language up to modern standards would blow the code," Grandyn said as he watched the assistants work the room, reading spine by spine, looking for the elusive volumes. Little by little, discoveries were made while Grandyn and Nelson tried to figure out a way to not have to check them all.

Fye, working from another location, remained holographically present through the AirViews. Grandyn introduced her to Nelson and admitted she was a List Keeper. Nelson raised an eyebrow. She was the first List Keeper he'd actually met, and the first real confirmation he had that the secretive group even existed. But what surprised him the most was that Grandyn had hooked up with the List Keepers.

They must be the ones who have helped him stay hidden all these years, he thought. *One day, maybe he'll tell me how they did it.* He noticed she was busy writing in a pad. *Maybe that's why they call them List Keepers,* he mused.

CHAPTER SIXTY-FOUR

"What do we know about Clastier?" Grandyn asked, trying to picture the man who had created so much trouble. A man almost unknown, compared to Nostradamus, and yet one who had predicted far more events and with astonishing accuracy.

"Not as much as I wish we did. The Vatican destroyed almost all information about the man. You've read about the Church?" Nelson asked, knowing it wasn't studied in schools any longer and the old religions were now even more obscure than the dead languages.

"My father had me read about many of the former great religions: Christianity, Hinduism, Islam, Judaism, Buddhism, and New Age Spirituality. I think I have a good grasp on the basics. I know a little of Vatican history, but why did they want to hide Clastier?"

"I'll tell you what Cope and Deuce have told me, because almost everything we know about Clastier comes from Booker Lipton. He was obsessed with Clastier and the prophecies, but that's another conversation." Nelson had a faraway look in his eyes and paused for a moment as if remembering something, but then turned back to Grandyn. "The Vatican didn't want to hide

Clastier's existence as much as they wanted to hide his work . . . erase it, really. And in those days, the first part of the nineteenth century, the Church had the power to expunge a man's entire existence. But Clastier was smart and obviously visionary, based on what he left behind, and the Vatican grossly underestimated him."

"Did they kill him?"

"No one knows for sure, but let me start at the beginning. He was born to a Spanish mother and a French father in the late 1700s and raised in the territory of New Mexico . . . "

After hearing the entire story of Clastier, Grandyn wondered what might have happened in the man's life to change him from being deeply committed to the Church to turning his back on it and his faith. Nelson didn't know why.

"So much of Clastier's life was lost to history."

"Look at the collapse of religion in the last hundred years," Grandyn said.

"You've studied religions, so you shouldn't be surprised that the Aylantik hasn't really been able to erase thousands of years of faith and worship from society with a simple stroke of the pen."

"People are still practicing?"

"Yes."

"Lots of people?"

"PAWN estimates perhaps eight million, but it's impossible to know exactly how many since they are doing it in secret, at risk of arrest."

"So Clastier spoke both Spanish and French," Grandyn said, returning to their objective. "Those were the dominant influences in the American Southwest at that time."

Grandyn looked over his list. There were still almost one hundred and fifty candidates, but as he scanned for titles that related to French or Spanish authors, one immediately stood out.

"Of course," he said. "I can't believe we didn't get this one earlier. *The Ingenious Gentleman Don Quixote of La Mancha* was an extremely influential book for centuries, a Spanish novel by Miguel de Cervantes Saavedra.

"One of the many islands Deuce inherited from his grandfather is called Cervantes," Nelson said. "Maybe Booker solved some of these clues long ago."

"The thought crossed my mind, but then why doesn't Deuce know? Why does he need us?"

"I don't know. Maybe Deuce doesn't know he already has the answers, or maybe Booker didn't want Deuce to know . . . Booker obviously had some method of seeing, or at least predicting, the future. If it wasn't the prophecies, I don't know what it could have been, but evidentally he knew Deuce would need help."

"Money and power are never enough, or all the great empires of history would not have fallen."

"I'm counting on that with Aylantik. They make all the empires of the past look like peasant villages," Nelson said.

The assistants were busy stacking up books on two tables they'd cleared for the pre-1847 candidates as they were found. Grandyn and Nelson were so excited about *Don Quixote* that they went to look for it themselves. Less than ten minutes later an assistant found it, an edition that had been published in the 1940s. Grandyn rushed to feed the data to Fye. After a few minutes, she announced a match.

CHAPTER SIXTY-FIVE

They now had the *Iliad, Paradise Lost, Hamlet*, and *Don Quixote*. They kept testing pre-1847 titles as soon as they found them, but it was hours before they got another hit, Edmund Burke's *Reflections on the Revolution in France*.

"Lest we forget, our man Clastier was a revolutionary," Nelson said, stepping outside for a celebratory bac.

"And part French," Grandyn added. "Then we should check Thomas Paine's *Rights of Man*. It's a response to Burke's work on the Revolution."

By the time Nelson came back inside, Fye had confirmed their sixth match.

"When did you get so smart?" Nelson asked.

Fye's hologram walked into the room and answered before Grandyn had a chance. "Since he fell in love with me."

"Is that so?" Nelson said. Knowing Fye was a List Keeper, he didn't doubt it. The enigmatic group was mostly a mystery to him, but he'd heard enough during his lifetime as a rebel to know that the List Keepers were all supposed to be super smart – Imp-smart, but without the implant. List Keepers' shadowy reputation had

left Nelson with the definite impression that they could beat Blaze
Cortez in an intelligence duel.

Grandyn ignored Fye's comment, but blew a kiss to her hologram. Hours went by without any more progress until a random
test produced another winner. *The Federalist,* a collection of 85 arti-
cles and essays written by Alexander Hamilton, James Madison,
and John Jay.

"Once again, Clastier is a revolutionary," Grandyn said.

"It's deeper than that, the *Federalist Papers* is really an attempt
to bring order out of the American Revolution," Nelson said.
"They wanted to influence and promote the ratification of the US
Constitution. Clastier was an interesting man, that's for sure."

"Carrying with the French and Spanish themes, I see several
French books, or books about France, but now that we already have
Burke's contribution and Paine's *Rights of Man,* I'd say Clastier's
father is more than well represented. Nothing else Spanish on the
list matched," Grandyn said. "The man was in spiritual crisis, parting
with his Church and discovering prophecies that made him question
everything about his life, not to mention changing his perception
about human existence in general. I'd have to guess he would go for
something more philosophical, something like that," Grandyn said,
stabbing his finger into the AirView containing the list.

"*Meditations,* by Marcus Aurelius," Nelson said, reading the
title Grandyn had pointed to.

"I think so. Let's check it."

Less than ten minutes later, Nelson smiled. "We have the
eighth book! Shoot Grandyn, your dad would be so proud. Your
mom, too." Nelson smothered Grandyn in a bear hug.

"We're almost there." He smiled. "But I'm not sure Hamlet is
part of the prophecies."

"Why wouldn't it be? Why else would it have an altered
pattern?" Nelson asked.

"Look what we have," Grandyn pointed to a list.

1. *The Iliad*
2. *Paradise Lost*
3. *Hamlet*
4. *Don Quixote*
5. *Reflections on the Revolution in France*
6. *Rights of Man*
7. *The Federalist*
8. *Meditations*

"One of these books has to be the key to the code," Grandyn said.

"True," Fye said "The books are useless to us without the key. Until we get that, all we can do is read them, like anyone else. The hidden message remains buried in the original arrangement of letters."

"One of the last things my dad told me was that Hamlet was important to the prophecies. I think it might be the key."

"But maybe the eight works are seven messages and one key," Fye said, furiously putting down numbers and letters in her pad.

"I get what you're saying. We have the books, but how do we access the code?" Nelson asked. "I really don't know."

"Clastier was a priest, right?" Fye asked rhetorically. "He was raised by the Church. There is only one thing he would have used to set the code . . . the Bible."

Nelson and Grandyn stared at her.

"Bible codes have been used by others throughout history to hide messages, including other purported prophecies," Fye said, "but even assuming I'm right, we still need a check digit."

"Wait, explain that slowly," Nelson said.

"Although most early examples come from the Hebrew text of the Torah, there are many ways to do it. By using every 50th letter of the Book of Genesis, beginning at the correct point, you'll find the Hebrew word "torah" spelled out. The Book of Exodus produces the same result."

"Cool," Grandyn said.

"But we're not talking about text hidden in the Bible," Nelson said.

"Right, what we're interested in is using the Bible as a key, but think about it. There are not many things that Clastier had access to that we can also find still unchanged nearly three hundred years later. He might not have known that the books he used for the prophecies would exist in a simple form, but he needed to be confident that the object he chose for the key would be easily available and in multiple copies. What else but the Bible?"

"Okay," Nelson said, lighting a bac, "but how's it work?"

Fye started coughing and asked him to put it out, which he did.

Grandyn laughed. Fye was there only as a hologram and could not have been affected by the smoke. Nelson missed the joke.

"How do we unlock the Bible code?" Nelson asked again.

"Ah, that is the question," Fye said. "Clastier was obviously a bright man, but he still would have had little access to complex methods of creating a code. One possiblilty he might have known about, or even devised a version of himself, would have been the Equidistant Letter Sequence or 'ELS.' It's a fairly simple way to go, as long as you know where to begin and have the right skip number." She pointed to text from a transcript of the zoom detailing the recent AOI attack on the PAWN facility. "Here, assume my starting point is a particular word, and my skip letter is five. I would take every fifth letter and a message would soon appear. Negative numbers can be used and, to make it more complicated, even sequences, such as, five, four, one. In that case you first skip five, then four, then one. They can get even more complex by adding dumb numbers or shifting sequences. The INU can detect the patterns if we have the start number."

"So there could also be multiple messages contained in one book?" Nelson said.

"Oh yes. Theoretically, if the codes are applied after the book is published, there could be hundreds of books and thousands of messages, even millions contained in each book. All the code is doing is creating a new way of reading the assembled letters."

"So that's how they could change," Grandyn said in an awed tone.

"Exactly."

"I've actually come to this conclusion by more than just deducing. I've run six thousand twenty-nine possible codes through the system using the *Iliad,* and I'm very confident about the ELS. We just need to confirm it with another book and we need the skip number."

"The influence of his parents is profound," Grandyn said. "What else was important to Clastier? His name. It was the only thing his father gave him. Even though his father left before he knew him, a son never forgets his father."

Nelson nodded sadly and gave Grandyn a knowing glance.

"It holds eight distinct letters," he continued.

Fye tried it, but it didn't work. They kept analyzing what they knew about Clastier, about the Bible, anything at all. They worked for another hour and a half, running every possible number sequence they could dream up with the help of the INU, but nothing came. Deuce walked in and they quickly told him where they were.

"My grandfather also believed the Bible contained a code which would lead to the books in which the prophecies appear, but he'd never been able to find it," Deuce said. "I've thought a great deal about it and studied everything we know about Clastier and his times, and I don't think he would have used the Bible because by the time he wrote the codes, he had rejected the Church."

"But he couldn't have counted on his writings surviving," Grandyn said.

"He could if he could see the future," Nelson replied.

"Let's remember he didn't create the prophecies, he merely

interpreted them and, in the case of his Divinations, he only recorded them," Deuce said. "Those, we call his stagnant prophecies have already come to pass. The ones we're looking for, called the *Justar Journal*, are something entirely different. His attempt to preserve them for us was based on what he saw of the Banoff and its aftermath. He wanted us to have a way out, a chance to fix it."

"So where did he hide the key?"

"I believe the only clue he possibly gave was in a letter he sent to a follower, which read, "To unlock the eternal mind of existence, the *Justar Journal*, one must go one, two and possess it, next . . . one must cope."

"I know how to read the prophecies!" Grandyn shouted.

CHAPTER SIXTY-SIX

Blaze sat with his knights gathered at the round table. "The trouble is too much for us," he said, resigned in the most un-Blaze-like manner.

Morholt nodded. "Unfortunately, the trouble will be multiplied greatly by our own allies." He paused and looked around slowly at the others. "The Imps have grown restless. They are impatient with the traditionals."

Traditionals were actual humans without implants, and the traditional he was most likely referring to was Lance Miner. Morholt, being a CHRUDE and speaking about the Imps that way, while so many were in the room, was going to create an argument that Blaze was not in the mood for, but had nonetheless known was coming.

"Morholt, I do respect your knowledge. You are programmed at the highest level and able to simulate reason and access massive amounts of data, but you are not human, nor an Imp," Galahad said, "so please don't speak for us."

"It was merely an observation, and an accurate one," Morholt shot back.

"CHRUDEs are in many ways superior to Imps," Bors, another CHRUDE, said. "We have complete control over our emotions."

"Your emotions are artificial," Lucan the Butler snapped.

"Please," Blaze said, slapping the table. "Please don't let this disintegrate into an 'Imps are better than CHRUDEs' debate. As far as I'm concerned, you're all a damn close second to me, so let's carry on."

Most of them laughed.

"My point is still on the table," Morholt said.

"And so it is," Blaze muttered.

"You all may not like my analysis," Morholt continued, "but that doesn't mean it isn't true. The Imps here will surely agree that Imps have seen things, understood things about the world today . . . and yesterday. The Aylantik cannot stand, its foundations are far too weak, built on the lies and manipulations of billions dead."

"Your assessment, please," Blaze said, as he could see the Imps ready to pounce.

"We are at a presage to war. At this point there are many sides, which will surely consolidate if hostilities deepen further. I'm saying the Imps will create a new side . . . their own side."

"Outrageous!" Galahad said, leaping to his feet.

"Your programming is obviously contaminated," Percival said, slapping the round table and pointing at Morholt.

"Your reaction is an indication of your knowledge of the conspiracy," Bors said.

"Conspiracy is it?" Lucan the Butler asked bitterly. "The CHRUDEs may be the ones with a conspiracy against us Imps."

"What is this?" Blaze called loudly, holding out his hands in a gesture of confusion. "My knights do not quarrel among themselves, and they certainly don't scheme without my consent. I'm the schemer in this world." He stared around the table, letting a stern gaze linger on Galahad. "If the Imps open yet another dimension to this dispute, then I shall not be an ally."

"Are you short on logic?" Galahad asked Morholt. "The Imps are *vastly* outnumbered by the AOI, BLAXERS, Enforcers, and PAWN. Do you take us for fools? Even if we had cause for revolt, we could not win with such odds."

"You outnumber any of the sides with brain capacity and access to realms of higher intelligence," Morholt said calmly. "And you would obviously begin any conflict in an alliance, which you would, if things go your way, betray."

"Instigator, subversive!" Galahad shouted. "Remove him!"

"Do you have any proof for your allegations?" Blaze asked Morholt when order was finally restored.

"It is only beginning. There is not yet proof. We will know more in the coming days." He turned to Blaze. "Another issue of urgency is the AOI . . . they will not ignore the Imps much longer."

The Imps erupted again. It took Blaze some time to calm things down, with an agreement to drop the subject until the next meeting. The discussion shifted to the AOI and whether they could prevent war much longer. Eventually, Bors brought up Lance Miner's influence in the AOI and the conversation circled back around to Imps. Miner had been increasingly employing Imps for information and strategy, but there had been a falling out. Morholt pointed to this as a factor in the growing Imp discontent. Blaze adjourned the meeting before things deteriorated again. He needed time to look into Morholt's information.

As the knights were standing to leave, Blaze added one last thought. "If and when the AOI turns their attention onto the Imps, either for prosecution or assistance, we'll have arrived at a very dangerous precipice, one I'm not sure we will be able to cross, or even see over."

The AOI Chief looked at her blinking INU with trepidation. She'd seen the zoom, dreaded it actually, but not because the A-Council Chairman intimidated her. Quite the contrary. She knew that although he was a very bright man, he didn't understand the intricacies of the impending revolution.

"Are you going to be able to stop this thing?" he asked, jumping right in.

"Mr. Chairman, I assure you that we're doing everything we can."

"It doesn't look like it's enough. Can you explain to me why this is so difficult? Why on earth are there more than a handful of crazies wanting to overthrow the government that has given them everything?"

She started to answer but he plowed on.

"We have brought these people from the brink of human extinction to a prosperous utopia. Lifetime employment, full health coverage, the longest life expectancy in history. We've eliminated war, poverty, hunger, and fossil fuels . . . fossil fuels, that means we've also eliminated pollution. I mean what more do these torgon people *want?*"

"You know what they want," she said, more than a little impatiently.

"No, I don't. I'm at a complete loss."

"They want the truth!"

"Truth? Why would they want the truth when they have entertainment and sports beamed to their INUs twenty-four hours a day?"

"It's hard to believe," she said sarcastically.

"They don't really want the truth. The *truth* would just confuse them, the *truth* would make them start to think that there might be something better. They don't even know how good they have it. They're bored. It's time for a change, something new . . . well, screw them! We're not letting PAWN, or a bunch of Creatives, or a damn TreeRunner, or anyone else take us back to the dark pre-Banoff world."

"No, sir."

"The Council is getting worried. We're wondering if you can contain this thing."

"It's got lots of moving parts, but I believe we're still out front."

"You crush this thing, and you make sure no one is left to start again. The Doneharvest has to be as close as we ever get to war."

"I understand the objectives, sir."

"Make torg sure you do."

"Sir, my attentions are required elsewhere. I address the full Council in forty-eight hours. We can certainly go more into this at that time," she said curtly. "Peace prevails, always."

"See that it does!"

CHAPTER SIXTY-SEVEN

Everyone looked at Grandyn.

"My dad gave me the clue, but only the part that related to Hamlet," Grandyn explained. "Now it makes perfect sense. To unlock the eternal mind of existence, the *Justar Journal*, one must go one, two, that's Act One, Scene Two of Hamlet. Possess it, next, not only confirms that Hamlet is the correct play, but it also gives the starting point for the code."

"And the check digit?" Fye asked.

"Four," Nelson said before Grandyn could respond. "Four digits in Cope."

"Right," Grandyn said.

"But why Cope?" Fye asked.

"I can answer that one," Deuce said. "Clastier saw three people as instrumental in preserving the message of the *Justar Journal*. Spencer Copeland was a mystic who lived a hundred years ago. Nathan Cope Ryder, also a mystic, was named for Copeland, and finally Cope Lipton, named for both men, who became a mystic and passed on much about the prophecies . . . one must cope." Deuce smiled.

"Well, let's see if it works," Fye said, scrawling out scores of lines of text in a pad as if her hand belonged to a secretary doing shorthand.

Munna walked into the large room. "Am I in time?" she asked, smiling.

"Always," Grandyn answered.

They set up a giant AirView for each book. The text filled the nearly-three-meter-high screens. Like the paper pages it emulated, the background was an opaque white while the text was a vibrant black.

"The INU will overlay the pattern from the Hamlet code and apply it to the text of this book, picking the letters and giving us a new book, so to speak," Fye said. "It will automatically fade back the old text."

They started with the passage from Hamlet on the first AirView:

"To be, or not to be: that is the question:
Whether 'tis nobler in the mind to suffer
The slings and arrows of outrageous fortune,
Or to take arms against a sea of troubles,
And by opposing end them? To die: to sleep;
No more; and, by a sleep to say we end
The heartache and the thousand natural shocks
That flesh is heir to, 'tis a consummation
Devoutly to be wish'd. To die, to sleep;
To sleep: perchance to dream: ay, there's the rub.
For in that sleep of death what dreams may come . . ."

Once the check digit was plugged into the program at the starting point in Hamlet, all the books, linked through INUs, miraculously began shuffling the letters. They looked like tens of thousands of ants racing across the sand.

"Look at that, it's picking the patterns, it's changing!" Grandyn whispered in awe. "It's really working!"

"Can you imagine if someone had to do this by hand?" Nelson mused. "It would take months, maybe years, to decode the scramble."

Surprisingly, the text of all eight books moved. They had not expected anything from Hamlet, and it didn't move for long, but it revealed a very important piece of information. The other seven books were each a chapter of the *Justar Journal*. It presented the following list:

Meditations, by Marcus Aurelius
  Health and Birth
  Spirituality and Death

Reflections of the Revolution in France, by Edmund Burke
  War and Peace
  Wealth and Power

Paradise Lost, by John Milton
  Earth and Nature
  Planets and Stars

The Federalist, by Alexander Hamilton, James Madison, and John Jay
  Science and Technology
  Art and Creativity

The Ingenious Gentleman Don Quixote of La Mancha, by Miguel de Cervantes Saavedra
  Time and Thoughts

Dreams and Wishes

The Iliad, by Homer

Rights of Man, by Thomas Paine

"It would seem that each one of your books deal with one aspect of the prophecies," Munna said.

"But the *Iliad* and the *Rights of Man* have not come through yet," Grandyn noted. "And look," he pointed, "those two screens are still scrambling while the others have settled on readable text."

"What good is a book with two missing chapters?' Nelson asked.

"The two final chapters at that," Deuce added.

They didn't have time to ponder the meaning of two lost chapters, and collectively hoped they might still come through. Each had independently begun reading the screens and no one, at that moment, could imagine needing more information.

Each book had fascinating insights and predictions for the near future. *Paradise Lost* described a meeting between intelligent life forms and humans, and based on the descriptions, it would happen in eleven years, in 2112. That seemed to be about as far out as the prophecies went, but the monumental meeting, dreamt about since humans started looking to the stars, would come at a time of complete devastation for Earth. Hardly anyone would be left. Deuce and Grandyn had coincidently been reading that one, and both of them stood stunned. At the same time, Fye was reading a similar fate in *Meditations*. Nelson found himself absorbed in *The Federalist,* and he too discovered that the end of the world was near. Munna finished reading a page from *Don Quixote* and smiled.

"Think we can stop it?" she asked the group.

They all turned to *Reflections of the Revolution in France* and saw the war described in detail. It hadn't begun in Portland or the Amazon as they feared, but it led to the near complete destruction of the human race.

"We can't let this happen," Deuce said, bringing up two of his own AirViews and madly motioning a series of commands.

"I have to talk to Drast," Grandyn said.

"What can *he* do?" Deuce asked.

"Don't you see? It's telling us that the war starts in nine days . . . from the prisons!"

"And you think Drast is behind it."

"I know he is!"

"It doesn't matter how it begins," Nelson said. "It is going to begin, but now we have the tool needed to make sure it doesn't go this way. The outcome will be different if we win."

"The *Justar Journal* cannot be used for war," Munna said firmly.

"How can it not?" Deuce asked.

"You gave me your word," Munna said.

"That was before I saw what happens. Look at this! Ten years of war and destruction and we're wiped out," Deuce said, motioning to the AirViews.

"Look!" Nelson interrupted. "It's changing."

Suddenly the scenario was different, some events erased and new ones appeared. The end result was still almost total annihilation of the species, but now it ended two years sooner.

"What just happened?" Deuce asked. He pulled up another AirView, this one showing up-to-the-moment satellite-monitored news collected from unauthorized internal AOI feeds, including Seeker, zooms and Field data. It only took a second to spot a major event. Two PAWN POPs had been raided in France and Pennsylvania Areas. "As soon as these events happened, the prophecies transformed."

"They're still changing," Grandyn said, pointing to all the screens.

"Incredible," Nelson said, staring as the lines continued to rewrite themselves. "Then it's true. The prophecies *do* change."

"But how? How can they?" Grandyn asked. "I've got to get to Drast."

Suddenly, BLAXERs appeared from concealed panels behind the still half-empty shelves. The doors locked and the connection to Fye was terminated. Grandyn watched helplessly as her hologram dispersed into the ethers.

"No one is leaving here," Deuce said.

CHAPTER SIXTY-EIGHT

Munna turned to Deuce and appeared almost to glide toward him. Only centimeters from his face, although much shorter, at that moment she seemed equal in stature. "You let Grandyn go!"

"I can't do that," Deuce said, unable to shake her stare.

Munna waved a hand above her head and the five AirViews displaying the decoded chapters went blank. Only Hamlet and the two scrambling screens remained active.

"What did you do?" Deuce snapped.

"You will not use the *Justar Journal* for war!" Her gravelly whisper had the effect of a shout. The rest of the room reverberated silence.

"Munna, please. I'm on your side," Deuce said. "I'm trying to save us all from what we just saw up on those screens. We need to win this war. You saw what happens if we let them beat us."

"You can not save us through war," Munna said, looking at Deuce, her hand still in the air. She turned to Nelson. "Winning a war is not possible."

"Munna, I don't know how you've hijacked the INUs," Deuce said, "but I manufacture them, my family invented them, I will get back control."

"Booker did not invent them, he merely borrowed the technology," she replied. "I'll enjoy watching you try to get back in." She turned to Grandyn. "Go, TreeRunner, go!"

Grandyn looked at the BLAXERs.

"They will not impede you," she said firmly.

Grandyn jogged to the door and as Munna stared at them, two BLAXERs stood back, and the door unlocked. He turned back and looked from Munna to Deuce. The trillionaire seemed resigned to having to operate under the whims of an old lady. Grandyn spun and headed out the door.

"Grandyn!" Nelson yelled.

He stopped and looked at his uncle.

"Be brave and true."

Grandyn nodded and left. A few minutes later, he was on a boat heading toward Ryder Island. He wasn't sure how he was going to get back to the mainland from there but, to his surprise, a man met him at the dock and said Deuce had given instructions to fly him wherever he wanted to go.

Munna just *might be powerful enough to defeat Aylantik without a war,* he thought, shaking his head in wonder. He told the pilot where to take him. The man was surprised, and told him to prepare for a long flight.

Once the Flo-wing lifted off, he reconnected with Fye. "Munna somehow stopped the INUs from processing the chapters," Grandyn told her. "But if Deuce gets back on, doesn't he need your program to re-start them?"

"He's already got it. While we were connected, he would have easily copied it."

"Maybe Munna can keep him from getting back in. At least until I can have a conversation with Drast."

"Do you have a plan?" Fye asked. "The AOI is on the highest alert level. There are still checkpoints everywhere. What might have been simple a few days ago is now likely to get you killed."

"I just need to show him something."

"He is in a maximum security *prison*."

"I know that, but I have no intention of talking to him directly."

"I'm glad to hear that."

"But it won't be easy. It's about so much more than just getting Drast to stop his rebellion. I'll need Chelle to cooperate."

"You want Chelle to help you stop the war she so badly wants?"

"It was a war I wanted too until I read the prophecies."

"But *she* hasn't read them. And even if she did, she'd be like Nelson and Deuce. She'd just want to use the *Justar Journal* to win."

Together they devised a risky plan. Fye went to take care of her part, while Grandyn, still in the air, zoomed Chelle. She sat next to him holographically as the Flo-wing continued its flight. He told her about the scene on Runit Island.

"So Deuce is going to keep them to himself?" she asked.

"I don't know if he just wants time to figure it out, or if he intends to hold the power exclusively for his agenda."

"So it just showed us losing. There's nothing on how we could win?"

"I don't think there is any question it can show us what needs to be done to avoid that horrible fate we're heading toward now," Grandyn said, "but we've just started."

"You said you needed me to do something."

"My father thought I was asleep the night before . . . that final night. I heard him whispering these words from Hamlet: 'Doubt thou the stars are fire, Doubt that the sun doth move, Doubt truth to be a liar, But never doubt I love.' It was a message."

"To me?" she asked.

"No. I mean, I'm sure he loved you, but repeating lines from Hamlet was him trying to decode the prophecies."

"Do you think it could lead to the last two chapters? The ones you said were still scrambled?"

"I don't know, but before we can discover the rest, or figure out how best to use the *Justar Journal*, I need your help with something in the Amazon."

CHAPTER SIXTY-NINE

Miner watched as the rain began. Within two hours, the deluge would be heavy enough to put out most of the fires. It would take days more to stop the downpours. Sending that much water into the Amazon during the dry season shouldn't cause any major problems, at least for the trees, but things could go wrong and the rains could last weeks. Weather-making was still an inexact science.

Chelle Andreas, of all people, had made the request, and he still couldn't decide if he'd done the right thing.

"Putting out the fires is a good move no matter what," Sarlo said.

"That's what I think. It's just that she wants a war and I don't, so doing what she requests is counter to my interests and against my better judgment."

"But she said they had the prophecies."

"Yes."

"Do you believe her?"

"I think I do. And if she is telling the truth, then the Amazon burning leads to a war which results in Armageddon."

"Your greatest fear."

He thought of the years of nightmares about war that had plagued him, both in his sleep and during waking hours. Some might accuse him of using his power and wealth to accumulate more power and wealth and, to a great extent, that was true. But mostly he had spent his life desperately trying to avoid war. Others could question his motives, but not his resolve.

He simply nodded, consumed by his mental wanderings.

"The irony is that the prophecies may unite us all."

"I hope so," he said, surprised at his response. "Munna was right, she might be my best hope. But if Deuce and Nelson Wright have seen the potential result of their revolution, they may think differently." He was silent for a moment. "Getting them to live quietly under Aylantik rule . . . even with what they know about the future . . . I don't think it's ever going to happen. They can't change that much."

"Maybe we have to change some too."

Before he could reply, their conversation was interrupted by another zoom, this one not as unlikely as Chelle's had been, but the consequences were far more dire. As it would turn out, it was a zoom he'd been hoping to receive for years.

"Look at your INU, pull up the file named 'gold'," Blaze said, smiling as the image view opened.

"I don't have a file called gold." But as Miner said the words, the gold file appeared in his secure section. "How the—"

"You're going to like this very, very, *very* much," Blaze teased.

"This is an AOI personnel file," Miner said, annoyed and bewildered. "Who the hell is Ander Terik? And how did you get into my torgon INU?"

"It will cost you one billion digis to find out who Ander Terik is. To find out how I put the file into your INU would cost more money than you have! Only Deuce could afford information like that." Blaze loved pushing Miner's buttons.

"Are you out of your mind? Why do I give a damn who this guy is?"

"Two billion."

"What? Are you serious?"

"Three billion."

"Stop talking! You're crazy!"

"Four."

"Blaze, I'll pay! Damn it, I'll pay!"

"Five billion."

"I said I'll pay!"

"Say you're sorry or it'll be six."

"Blaze, you're asking me for five billion digis to find out something, but I don't even know what I'm buying!"

"If I told you first, you wouldn't have to pay for it would you? Six billion digis, normal procedure. Zoom me once it's done."

"*Six?*"

"You didn't apologize. Should we make it seven?"

"No. I'll be back to you in less than ten minutes."

"Make it less than nine minutes or I'll make you throw in that silver dollar of yours too," Blaze said without even the hint of a smile as he vanished, ending the zoom.

It took just over four minutes for Miner to initiate the transfer of funds and for them to be received and verified on Blaze's end. "If only this is true," Miner said, as he ended the second zoom with Blaze and opened a series of AirViews and issued orders to PharmaForce leaders all over the Pacyfik region. Once everything was in motion, he and Sarlo boarded a jet for Oregon Area. The rain continued to pour across the Amazon as their plane punctured the sky.

"With any luck, he'll be in custody by the time we arrive," Miner said.

"I still don't believe it. All these years, Grandyn Happerman has been hiding in the AOI, undercover, as an actual AOI agent . . . what's the name he's been using again?"

"Ander Terik."

CHAPTER SEVENTY

The soldiers were not AOI, he knew that for certain. They had violated AOI protocol on no less than eight occasions since his arrest. On top of those violations, he found it curious that he had not been searched for a neuro-cap, which he did, in fact, have in his mouth. He was encouraged that he hadn't already been executed and, if they didn't know enough to prevent a neuro-cap brain-erase, perhaps he'd live through the day.

Ironically, his capture had come on the edge of a great forest, just far enough in that he'd thought he'd be safe, but he should have been more careful. The soldiers had somehow been tipped off to his whereabouts. Who had betrayed him? He tried to think. It could only have been one of four people who knew what Terik had been doing.

They shoved him to the floor and removed his blindfold and restraints. Before he could react, they'd sealed him in the tiny cell. Not really a conventional cell. The room, the size of a small walk-in closet, had three glass walls. He looked out onto what was clearly a research lab at a large corporation. There were medical disposal containers, glass beakers, and test tubes, and based on the INU AirViews left monitoring heating and cooling containers, it was clear this was a PharmaForce facility. That answered his question: the soldiers had obviously been from the Enforcers. He'd learned about PharmaForce's private army while at the AOI. The agency sometimes worked with "the Force," but mostly they were a concern for the AOI leadership. The Force had been tolerated only as a counterbalance to Lipton's BLAXER army.

A man approached the glass wall. Grandyn recognized him immediately. He'd even passed him in the hallway at AOI headquarters in Atlanta once, a couple of years earlier. The PharmaForce CEO was a well-known public figure. A hero, even.

"Funny how much you resemble Ander Terik," Miner said, pointing to a projected image of the AOI agent. "You really don't look a thing like Grandyn Happerman."

"Torg off."

"Hmph," Miner laughed. "According to records I'm privy to, the AOI has executed six people in the past three years who claimed to be Grandyn Happerman. Doesn't that make you feel just awful?" Miner gave him a hard look before continuing. "I know if friends of mine had died so that I could live, I'd have a hard time sleeping at night."

"I doubt you ever have trouble sleeping Miner." Grandyn squinted at the man he had long considered to be the face of evil. "I mean, really, how do you sleep knowing your family killed billions of people so that you could live in obscene Pharaoh-like luxury?"

"You don't know what you're talking about. You have no idea how bad the world was and how it came to be so good." Miner scowled. "You hear rumors and believe propaganda concocted by rabble-rousers and scalawags bent on destroying the utopia we've created."

"Save your lies for your doped-up public. I know the truth."

"You're a foolish young man." He stared. "Don't you wonder how we cracked your identity? Aren't you curious who betrayed you?"

"I don't think anyone betrayed me. You just have better technology than we do."

"Really? Better than the List Keepers?"

"Let me out of here!" Grandyn yelled. "Face me like a man, Miner!"

"Grandyn, I don't bother with people like you." Miner tapped the glass with his silver dollar. "You see, you're replaceable. You're just another cog in the wheel of the pharmaceutical economy. We require only four things to power this great society: people to be born, to grow into workers slash consumers – earning and spending, to get sick, and finally . . . to die."

"*You* make me sick!"

"Yes, well it's a little late for that. I think you missed some of your shots. Come to think of it, you never grew into much of a worker or spender. We don't tolerate loafers like you not doing your part."

"Open this door and I'll show you how I work, you bastard!"

Miner shook his head slowly. "No, not going to be your luckiest day." He made small moves with his fingers on an AirView. "I guess you'll never know how I found you."

A slight hissing sound filled the tiny space and Grandyn quickly discovered the source, six small vents in the floor. He could feel the forced-air streaming in, and although it was odorless and colorless, he knew where he was, a PharmaForce lab, and he knew he wouldn't be leaving alive.

Grandyn pounded the glass. "You're a torgon coward!"

"I'm sure you see it that way. I prefer to think of myself as efficient."

"The Aylantik and AOI are doomed, even without me. It's too late, Miner. You've already lost!"

As the gas filled the space, Lance, with a slight smile on his face, looked and found Grandyn's eyes. He spoke into the microphone one last time. "Say hello to your mother and father for me."

Grandyn looked away. He had done his part. Grandyn always

said being a fighter, brave and true, was more important than living a false life. It was true. The lost TreeRunner bit into his neuro-cap and crumpled onto the floor, finally free.

Miner didn't immediately report Grandyn's death, knowing Deuce would find out the minute it hit the AOI system. He needed to review Grandyn's brain scan and learn the secrets of the last Happerman. Miner expected a wealth of information from the TreeRunner's mind. After all, he'd been involved since the start of the Doneharvest, and he had skirted the uprising on both sides.

After all the hunts and false deaths, Miner couldn't believe he had finally taken Grandyn out. He had the body to prove it. It had been the best money he'd ever spent buying that information from Blaze. Only the two of them knew that Grandyn Happerman had been Ander Terik, a star AOI agent. What would the Council think? And the Chief? He could hardly wait to leverage all this. The great TreeRunner was dead.

He stretched out on an over-hold. The furniture instantly contoured from a chair to a gliding sofa and applied massage and aromatherapy. His mind fought for focus. There were so many pieces, so much at stake. He was excited for the test results. Grandyn likely knew the location of important rebel bases, and his Said-scan could lead them to Chelle and Munna. Miner rubbed his hands together, smiling.

The pressure had been taking its toll for years. He longed for an ending, and that was finally in sight. One of his five great enemies had been destroyed. Now, only Chelle Andreas, Nelson Wright, Munna, and Deuce remained. Munna couldn't live much longer, and Deuce would soon be cornered by his own actions. As the rebels gained ground and war grew closer, the A-Council would no longer be able to ignore Deuce's flagrant support of the opposition groups, but Miner was freshly optimistic that war could be avoided.

CHAPTER SEVENTY-ONE

"Ander Terik is dead. Neuro-cap deployed. Mind erasure complete." The cold voice from her INU caught Fye by surprise, and it felt like she was being strangled until a primal "ohhhh" escaped her lips, her eyes instantly wet with tears. Fye fought the emotions so as to not upset the baby growing inside her, but it took a while to deal with the shock. Even though she'd always known it could happen, the realization that the AOI had discovered that Terik was an alias of Grandyn meant more than just the loss of their greatest asset. It meant there was a leak somewhere, and it could only be from Blaze or one of his infallible "Knights."

"Ah, Fye, looking loving as always," Blaze said, smiling as he answered her zoom.

"Wipe that torgon smile off your two-faced face, Blaze!" Fye clutched her Eysen as if it were his throat.

"Back up love, you look like a fish when you get in that close," Blaze said, smiling wider. "Anger becomes a woman, but the wrong angle never does."

"You smug bastard," she said swiping at his holographic image projected less than half a meter away.

"Are you trying to saw me in half? Because I'm working on

technology that might make physical contact possible over a zoom. Would you like that, kitten? All kinds of naughty applications."

She shook her head, resisting the urge to spit on his avatar. "Ander Terik is dead!"

"Yes, I thought that might be the reason for your call. Really, such a shame. Such a damn shame. I imagine you're upset. He really was quite the man, but not much use now."

"How did you get this way?"

"Years in the making. Did you know that many people think I'm an Imp? That would explain quite a bit, wouldn't it, love? Thing is, I take that as a compliment. But no matter, enough about me, well rarely, but in this case . . . I think you were mourning Ander Terik."

"Also known as Grandyn Happerman!"

"Oh, yes. Really? Hmm. Is that why you're overreacting to this bit of news? Because it is but one death. You're aware that the Aylantik killed billions in the Banoff . . . *billions*. Now that is a number worth grieving over, and yet it is only history now. Deaths as a part of history hardly hurt at all. Have you ever noticed that once everyone has died who knew any of the victims personally, it quite changes the viewpoint on the tragedy?"

"Shut up Blaze! Just shut up!"

"You do recall that you initiated this zoom, don't you?"

"Are you drunk?"

"No. Would you like to get drunk?"

"Yes, I would, but not with you."

"Right, you're too upset. Grandyn Happerman is dead."

"You did this, didn't you?"

"Well, you know I could never confirm something like that, but yes, of course I did."

"Why?" Her anger prevented tears for the moment.

"Terik, in his position with the AOI, was very valuable indeed, but that very value made him even more valuable as a bargaining chip, and I love to bargain. You knew that about me, I assume. Of course you did. And bargaining is about strategy or vice versa. But my point, luscious Fye, is that we're days away from the revolution, wouldn't you agree?" He didn't wait for an answer. "Therefore it was time to use that chip. As highly intelligent as you are, and I do have even higher respect for your extraordinary genius than I do for your remarkable beauty, I wouldn't expect you to understand the complex strategy of this situation."

"You are such a— "

"Wait a minute, love." Blaze said, suddenly looking concerned and serious. The smile left his face as his image walked over to her and reached up to touch her face. Even though it wasn't really there, she instinctively batted his hand away as if he were a rapist. "Tsk, tsk. Such anger. A shame you're spoken for, and pregnant. My goodness, you're pregnant!" He seemed more pleased with his ability to detect that than with the news itself. "Is the baby Grandyn's? Because, unfortunately, it isn't mine, but perhaps you played around, in such poor taste, all those long months when Grandyn was away."

She scowled, shaking her head, disgusted. His ability to see her pregnancy bothered her, but it certainly came as no surprise. Blaze, however revolting, was a gifted man. She'd long referred to him as "the wizard" behind his back, never to his face. He would have liked it too much.

"But that is why this news has you so extra upset." He stood back and regarded her. "We'll be in the middle of a full-blown war when this baby is born . . . bad timing, Fye. This wasn't planned, was it? That's illegal you know. The AOI will come looking for you." He laughed at his own humor. "But you do know, don't you?"

"What?" she exclaimed, exhausted by his Dr. Seusserisms.

"About Ander Terik."

"I know all about Terik. I sent him in, and I—"

"Yes. You programmed him." Blaze nodded. "It just seems

strange, even with the pregnancy, that you would be this upset over a CHRUDE. It's not as though Terik was really Grandyn, or even human for that matter."

"Do you know it wasn't Grandyn?"

Blaze feigned confusion. "CHRUDEs only seem real. They may act like people, even better than them, but they are not human. They are beautiful in that way. Better than people, but legal to kill."

"Grandyn could be dead!" she screamed, exasperated.

"Terik was a CHRUDE," Blaze said. "Do you get them mixed up? Have you made love with the machine by mistake? Is it the CHRUDE's baby? Is that even possible?"

"Shut up, damn you!" she shouted. "Long before we put the CHRUDE in, Grandyn was using Terik's identity. It was extremely dangerous. If you recall, that's *why* we put the CHRUDE in."

"Yes, that's what I'm saying. Terik was a CHRUDE," he repeated.

"Maybe, but we don't know for sure."

"Wait, was Grandyn still using Terik's identity?" Blaze said, showing concern for the first time.

"Yes. He went into the prison as Terik to see Drast. He didn't want to trust the CHRUDE, and whenever he had to go to AOI functions, he went himself. He only used the CHRUDE for field work."

"That was a big mistake," Blaze said. "The CHRUDE could have handled any of that. Have you tried contacting Grandyn?"

"Of course I have. Nothing," she said, trying not to cry. "And even if it was the CHRUDE that got killed, thanks to you they've linked Terik to Grandyn, and once they find out that Terik is a CHRUDE, it will unravel his whole chain of protection."

"Yes, it might. It's a good thing you're so smart because, assuming he's alive, I know you'll think of another way to protect young Happerman, future father of your child. And . . . if Grandyn really is dead this time, think of me."

"You?" she asked, disgusted.

"Not for sex if that's what you were thinking, kitten. No, I'm talking about CHRUDEs. My greatest invention, and the AOI doesn't even know they exist."

"But they will know when they dissect Terik!" she yelled, clinging to the hope that the Terik they killed was a CHRUDE. "Why, Blaze? Why did you do it?"

"I told you. It's about strategy."

"What strategy?"

"Ever try to teach chess to a monkey? It can't be done."

"Why are you such a pig?"

"Please don't insult me, Fye. I have the utmost respect for you, really, in spite of your ill-timed pregnancy."

Fye shook her head. "I have a favor to ask."

"Anything, love. Ask away."

"If he's still alive, you have to stop your games. You don't need the money, and you have no reason to put us at risk."

"Is that your favor?"

"Please, *please*, don't lead them to Grandyn."

"Why would I do that?"

"Strategy? How should I know?"

"Knowing is not the same as understanding."

"Is that an answer?"

"Yes, but not precisely to the question you asked. People seldom ask the correct questions, so I'm forced to edit and rewrite our dialogues in order for any of it to make even a semblance of sense."

"I'm just asking you, as an old friend, and on behalf of my unborn child. Don't let them find Grandyn."

"Are we friends Fye? Really? That's sweet you think so." His image went to move a strand of her hair. She did not push him away, but the pixels passed through her sandy blonde strands with less notice than the sunlight. "And you might recall, babies make me laugh. They do funny things, but I'm not sure they are legally allowed to make requests such as this, particularly from the womb. However, I will tell you this, dear woman. I do not currently know where the lost TreeRunner is, but I continue to look for the same reasons as everyone else."

"And if you find him?"

"Again with the wrong question. If someone else is going to find him before I do, then he may have to die. But if I'm the one to find Grandyn, he will be quite safe."

"So you want me to tell you if he comes back? You want me to tell you in order to save him? Is that all part of your strategy?"

"My strategy is not nearly that simple. I see the entire chess match in my mind in less than a tenth of a second after the first pawn moves." He paused. "You don't trust me enough to ever tell me where Grandyn is, nor should you, although there may come a day very soon when I'm his only hope of survival. I wish you the wisdom to make the right decision when we arrive there. Until then, take care that no one else finds the lost TreeRunner . . . if he's even still alive."

CHAPTER SEVENTY-TWO

Deuce had a decision to make. He sat in a small room on Ryder Island. The ceiling swirled with a planetarium view of the outer reaches of the Milky Way as Billie Holiday's voice delivered "All Or Nothing At All."

With the prophecies finally in hand, and seeing them on the AirViews for the first time in his life, he knew for sure that his grandfather, Booker, and UC were right. There is something beyond what we see, something extraordinary, and with that knowledge comes an endless array of possibilities. They could change everything, the Aylantik could be defeated, and maybe without the need for a horrendous war, but what exactly was that power? How could it be harnessed? And, more importantly, how could it be kept out of the wrong hands?

"How is Munna controlling the INUs?" he asked himself as he stared into faux stars. Deuce missed UC. He would have known what to do. He would have been able to reason with Munna. *Maybe he would have been on her side*. "Why aren't I on her side? Because she's a crazy old lady who won't even allow anyone to kill a spider. What if there is a way to avoid war and she won't let us look into the *Justar Journal* to find it?" he asked out loud.

Maybe there isn't a way to avoid war, and that's why she won't let us see it.

His INU lit up, interrupting his thoughts. The zoom had not been expected but didn't surprise him.

"Deuce, we need to talk," the Chief said as she holographed into his space. She looked above, unsmiling. "Interesting stars."

"I've got two minutes."

"This won't take that long. I know you have Munna and Nelson Wright somewhere. You're probably also hiding the Tree-Runner." She hesitated, then added bitterly. "We've killed Grandyn at least half a dozen times, yet he still keeps running like a stupid dog looking for a soggy tennis ball."

"Are you accusing me of a crime?"

"Oh, not you Deuce. Give me some credit. I know you're above the law. I'm merely warning you."

"I'm listening."

"I will not allow this to turn into a war. Do you understand what I mean by that? If your BLAXER army even appears to be helping the rebels, I will crush them. I think you know we have weapons at our disposal that are not meant to fight a war, but rather to end it."

"I understand."

"Don't let this start," she hissed.

"Is that all?"

"For now." She faked a smile. "Peace prevails, always."

After the zoom, Deuce walked into his son's room. Twain, still weak, but talking more now, smiled when he saw his father. "How are you feeling?" Deuce asked.

"Better than you," Twain replied, smiling with his eyes. "What's wrong?"

"Your pal Munna is playing a dangerous game with me."

"That doesn't sound like her." He studied his father for a moment. "She might be trying to save you from yourself."

"Really? I don't need a crazy old lady to interfere with—"

"Dad, Munna is not some freak. She's us."

"What's that mean?"

"She is the example of what we could be if we'd taken a different path. Instead of following money and things, we could be there. We could be her."

"I know," Deuce said, sitting on his son's bed. "It's why I'm in this thing. PAWN wants to get rid of Aylantik so we can go back to multiple governments around the planet. Grandyn wants revenge . . ." Deuce paused and thought of his own father, killed by the AOI, and fought his own lingering wishes for vengeance. "Chelle and Drast want to right the wrongs of the Banoff . . . the Creatives, the Rejectionists, they all have differing reasons for the change, but I'm after the same thing Munna wants. I'm trying to bring Booker's vision into reality."

"Booker sent Munna."

Deuce looked at Twain, surprised.

"She knew him, they worked together."

"That much I knew."

"He told her that one day she would need to help you and me, to show us how to get through."

Deuce nodded slowly. After a few moments, he spoke. "Then why isn't she showing me? Why won't she let me see the prophecies?"

"Because you're still looking at things the wrong way. You still think that power is external," Twain said softly, looking tired again. "The real power is inside. Look at her. Can't you see it? She is showing you."

CHAPTER SEVENTY-THREE

Grandyn arrived, looking beleaguered, dirt-covered, and with bits of leaves, twigs, and bark in his hair. He fell into Fye's arms.

"What happened?" She asked, kissing him, crying tears of joy. "Are you hurt?"

"Did you hear about Terik?"

"Yes, I thought it might have been you."

"It was the CHRUDE." He kissed her softly, and then rested his forehead on hers, staring into her eyes. "I'm alive. Nine lives, remember?"

She wiped her tears. "I think you've used them all up."

"I'll have to be careful now then, won't I?"

She patted her belly and gave him a serious look.

"I know," he whispered. "I promise you I'm not going to die."

She looked at him quietly for a long moment.

He nodded, acknowledging the seriousness of his promise.

Finally, she spoke. "But how did you hear about Terik?"

"Drast."

"How?" was all she could manage, hoping he would answer all of the questions contained in that single word. How did Drast know about Terik already? How did Drast get word to Grandyn, the *real* Grandyn? And how did Grandyn escape from whatever ordeal he'd been through?

"We now have our case for the masses." Grandyn looked at her for a moment and then slid into a chair by the window. "The Terik execution was recorded. The unit relayed a digital capture showing Lance Miner killing Ander Terik at a PharmaForce facility."

"Incredible. I had no idea it could—"

"It gets better. After Terik 'died,' they were taking his body to a medical room for a brain scan and it exploded. Killed three people and partially destroyed a wing of the building."

"Miner?"

"No, he was in another part of the facility. But it gets even *better*. A team of rebels stormed the building at the same time, did some more damage, and escaped in a Flo-wing before one of Miner's Enforcers units could overpower them."

"What were they doing there?"

"Getting Terik's body so it couldn't be brain-scanned."

"But it blew up."

"Right, but Miner doesn't know it blew up. He thinks the rebels sent in explosives to cover their extraction of Terik."

She looked at him and smiled. "So Miner doesn't know that Terik was a CHRUDE?"

"Exactly. But it still gets *even better* . . . Miner thinks Grandyn Happerman is really dead."

"Yes!" she squealed. "So Blaze sent the rebels?"

"I would have thought so too. But it wasn't him."

"Then who?" she asked genuinely surprised. "Only Blaze, you, and I knew about Terik."

"Drast."

"Polis Drast?" she whispered, as if it was too unbelievable to be spoken out loud. "How could he send an attack from prison? How did he know? Who is still taking his orders? How did you find out? What—"

"Slow down. I'll tell you."

"But you're such a mess. Are you really okay?"

"I'm a mess because after what happened to Terik I couldn't risk a LEV, so I ran here, through the forest, from the coast. It's more than seventeen kilometers."

"Good thing you're a TreeRunner," she said, smiling sweetly, happy he was all right, happy he was back with her. "Now tell me everything."

"It's really quite amazing." He poured a glass of water and gulped it down. "Once Chelle convinced Miner to bring rain to the Amazon, I knew the prophecies would change again, but I didn't know by how much, so I still had to go through with our plan to stop the prison uprisings."

Grandyn thought back three years earlier when the List Keepers agreed to protect him. They went through a difficult and tedious process to erase every photo or identifiable trace from all AOI databases, then inserted new photos and identification so that the AOI was searching for someone who looked nothing like Grandyn. Then they created Ander Terik and gave him Grandyn's true appearance so Grandyn was free to move around and even become an AOI agent. But as he thought about the controversial part of the plan, his heart sank.

Eight people had died for him. Look-alikes were dispatched around the world, not just to throw the AOI off his trail, but to take resources and distract the agency. It had worked perfectly, but the deaths were hard for him to live with.

"There was another Grandyn death in the Amazon," he said.

"Oh no . . . I'm so sorry," she said, knowing what it did to him.

"Drast, of course, knew about Terik," he said, returning to the subject as to not dwell on the loss. "But he wants a war, so our decision to not ask him to stop the uprising was right, at least until Terik was destroyed. That's when I deviated from our plan."

"How?" she asked, gazing in amazement at the man she loved. Oddly, in that moment she smiled, realizing again what a wonderful father he would be and wishing she had met Grandyn's dad.

"I was halfway to the AOI's prison in the Illinois Area to talk to Drast's inmate buddy Tiger, when my INU lit up with the news of Terik. Now, I couldn't very well go into an AOI prison as AOI agent Ander Terik when he'd just been killed by Miner. I didn't know that the AOI didn't know yet, so instead I went back to Runit Island."

"You could have told me."

"I didn't want to compromise you, or the baby," Grandyn said. "I was traveling as a dead AOI agent. It was too risky."

Fye nodded. "Why do you still have that?" she asked, pointing the AOI pin he was mindlessly fiddling with.

"It's a symbol," he said, "of something we can't ever forget. I'm keeping it until all the lies and corruption are exposed."

"You might have it a long time . . . "

"I know." He thought of his parents, then gently touched Fye's belly and resumed the story. "On the way, I had to take a chance on Drast."

"How?"

"I got into Osc's system using Terik's credentials, and Osc arranged a double-blind zoom." The term described a non-visual zoom of very short duration so that a satellite lock on the location of the INUs could not be determined.

"So you had eighty-two seconds."

"Exactly. I told him we'd seen the prophecies and that if his war started in the prisons, he would lose. He believed me, at least enough to delay things until I can get him more information. That's when he told me about the raid on PharmaForce."

"All that in eighty-two seconds?"

"We talked fast."

"Chelle is going to want to get him out," she said.

"Probably, depending on the *Justar Journal*," he said. "Anyway, I got back to the island and found Nelson and Deuce in the middle of a huge argument and Munna still freezing the screens. I told them about Terik, and about the raid and Drast. Munna opened the AirViews again, and everything had changed."

"What did it look like?"

"It was messy, we were still at war, years and years of war, but it had gone much better. Munna was still alive, PAWN was winning. But . . ."

His hesitation worried her. "What?"

"Chelle was dead, and . . . so was I."

"I'm not losing you," she said, holding her belly.

"There may be only one way to avoid it."

"Tell me."

"It's the one thing that you've sworn never to do."

She shook her head in disbelief. "How has it come to this . . . Is there no other way?"

"I don't think so," he looked at her with his gravest expression, as if the crushing weight of the entire corrupt Aylantik system were pushing him. "The List Keepers must come forward and show the world the truth."

END OF BOOK TWO

The List Keepers, book three of the Justar Journal available here.

The thrilling conclusion to the Justar Journal!

For longer than anyone knew, they were there. Before half the world died, before the lies became the truth, before anyone understood, the List Keepers were there . . . waiting.

.   .   .

Inside the books, it had predicted everything, the Banoff, the Aylantik, the AOI, the Doneharvest, the end, and even itself. The Justar Journal had always been there . . . waiting.

With so many secrets hidden, Grandyn discovers something more extraordinary than he ever dreamed. The AOI must stop him from sharing it; they are far from his biggest problem. Blaze, Deuce, and Lance all need to control the secret. But the greatest danger may be the Trapciers, who must destroy it. He can only count on one person. She's been waiting . . . and she belongs to the List Keepers.

When searching for the truth, you may find it never existed.

The List Keepers, book three of the Justar Journal available at here.

A NOTE FROM THE AUTHOR

Thanks for sharing the adventure!
Help spread the word
If you enjoyed this book, please take a minute to
post a review wherever you purchased it
(even a few words).
Reviews are the greatest way to help an author.
And, please tell your friends.

I'd love to hear from you1
Questions, comments, whatever.
Email me through my website.
I'll definitely respond (usually within a few days).
Join my Inner Circle
If you want to be the first to hear about my new releases, advance
reads, occasional news and more,
join my Inner Circle at: BrandtLegg.com

ABOUT THE AUTHOR

USA TODAY Bestselling Author Brandt Legg uses his unusual real life experiences to create page-turning novels. He's traveled with CIA agents, dined with senators and congressmen, mingled with astronauts, chatted with governors and presidential candidates, had a private conversation with a Secretary of Defense he still doesn't like to talk about, hung out with Oscar and Grammy winners, had drinks at the State Department, been pursued by tabloid reporters, and spent a birthday at the White House by invitation from the President of the United States.

At age eight, Legg's father died suddenly, plunging his family into poverty. Two years later, while suffering from crippling migraines, he started in business, and turned a hobby into a multi-million-dollar empire. National media dubbed him the "Teen Tycoon," and by the mid-eighties, Legg was one of the top young entrepreneurs in America, appearing as high as number twenty-four on the list (when Steve Jobs was #1, Bill Gates #4, and Michael Dell #6). Legg still jokes that he should have gone into computers.

By his twenties, after years of buying and selling businesses, lever-aging, and risk-taking, the high-flying Legg became ensnarled in the financial whirlwind of the junk bond eighties. The stock market crashed and a firestorm of trouble came down. The Teen Tycoon racked up more than a million dollars in legal fees, was betrayed by those closest to him, lost his entire fortune, and ended up serving time for financial improprieties.

After a year, Legg emerged from federal prison, chastened and wiser, and began anew. More than twenty-five years later, he's now using all that hard-earned firsthand knowledge of conspiracies, corruption and high finance to weave his tales. Legg's books pulse with authenticity.

His series have excited nearly a million readers around the world. Although he refused an offer to make a television movie about his life as a teenage millionaire, his autobiography is in the works. There has also been interest from Hollywood to turn his thrillers into films. With any luck, one day you'll see your favorite characters on screen.

He lives in the Pacific Northwest, with his wife and son, writing full time, in several genres, containing the common themes of adventure, conspiracy, and thrillers. Of all his pursuits, being an author and crafting plots for novels is his favorite.

For more information, please visit his website, or to contact Brandt directly, email him: Brandt@BrandtLegg.com, he loves to hear from readers and always responds!

BrandtLegg.com

BOOKS BY BRANDT LEGG

Chasing Rain

Chasing Fire

Chasing Wind

Chasing Dirt

Chasing Life

Chasing Kill

Chasing Risk

Chasing Mind

Cosega Search (Cosega Sequence #1)

Cosega Storm (Cosega Sequence #2)

Cosega Shift (Cosega Sequence #3)

Cosega Sphere (Cosega Sequence #4)

Cosega Source (Cosega Sequence #5)

CapWar ELECTION (CapStone Conspiracy #1)

CapWar EXPERIENCE (CapStone Conspiracy #2)

CapWar EMPIRE (CapStone Conspiracy #3)

The Last Librarian (Justar Journal #1)

The Lost TreeRunner (Justar Journal #2)

The List Keepers (Justar Journal #3)

Outview (Inner Movement #1)

Outin (Inner Movement #2)

Outmove (Inner Movement #3)

ACKNOWLEDGMENTS

Thank you to each of you who has posted positive reviews. Thank you to all the readers who have contacted me. I know everyone leads busy lives, so when you take the time to review my work or to email me your thoughts or questions, or to tell me your stories, it means more than you could know. I would also like to acknowledge two teachers from so long ago . . . Mrs. Snare, for handling me just right at a difficult time, and Mrs. Grenfel, for reading so many great stories to us, especially because you chose such wonderful science fiction. To the best schoolteacher I ever had, Jan Anderson, thank you, I'm sure my books would be quite different if I had never been in your class.

There are many others to thank. I'm fairly certain that everything would be impossible without Roanne Legg, she has changed my world so that I can create new ones on paper. Special gratitude to my mother, Barbara Blair, who instilled the magic way back when, and to my father, Bill Legg, who took the time to lead a young bunch of "TreeRunners," in the forest of Kemper and many other interesting places. You both can be found on countless pages of all my books. Bonnie Brown Koeln, a member of the family, who is always willing to help. Elizabeth Chumney for being a very loyal friend! Extra thanks to Melanie C. Hansen for reading it again. And finally to Teakki, who patiently waited for spells, talk of wizards, and sword fights, until I finished writing each day.

This book is dedicated to Teakki and Ro

GLOSSARY

A-Council – Secretive group that controls the economy and decides who will be elected.

ACE – Aylantik Commission on the Environment.

ADAM – Atom-Displacing-Adjusted-Molecule technology – Reduces the weight of objects.

AirSlider – Jet-propelled scooter, sometimes equipped with laser munitions.

AirView – Virtual INU (computer) monitors.

AOI – Aylantik Office of Intelligence.

AOI Chief – Top AOI official.

Android – An artificial being, advanced robot, with approximate human appearance. Manufactured to replace humans in many jobs.

Aylantik Government – Group running the world since the end of the Banoff War.

Aylantik Records Circle (ARC) – Manages ID chips.

Aylantik region – One of twenty-four regions governed by the Aylantik.

Bacs – Privately made cigarettes.

Banoff Pandemic – Plague which wiped out more than half the world's population in 2025.

Banoff War – War which followed the plague. In which the Aylantik coalition secured power.

Bearing rights – Rights to have one child could be sold for up to 20,000 digis after age eighteen.

BLAXERs – Deuce Lipton's private "security" army.

Breeze-Blowers - Dust-sized computers, equipped with video transmitters, that blow in the breeze.

CAAP – Corporate Assets Acquisition Parity Board.

Chamber-slot – Plan to breach all AOI prisons at once.

Chiantik region – One of twenty-four regions governed by the Aylantik.

Chicago85 – Company that sells spy, intelligence, and surveillance technologies to the government.

CHRUDEs - Cloned Human Replacement Unit DesTIn Enabled – Human-like robots.

Collins-HG3 – Autonomous flying weapon.

Com – Universal language that has replaced all other languages, including English.

Courier – People who personally deliver confidential messages or small parcels.

Creatives – Writers, artists, musicians, etc., who tend to have liberal views and prefer total freedom.

Cyborg – Cybernetic Organism constructed from organic and biomechatronic parts.

DACAR – Data Arts Correction And Revisions Project.

DesTIn - Design Taught Intelligence, or "DesTIn," an advanced artificial intelligence program.

Digi-link – World Central Bank.

Digis – Form of digital currency.

Digital-drapes – Where people download books, movies, music, or whatever data they desire.

Doneharvest – AOI martial law style crackdown.

Earth Parks – Replaced National parks and protected lands.

ELS – Equidistant Letter Sequence – Type of code for hiding messages in text.

Enforcers — Security unit of PharmaForce and Lance Miner's private army.

Exchange – Code word for the second start of the revolution.

Eysen-INU – Leading type of Information Navigation Units.

FA – False Audio equipped micro-whistler-FAs.

Field – What the Internet evolved into – Everything is connected.

Field-View – Secure videoconference.

Flash – Equivalent to email/text/instant message.

Flo-wing – Super-fast vertical takeoff mini aircraft – The evolution of helicopters.

FRIDG – Facial Recognition Identification Grid.

Grunges – Slang for AOI agents.

Health-Circle – Or AHC – Aylantik government agency responsible for health care.

Hops – State run health and fitness facilities.

ID chip - Secured into every Aylantik citizen. Details all personal data.

Implant – AI computer brain interface implanted in humans resulting in super intelligence.

Imps – Slang for people who have computer implants.

INU – Information Navigation Units – Powerful marble-sized computer/communications device.

InvisiLine – Secret bank and currency control.

ISBN – International Standard Book Number – Unique book identifier system.

Lasershod – Advanced handgun.

Laserstiks – Advanced, highly accurate, long-range weapon.

LEVs – Levitating Electro Vehicles – Solar-propelled floating vehicles.

Micro-whistler-Mimics (MWM) – Device that fits into mouth – Blocks conversations, broadcasts a false audio.

Micro-drones – Bug-sized drones, used individually or in swarms.

Media no-list – Topics not allowed to be covered by the media – PAWN, Rejectionists, etc.

Medical Sensor – Small coin-sized patch worn to monitor all health data.

Monitoring-mimic-drones – Bird-sized, sophisticated drones. Almost impossible to detect.

Nano-camo – Tarps that automatically change to the surrounding landscape like a chameleon.

Nano-tracers – Seeker-defeating microscopic decals applied to the face.

Neuro-cap – Erases data and memory from both human, cyborg, CHRUDE, and Imp brains.

Neuron-mites – Mind reading nano-sized INUs.

Nusun – Single nation utopian Earth.

Over-hold – Instantly contouring chair/gliding sofa, which applies massage and aromatherapy.

Pacyfik region – One of twenty-four regions governed by the Aylantik.

PAWN – People Against World Nation – Leading revolutionary group.

Phantom-Shield Nano-device – Sends holographic image into the same path and trajectory.

PharmaForce – World's largest pharmaceutical company, controlled by Lance Miner.

Plantik – The naturally derived plantik that replaced plastic.

POPs – PAWN Operational Pods – Underground PAWN facilities.

Proof – A-Council's name for the generation that survived the Banoff.

Pulse-rods – Communication-disrupting weapon.

Q-lifts – Ultra fast elevator that uses atom-displacing-adjusted-molecule technology.

Red-1953 – Chemical used to burn books.

Rejectionists – People who rejected Aylantik rules and modern society.

Retina-synch - Allows wearer to access data through what amounts to a micro-contact lens.

Said-scans - Postmortem brain scans.

Sat-grids – Satellite monitoring system.

Scram Network – Emergency, secret communications system that operated apart from the Field.

Seeker – AOI camera network.

Shockers – A hand-held laser-powered pulse bomb about the size of a hand grenade.

Slide – Thumb drive-like data carrying device for INUs.

Sonic-bomb – Vibration frequency device that can shatter everything within a specified radius.

Sophisticated-GPS – Tracking program able to predict where an object is heading or came from.

StarFly – Largest company in the world's fourth biggest industry: Space. Owned by Deuce Lipton.

Swarm-Drones – Bug-sized drones, equipped with cameras – Can go anywhere a flying insect can.

Tech-tracing – Can track the fingerprint of any electronic device from the web of satellites.

Tekfabrik – Multipurpose nano-fabric capable of changing color, size, and texture. Self-cleaning.

Thread – High capacity memory stick about the size of a short piece of angel hair pasta.

Torgon – Curse word in the com language. Also used as torg, torgged, or torging.

Traditionals – Name used to describe ordinary humans without implants, etc.

Trapicers – Mysterious revolutionary group.

Tru-chair – Chair that conforms to the sitter's anatomy and delivers acupressure. Uses energy by harvesting body heat.

Wavesuits – Tekfabrik suits equipped with tracking-blocking capabilities.

Whistler – Tiny device and app that blocks AOI monitoring of INUs.

World Premier – Elected leader of the United Earth and head of the Aylantik government.

Zoom – Similar to a phone call with video.

www.ingramcontent.com/pod-product-compliance
Lightning Source LLC
Chambersburg PA
CBHW050919250626
47155CB00001B/300